D0289557

Whiskey
with a
Twist

ALSO BY NINA WRIGHT FROM MIDNIGHT INK

Whiskey on the Rocks
Whiskey Straight Up
Whiskey and Tonic
Whiskey and Water

YOUNG ADULT BOOKS BY NINA WRIGHT

Homefree
Sensitive

A Whiskey Mattimoe Mystery

Nina Wright

Midnight Ink
Woodbury, Minnesota

First Edition
First Printing, 2009

Book design and format by Donna Burch
Cover design by Lisa Novak
Cover art © 2008 Bunky Hurter
Editing by Connie Hill

Midnight Ink, an imprint of Llewellyn Publications

Library of Congress Cataloging-in-Publication Data (Pending)
ISBN: 978-0-7387-1470-7

Midnight Ink
Llewellyn Publications
2143 Wooddale Drive, Dept. 978-0-7387-1470-7
Woodbury, MN 55125-2989 USA
www.midnightinkbooks.com

Printed in the United States of America

For the 17-word man from the 80,000-word woman.

ACKNOWLEDGMENTS

Warmest thanks to the following writers and readers for skillfully and generously critiquing my drafts: M. K. Buhler, Rebecca Gall, Greg Neri, Teddie Aggeles, and Richard Pahl.

Hugs to Clooney and Redford, the four-leggers.

Eternal gratitude to Flannery, Lola, Endo, and Talley for their unconditional love and infinite inspiration. See y'all in another novel. . . .

Cheers for my nonagenarian father, who makes sense of life—and makes me laugh—every single time we talk.

ONE

"SHE *BREEDS* AFGHAN HOUNDS?" I asked. "Then why would I want to meet her?"

I was drinking with my ex-husband, who looked good in the autumn sunlight slanting across Mother Tucker's oak bar. So good that I strained to remind myself of the pain that must have surrounded our divorce. At the moment I could recall none at all.

"I already have an Afghan hound," I said. "One is too many."

Jeb Halloran sipped his scotch, a fine single malt that he could only recently afford. "Susan Davies has connections."

"Will she take Abra?" My voice rose in hope.

"She sells dogs, Whiskey. She doesn't collect them. But she might introduce you to her husband."

"Will he take Abra?"

"No, but he might help you make money. Liam is a builder."

"The real estate market sucks."

It was my turn to drink. But unlike Jeb, I didn't sip. I gulped. The Pinot went down way too easy.

Jeb signaled the barkeep to pour me another. "It's not that bad."

"It's *not that bad* if you're a buyer with financing. If you're one of them, you got plenty to choose from. Thanks to all those foreclosures..."

Real estate values were in the toilet, even in Magnet Springs. A downsized job market and mortgage-lending crisis had tightened screws on homeowners everywhere. Michigan and other industrial states were especially hard hit. Locally, though, we had an advantage: ours was a resort region, scenic and sports-oriented the whole year round. We were a playground for the Midwestern rich. Particularly those from Chicagoland, a mere one hundred miles across the Greatest Great Lake.

Jeb said, "Knowing Susan and her husband might help. He's negotiating with the Shirtz Brothers. Money will be made."

I knew about Susan Davies' husband and his builder-developer machine. Rumor had it that Liam Davies Ltd. was conferring with a local farm family to purchase an eighty-acre parcel at the north end of town.

"No real estate commission to be made on that transaction," I said.

"Ah, but what happens next?" Jeb tossed me a teasing look. The kind that usually led to action in the boudoir.

"What?"

He grinned maddeningly. "Meet Susan. You know how things work."

I knew this much: during economic downturns, the poor get poorer, the middle gets squeezed, and the rich scoop up real estate bargains. Chicago-based Davies had built his fortune turning land in Illinois and Indiana into industrial compounds, office parks, and subdivisions. His plan for the land along Uphill Road remained a mystery. Although the property was zoned agricultural, anything was possible.

"Start pouring. The drinks are on me!" announced a voice rich with a Tongo accent and real estate commissions.

Odette Mutombo, the best Realtor on this side of the state, slid onto the bar stool next to mine. Ignoring me, she fixed her sparkling black eyes on Jeb.

"Don't let Whiskey sing you any sad songs. I'm here to change her tune."

"I leave the singing to Jeb," I quipped, referring to my ex-husband's rising career. "You've got good news that involves real estate?"

"I have amazing news. Opportunity knocks for those who can hear it: me."

Folding her manicured hands on the bar, Odette smiled languidly. "I just took a meeting with Liam Davies' people. They want Mattimoe Realty as broker of record for their new development."

Before I could gasp, Jeb's cell phone sang out his own version of *Itsy-Bitsy Spider*, now available wherever music was sold. He turned away to take the call.

"She'll need something stronger than that," Odette informed the barkeep when he presented a fresh glass of Pinot Noir. "Pour her what her boyfriend's drinking, and make it a double."

"He's not my—" I protested. Odette made the rude raspberry sound she favored when calling my bluff.

"For this news you will require sedation. Liam Davies' people want me to handle the project, start to end. And it's a whopper. Will you sulk?"

Once upon a time I would have. Back when the market was stronger than my ego. Before I'd accidentally absorbed enough New Age wisdom to sort out my priorities. Now I accepted both my own limitations and Odette's astonishing strengths. The woman could sell saltwater to sharks. Ergo, she could make money in a down market. Although I owned and operated Mattimoe Realty, sales wasn't my forte. Which was why I gave thanks every day that Odette worked for me and not the competition. Anything she brought in the door fattened my company coffers.

"I should buy *you* a drink," I told her.

"Oh, you will. Plus dinner and assorted high-end gifts of gratitude. Not to mention the colossal commission checks you'll sign. But tonight I'm buying. Drink up."

The barkeep slid a double Glenfiddich my way. I would have preferred to stick with Pinot Noir. Hard liquor tends to get me in trouble, especially trouble of the sexual sort. My engine was already revving too high. Seven mostly happy years after divorcing Jeb—which included my brief but blissful marriage to the late great Leo—I was seeing Jeb again. Translation: we were having sex. Hot sex. Frequent sex. Better-than-ever sex. And it was scaring the shit out of me. I must have had plenty of reasons for divorcing him way back when. Yet, in the throes of renewed passion, I couldn't remember a single one.

When the short-term lease on his house ran out at the end of July, Jeb had suggested I let him move in with me. Instead, I found him another rental. But now, two months later, he hardly ever went home. He spent most nights with me at Vestige, the lakefront home I had lovingly built with Leo. The lonely, horny part of me wanted to give Jeb his own key. But the sane, self-protective part wanted him to hit the road on another music tour while I cooled my jets. After a whole season of intense sex, I needed to separate my brain from my libido and decide which one was my friend. Even in the midst of Odette's thrilling news, I caught myself eyeing Jeb's ass.

"You'll love Davies' plans for developing the property," Odette purred. "A two-phase, two income-level *super*-subdivision: Little House on the Prairie *and* Big House on the Prairie—Little House for the common people, Big House for the rich. Separating the two will be a manmade lake. And in the middle of the lake will be an island with tall, thick trees."

"So the people in the big houses don't have to look at the people in the little houses," I guessed.

"You're catching on!" Odette clinked her chocotini glass against my tumbler of scotch. "Mattimoe Realty will be the listing agent for fifty homes that sell for under two hundred thou, and fifteen homes that sell for more than one-point-five million. Cheers!"

I clinked back and chugged my scotch. It was alarmingly smooth. "But the economy—"

Odette made the raspberry sound again. "The rich always have money! Davies will start on *that* side of the lake."

"Did you say 'Davies'?" Jeb rejoined the conversation.

Odette summarized her latest coup. My ex congratulated her and told me to expect a call.

"From who?"

"The other Davies. She phoned me, looking for you."

"Did you ask her to take Abra?"

"No, but you can," he said as my cell rang. "That's Susan now."

The first zing from my free scotch hit me the instant I opened my phone. I was pretty sure I slurred my greeting. "This is Whiskey."

"Hello, Whiskey," said a warm female voice. "This is Susan Davies. I believe we're both fans of Jeb Halloran. He's told me so much about you and your Afghan hound. I hope you don't mind that I asked him for your number."

Scotch buzz notwithstanding, I had three instant questions, none of which I asked out loud. First, which horror stories had Jeb shared about me and my diva dog? Second, when and where had he shared them? Third, and this was related to Second, what did Susan Davies mean by claiming that she and I were both "fans"? As Jeb's former wife and current lover, I was way more than a fan. Was she? I suddenly remembered one painful reason for our long-ago divorce: Jeb liked to stray.

I took another slug of scotch. "How do you know my ex-husband?"

"He didn't tell you?"

"He didn't."

I glared at Jeb, who was leaning on the bar, laughing with Odette.

"Liam and I caught his act at the Holiday Inn in Grand Rapids. That was in August. Since then, my husband has been too busy to go back, but I've heard Jeb at least five more times."

"Five *more* times?"

"At least. Fabulous, isn't he?"

"That's one word for him." My voice was calm although my diction lacked crispness. Since I rate peace of mind higher than clarity of speech, I drank some more. "What keeps bringing you back to Grand Rapids, Susan? Surely not Jeb's music…"

"You're right. Hearing Jeb sing is a treat, but that's not why I'm in the area. He didn't tell you why?"

"Again—no, he didn't."

I frowned at my ex-husband, who was having too much fun to notice.

Susan said, "Besides my kennel in Itasca, I co-own six dogs in Grand Rapids. The other owner and I started a breeding program. Our bitch is in heat."

"How nice for you!"

"It is, actually. Which brings me to the reason I called. I have a request, Whiskey. It's unorthodox, not to mention short notice, but I'd like to stop by your home. Tonight. My co-breeder, Ramona Bowden, is with me, and we want to meet your dog."

"My *dog*?" I blinked. "You don't want to meet *my* dog."

"Oh, yes, we most definitely do."

"Why not meet a nice Afghan hound? Mine is a convicted felon."

"We know that."

Susan Davies didn't seem to get it. So I spoke slowly. "Abra steals things. Expensive things. She consorts with thieves and kidnappers. My dog has a criminal record."

"Her criminal record is why we want to meet her!" Susan said. "It's why we are inviting her—and you, too, of course—to participate in next week's Midwest Afghan Hound Specialty."

At least that was what I thought she said. Since it made no sense, I blamed the scotch, set my empty glass on the bar, and waited for Susan Davies to try again.

"Are you there, Whiskey?"

"We must have a bad connection. It sounded like you want Abra to be in a dog show. Because she's a criminal." I giggled.

"That's right. Ramona and I are in charge of Breeder Education. We believe that the most effective way to teach grooming and training is to show how *not* to do it. Abra is the worst example we've ever found."

TWO

Until Odette convinced Liam Davies to sign with us, business had been deadly dull at Mattimoe Realty. Which explained why I was participating in a not-so-happy Thursday afternoon happy hour at Mother Tucker's Bar and Grill: I had nothing better to do. And no better place to do it.

The office phones weren't ringing. A couple new agents had recently quit for lack of commissions or the promise of any, anytime soon. My part-time agents weren't getting results, and my senior full-time agents were getting restless. Unless you counted foreclosures, nothing much was happening on the local real estate scene.

But now, thanks to Odette, my company had reason to celebrate. And I had a reason to comply with Susan Davies' ridiculous request regarding my diva dog. We ended our phone conversation by setting an appointment for her to come by and meet Abra: in two hours, exactly. That gave me sufficient time to get sober enough to drive home. And then try to locate my hound.

The barkeep replaced my empty rock glass with a mug of black coffee. I set my cell phone on the bar next to Jeb's.

"You knew about the dog show thing, didn't you?"

"Susan might have mentioned it."

"When?"

What I really meant was "How often do you see this woman?" Fortunately, I stopped myself from sounding like the jealous shrew I am.

"We run into each other now and then. In Grand Rapids. It's not that big a town."

Way bigger than Magnet Springs, I thought, which automatically qualified it for romantic trysts. I forced myself to choke down half the coffee. During the intervening silence, Odette offered a troubling tidbit.

"Susan and Liam have one of those on-again, off-again marriages. Or so I hear. They've separated a few times but never gone through with the divorce." She turned to Jeb. "Is the marriage on or off these days?"

When he shrugged, I didn't buy it.

"You don't know the marital status of your number-one fan?"

"I thought *you* were my number-one fan." He grinned. "As for Susan and Liam, I think they're working on it. I think they're always 'working on it.' At least that's the official line."

"Rather like Fenton and Noonan," Odette said, referring to our local New Age gurus. Fenton Flagg and Noonan Starr considered themselves "permanent spouses." In other words, soulmates. They had married long ago, split up almost immediately, yet never bothered to divorce. Why? Because they liked each other and had so much in common, including the Seven Suns of Solace step-program for inner peace. That didn't stop them from having affairs with other people, however. Fenton had almost had an affair with me—before I hooked up with Jeb again.

"Well, maybe they're like Fenton and Noonan," I said cautiously. "Except that Fenton and Noonan are ..." I mentally fished for the appropriate euphemism.

"Nuts?" Jeb suggested.

"Unique," I said and then gave up all pretense. "Are Susan and Liam crazy, too?"

"I haven't met Susan," said Odette, "but I can tell you that Liam is logical and blunt. When it comes to doing business, he's a straight shooter who wastes nobody's time."

She and I looked to Jeb for his assessment of Susan. He took a long swig of scotch. And remained silent.

"Well?" I prompted.

"I don't know what Susan's like when it comes to doing business. I only know her as my number-one fan."

I threw a cocktail straw at him. Even with two and a half drinks in his system, Jeb's reflexes were excellent. He snatched the straw in midair and lobbed it back at me. Only I didn't duck in time. Or even blink. The straw hit me right in the eye like a tiny javelin.

"Ouch!"

It really did hurt. Apparently I needed a lot more coffee. As well as some ice for my eye. And a couple aspirin. Jeb and Odette decided that I also needed someone to drive me home. My ex won the coin toss. At least I think he won; in any case, he provided the ride.

I resisted leaving my car at Mother Tucker's until Jeb promised he'd drive me to work in the morning. Translation: he planned to spend the night. With ice on my eye, I was in no position to argue. I just wanted to get through the damn meeting with Susan Davies and her associate. Presumably they needed to eyeball Abra in order to confirm that she was as awful as her reputation. I should have been mortified; their choice of her as the worst possible Afghan hound clearly condemned my skills as pet owner.

But I had an out. I'd come to accept that I didn't "own" Abra any more than I owned the wind. According to Four Legs Good (Fleggers)—the Ann Arbor-based animal rights advocacy founded by my veterinarian and my former nanny—all creatures were entitled to… some version of legal independence. To be honest, I couldn't quite follow their reasoning. If it got me off the hook when Abra broke the law, then I was on board. The Afghan hound was free to be her own "person." I just wished she could afford her own lawyer.

"Do you even know where Abra is?" Jeb asked once we were inside his shiny red Beamer, the first brand-new car he'd ever been able to afford.

"Uh, I saw her this morning."

"You don't have a clue, do you?"

"Nope."

And I doubted that I could locate her in time for the meeting with Susan Davies. Granted, I had in place a secure exercise area with an eight-foot-high fence and a doggie door that opened directly into my kitchen. I had also hired Deely Smarr, former Coast Guard Damage Control Specialist and nanny (hence "Coast Guard nanny") to train Abra. But those measures were less effective than they sounded.

Since my stepdaughter Avery had removed her charming infant twins and her charmless whining self from my home in July, I hadn't seen much of Deely. Funny how that worked: Avery no longer required the nanny's services once I stopped signing her checks. So Deely had to find a new full-time gig. She hired on as assistant to her veterinarian boyfriend and fellow Flegger, David Newquist. That left precious little time for her to drive out to my home in the country and work with my dog—I mean, the canine who lives with me.

I'd last seen Abra that morning when she scooted past me through the breezeway connecting my kitchen with my garage, and then bolted out the open door. A squirrel had caught her eye. She's a sight hound, after all.

I had neither the time nor the speed to chase her.

"In case you didn't know," I told Jeb, "Afghans can gallop up to thirty-five miles per hour, turn on a dime, and jump seven feet from a standing position."

"Impressive stats," he agreed.

"Damn straight."

I couldn't have competed with those numbers back when I captained my high school volleyball team. And that was sixteen long years ago.

I'd left the garage door open for Abra, hoping she'd return on her own. Her habit, however, was to find trouble before she found her way back home.

"She always shows up eventually," Jeb said.

"So far," I said.

There were times I wished she'd stayed gone even though she was my late husband's last misguided gift to me. When Abra stole precious jewels or a priceless painting, for example, some folks thought I'd trained her to do it. Please. I couldn't train her to come when I called.

By now Jeb and I were less than two miles from Vestige on a wide country road. He floored the accelerator, treating us both to a taste of fine German engineering.

"Hard to believe you owe this Beamer to Fleggers!"

I was referring to the phenomenal success of his recent *Animal Lullabies* CD, put out by Dr. David's group and then picked up by a major label. Deely had discovered by accident that Jeb's voice soothed the savage beast, a.k.a. Abra. Unlike his previous attempts at blues, Celtic, country, rock, and rockabilly, this CD did not land in remainder bins. This CD was a hit. Who knew there were so many affluent people with pets in need of musical solace?

As we approached my property, I removed the makeshift ice-pack from my right eye to fully enjoy the view. The late great Leo Mattimoe had launched me in real estate and the good life. I'd lost him far too soon. But he'd left me Vestige, a trace not only of the old farm that had once occupied this coastal promontory, but also of our love. Now the sun rode low over Lake Michigan, making the big water beyond my house glow like fire and sending spears of light through leaves turning yellow, orange, and red. It was late September, too deep in the year for water sports, but the perfect season for reveling in Nature's visual bounty.

"Is that Velcro?"

Jeb's question shattered my serenity. He could only be talking about the teacup-sized *shitzapoo*, technically *shih-poo*, that I'd recently returned to my neighbors after they'd tried to palm him off on me. Sure enough, a tiny black furball bounced across the lawn directly toward us. Yipping at top pitch and full volume.

Fortunately, a boy appeared behind the designer dog. The very boy to whom the dog now rightfully belonged.

"Hey, Chester!"

As I greeted my eight-year-old neighbor, Velcro circled my ankles in his customary frantic fashion. Now that he no longer lived with me, I could tolerate brief bouts of neediness. Velcro's, in addition to Chester's.

"What are you two doing here?" I said.

"We're locked out," Chester explained, and I knew he wasn't referring to my house. I had left the place wide open. For Abra's convenience.

"Your mom's … gone … again?"

He nodded. Then we all turned in the direction of an exuberant *woof.* Amber-gold Prince Harry the Pee Master loped across the lawn from the direction of the Lake. Prince Harry is Abra's illegitimate son and Chester's first dog. Suddenly I had three new roommates: one kid and two canines. Me, who tried to avoid all dogs and most children.

Chester's mother was Cassina, the single-named pop-harpist diva. She, her son, his father, and their ever-changing staff inhabited the Castle, a twenty-thousand-square-foot manor house just up the coast. Cassina toured frequently and imbibed more often than that. She was also on questionable terms with Chester's father, her on-again, off-again manager. As a result, Chester seldom enjoyed parental supervision. Rupert, his father, had hired MacArthur, known as "the cleaner," to look after loose ends at the Castle. I had also hired MacArthur to help me sell real estate. The man was versatile: a licensed Realtor *and* chauffeur *and* someone skilled at making sticky situations go away. Oddly, he was now living with my stepdaughter, or rather she and her kids were living with him, in his rooms at the Castle. Since MacArthur was a hunk, and Avery was a shrill screaming bitch, I could only assume she was blackmailing him.

"Avery and the twins are gone, too?" I asked Chester.

"Nobody answered the door. And I forgot my key. Again."

I suspected that Chester lost his key on purpose. No doubt he got lots more attention at my house than at the Castle. Besides, he adored Abra. He'd even had some success training her, using tips downloaded from the Dogs-Train-You-dot-com website. Now that I thought about it, having Chester around for a few days might be a good thing. If Abra came back. Assuming, also, that Chester could keep Velcro away from my ankles and prevent Prince Harry from peeing on my floors.

Honestly, though, I couldn't imagine a world in which having three dogs was better than having no dogs at all. I had just closed my eyes to recall the tranquility of life before hounds when a car horn rudely honked. Unfamiliar but expensive sounding. A foreign car, for sure.

"Hey, Susan!" Jeb called out.

I opened my eyes. The lashes on my right eye stuck together, but I could still make out my ex-husband's *other* number-one fan. Susan Davies had pulled her bright white Audi into my driveway. A whole hour early. With no Abra in sight.

THREE

As promised, Susan Davies wasn't alone. She'd brought along matronly Ramona Bowden, her *co-breeder*, a term I found faintly salacious. But Susan's opening remark canceled those speculations.

"Someone is trying to kill me."

Because she didn't scream it, I thought at first she was trying to be funny. Then I got my eyelashes unstuck and saw that her pallor was genuine. So were the bullet holes in her car.

Visibly shaken, Susan said, "Someone shot at us! About a mile up the road."

Her otherwise spotless Audi sported two black holes in the door near the left rear tire.

"I'm about to pass out from the shock," announced Ramona. And then she did, collapsing in my driveway like a deflated balloon. Finally I had met someone who fainted as easily as I did.

Jeb attended to Ramona. He was a gentleman that way. Since it was my driveway that she was lying on, I probably should have done something. In my defense, however, I was the one who usually fainted, so I didn't know how to respond when someone else did it. Jeb gently elevated her head, patted her wrist, and repeated her name until she came to. When she fluttered her cow eyes at him, I suspected Ramona of staging the faint. Uncharitable of me, I know, but she clearly craved attention, specifically of the male variety. As Jeb helped her sit up, she moaned and sighed, acting far weaker than a fifty-year-old woman of her plus-sized proportions should.

"Somebody, get me water," she gasped.

She had to say it twice before I realized that "Somebody" meant me. Ramona seemed to assume that I existed to serve. *Her*. Fortunately for both of us, Chester was faster and more motivated to please. He dashed into my house and quickly returned with a tall glass of tap water. Ramona asked Jeb to hold it to her lips so that she could sip it, slowly.

"I would have put ice in it," Chester said, "but Whiskey's ice-maker's broken, and she always forgets to put water in the trays."

"Yes, whiskey. A wee dram would be nice," Ramona panted.

Although Chester knew the meager contents of my kitchen better than I did, he generally deferred to me on the matter of my liquor cabinet. Out of politeness, rather than ignorance, I was sure. Given his parents' debauched lifestyle, he was probably well-versed in the types and effects of alcohol.

"Scotch or bourbon?" I asked Ramona.

"Johnny Walker Black would be nice," she sighed, never taking her eyes off Jeb.

Perhaps it wasn't Susan Davies who lusted after my ex, after all. I had barely had time to size up the builder's wife. This would have been the perfect moment to do so, while Jeb had his hands full of

Ramona. But it didn't seem right to dispatch an eight-year-old for a bottle of booze. So I had to go play barmaid.

A surprise awaited me on the sofa in my library-slash-bar: Abra the Afghan hound, fast asleep, missing all the human action. A day on the loose hadn't improved her hairstyle. Her tangled blonde tresses were now adorned with dried leaves and twigs.

"So *this* is the famous Abra!"

I jumped when I heard the voice behind me. Susan Davies had followed me inside and now beamed at the sleeping hound.

"More like the infamous Abra," I said. "Sorry about the state of her coat, but she got away from me today—"

"Why be sorry? This is what Ramona and I were hoping for. The dog is a complete and utter mess!"

As if to punctuate that pronouncement, the dog farted.

"Perfect," Susan murmured.

"Abra showed up about four o'clock," Chester announced, joining us in the library. "Whiskey, you forgot to put out food for her. Again."

"Wonderful!" Susan remarked happily.

"So I fed her," Chester told me. "I gave her fresh water, too."

"And who are you?" Susan inquired.

"I'm the neighbor. I come here a lot."

"I see. You have to let the dog in and feed her because Whiskey forgets to. This is almost too good to be true!"

If Susan got any more excited, I was afraid she'd have an orgasm in front of the kid. The color had returned to her patrician face. Her sleek chestnut hair and piercing blue eyes would make any man look twice. Then there was her body: trim but nicely curved. I imagined she was quite distracting in a tennis dress or golf shorts.

"Do you really think somebody's trying to kill you?" Chester asked Susan, sounding more like a reporter than a curious child.

"I'm sure someone shot at my car," she said evenly.

"Somebody doesn't like you," Chester observed.

Probably someone whose husband does like you, I thought. No question about it; Susan was a potential threat to most of the female population. Or could be if she liked to flirt.

"I'm a little nervous about going to the show this weekend," Susan admitted.

"What show?" I said.

"The one we've invited you and Abra to: the Midwest Afghan Hound Specialty. In Elkhart, Indiana."

"Elkhart?"

I wrinkled my nose. I had assumed the show would be in a real city. Like Chicago.

"Actually, it's just outside Elkhart. In Indiana Amish country," Susan said.

"Amish country?"

I sounded like a slow student. The kind who learns by repeating everything.

"Yes. It's being held at a convention hall in Nappanee."

"Nappanee?"

"That's what she said," Chester confirmed. "The Midwest Afghan Hound Specialty is in Nappanee, near Elkhart, in Indiana Amish country."

"Well, at least it's somewhere safe," I muttered, wondering how on earth I would kill time there. Shop for cheese?

"It's not safe at all," Chester said. "If somebody's out to get you, Amish country could be dangerous. Too many open spaces and very few cops."

I nodded, following his logic. "Plus all those Amish. They look alike, you know."

Susan and Chester frowned at me. Then Chester said to Susan, "I could recommend a bodyguard. If you're hiring."

"Oh no!" I said. "You're way too young for that kind of work."

"Not me," Chester said. "A professional. I was thinking of MacArthur."

"MacArthur? I thought he was a cleaner. And a driver and a Realtor."

"He is, but being a cleaner is mostly about being a bodyguard. That's his job when he's with Cassina and Rupert."

"Really?"

I was under the impression that MacArthur's main job was keeping Cassina sober.

"But MacArthur's not available," I said. "He works part-time for me."

Chester pulled a face. "Nobody's buying or selling real estate!"

He extracted a business card from the inside pocket of his school blazer and handed it to Susan.

"I happen to know that MacArthur is looking for work this weekend," he told her.

"You said he was gone," I protested. "You said nobody was at the Castle!"

"I said nobody answered the door. Cassina and Rupert are in Brazil for some R and R. They left their bodyguard at home."

"What about Avery and the twins? Where are they?"

"At a New Age 'Mommy and Me' retreat in Sedona," Chester replied. "MacArthur was probably taking a nap when I knocked. He gets bored when everybody leaves the Castle."

Before I could comment, three shots rang out in rapid succession. A woman, presumably Ramona, screamed theatrically.

What Susan, Chester, and I did next wasn't smart, but it was expedient. We dashed to the nearest window that faced my driveway and peered out. Sprawled on the pavement next to Susan's Audi lay a human heap. Jeb had flung himself on top of ample, prone Ramona, who appeared to be not only alive and unhurt but also capable of seizing the moment. Her bejeweled left hand gripped Jeb's firm ass.

Chester turned to Susan. "If you're going anywhere with that lady, or in that car, you'd better call MacArthur *now*."

"You can call the cleaner later," I told her. "First, we're phoning Jenx."

It was time, once again, to summon the Magnet Springs police force to my home. Fortunately, I had the chief on speed dial.

FOUR

To CALL IT THE Magnet Springs "police force" is an exaggeration. It's really the full-time chief and her trained canine, plus one part-time officer. The officer, Brady Swancott, is a nice enough, smart enough guy, but he's better suited to pursuing online degrees than felons. So I was glad when Chief Judy "Jenx" Jenkins answered her own phone.

"Whassup, Whiskey?"

I could hardly understand her.

"Are you eating?" I said.

"Yup. Dinner. It's that time of day. Somebody better be in serious trouble."

I assured her that somebody was and reported the gunshot incidents. Both of them. Jenx chewed thoughtfully.

"Nobody's hurt, right?"

"Right. Although there are bullet holes in a very nice white Audi. And a large, dramatic woman is lying in my driveway. She's attached herself to Jeb."

"Jeb can defend himself," Jenx said. "But we should probably do an incident report on the shootings. You think the shooter's on your property—or across the road?"

I hadn't thought about it. The question raised hairs on the back of my neck.

"Tell ya what I'm gonna do," Jenx said and burped. "Brady's out on rounds with Officer Roscoe. They checked in ten minutes ago from your side of the township. I'm gonna send 'em over to Vestige, siren off. Just in case the shooter's still around. Maybe we can catch him off guard. You know what you need to do, right?"

"Hire private security?"

"We'll talk about that later. For now, stay inside and keep away from the windows."

I took a giant step back from the large glass pane facing my driveway. Susan and Chester did the same. We were safer that way, but I hated to lose the view of Jeb and Ramona. Apparently either she or the car she had come in was the target of someone with a long-range rifle. And she desperately craved attention. My ex had never been fond of heavy women, or of females who required a lot of pampering. Hence his attraction to lean, mean, independent me. But for now he was stuck catering to zaftig, needy Ramona.

"Is Chester there?" Jenx inquired.

"As a matter of fact, he is."

"Let me talk to him."

"If it's about keeping him safe, I got it covered."

"This is police business, Whiskey. Chester is on active duty as a volunteer deputy. I want to update his instructions."

Since I was also a sworn-to-serve volunteer deputy, I asked for my instructions.

"You're on hiatus," Jenx said.

Like a professional, Chester excused himself to take the call in the next room. That left me alone with Susan, who seemed completely at ease with silence. I, on the other hand, had a lifelong compulsion to supply meaningless chatter. As Susan moved about my library, studying recumbent Abra from every angle, I considered several conversation starters. Unfortunately they all involved Jeb. Since I wasn't yet sure he was worth fighting for, I stifled my natural tendency to talk.

Susan stared at my still-snoozing canine. "How can she sleep through gunshots?"

"Practice," Chester offered, reentering the room. "We've all toughened up."

"Are you saying that *you*'ve been exposed to danger?"

Chester shrugged. "I've been kidnapped. I've fallen through the ice. I've worked undercover. If you hang around Whiskey, you take your chances."

"That's a fact," Jeb said from the library doorway. He looked none the worse for gunshots.

"Where the hell's Ramona?" I said. "Don't tell me you left her lying on her big fat—"

And then there was Ramona, leaning on Jeb.

"Whiskey," she whispered hoarsely.

"I am so sorry!" I said. "We haven't been properly introduced—"

"She means she wants whiskey," Jeb translated. "Did you forget her drink order?"

"Johnny Walker Black," Chester reminded me. To Ramona, he said, "Straight up or with a little water? Sorry, but Whiskey's fresh out of ice and mixes."

For the first time since her arrival, Ramona focused on someone other than my ex-husband. "Aren't you rather young to serve cocktails? Or are you one of those—oh, what's the accepted term?—'little people'?"

"I'm eight," Chester said. "But I have a lot of experience."

"He's in charge of Whiskey's dog whenever Whiskey neglects her," Susan piped up.

"I don't neglect Abra," I said. "I just... forget about her."

"Nurturing doesn't come naturally for Whiskey," Chester explained.

"That's not true," I protested. Although of course it was. "I took in my former stepdaughter and her twins, didn't I?"

Chester nodded. "But you hired Deely to take care of them. And you've hired Deely and me to take care of Abra."

Before I could object—and, really, how could I object?—Jeb said, "You do all right taking care of me. Most of the time."

He winked. I buried my face inside the liquor cabinet, where I searched high and low for Ramona's scotch. Most of what was in there I had inherited from Leo. Only when tempted by a man did I drink anything stronger than wine.

"It's the third bottle on the left, top shelf," Chester said helpfully.

So it was. He handed me a rock glass, and I poured a finger of the amber liquid into it.

"Better give her more than that," Chester whispered.

I doubled the dose. Ramona didn't respond when I asked if she'd like water, so I served the drink neat. She failed to thank me. Or even look at me.

That was when I recognized the behavior pattern: Ramona was determined to ignore me. Despite being at my house, leaning on my ex-husband, drinking my scotch, and evaluating my bad dog, she didn't think I mattered. I'm six feet tall, so ignoring me takes effort.

A series of strident yaps pierced the air. Before any of us could cover our ears, Velcro streaked into the room, followed by Prince Harry the Pee Master. Abra opened one eye, then closed it and pretended to go back to sleep. I wished I could do the same.

"What on earth?" asked Ramona. Her subtly highlighted blonde head followed the canine action as it circled the library.

"Are those your dogs, too, Whiskey?" Susan sounded so hopeful that I hated to disappoint her.

"Well, they were, for a while. But now they're Chester's."

"*Designer* dogs!" Ramona hissed the term as if it were the equivalent of "rabid."

"Well, one was by design," I said, referring to Velcro. "The other was a complete accident."

"A shih-poo and a Golden-Af, am I right?" asked Susan.

I nodded. "Although I call them the shitzapoo and the bastard."

"Appalling," Ramona said. "The trend toward designer crossbreeds dilutes the value of our purebreds and diminishes our breeding program."

"But here it's a good thing," Jeb said.

Everyone stared at him.

"It builds your 'how not to' case against Whiskey. For the dog show."

"So true!" Susan exclaimed. "She doesn't properly groom, train, or feed the dog. And she breeds indiscriminately."

In fact, Leo had tried to breed Abra with an Afghan hound champion in Chicago. But Abra didn't like *him*. Before Leo could find another stud for her, my dear husband died, and Abra eloped with Norman, the first good-looking Golden she saw. Prince Harry was the result.

Too tired to explain all that, I merely said, "I never intended to breed."

"And yet you did," said Susan.

"Abra's spayed. Now," I said.

"The woman is irresponsible!" Ramona declared as she sipped my top-shelf whiskey. Susan nodded her agreement.

I said, "I thought this was about 'Bad Abra.'"

"There's no such thing as a bad dog," Susan said. "Only a bad owner."

"As I've always said," Ramona intoned, "this is not a breed for those with low self-esteem. See what happens when an Afghan hound lives with a loser."

"Hey!" I cried.

Jeb stopped me before I could demonstrate what remained of the speed and strength I'd honed playing high school volleyball.

This gal still knows how to spike.

FIVE

It's not that Jeb was reluctant to defend my honor. It's just that I had a quick temper and generally took the shortest route to defending it myself. This time, though, the doorbell rang before either Jeb or I could respond to snooty Ramona.

The Magnet Springs police had arrived. Canine officer Roscoe, as dignified a German shepherd as you'll ever see, stood at attention next to human officer Brady Swancott. The human held a notebook.

"Come on in," I said. "Susan Davies can answer your questions. And her *co-breeder* can tell you about my low self-esteem."

"I don't need anyone to tell me about that," Brady said.

"Another dog!" Susan beamed when the cops entered the library. "This one appears to be in excellent condition."

"Beautifully bred," Ramona purred.

"Roscoe comes from a long line of police dogs," Brady said. "He was bred for athleticism, intelligence, and obedience."

Abra leapt down from the couch. In front of Roscoe she moaned and stretched provocatively. He kept his eyes fixed on the far wall. Undeterred, she salaciously sniffed his butt.

"She's trying to seduce him!" Ramona remarked, her voice dripping with distaste.

"She does that to most males," Chester piped up. He was seated in my leather club chair, cuddling both Velcro and Prince Harry. "Norman is her mate, but when he's not around—"

"Brady," I cut in, "why don't the rest of us leave so that you can interview Susan and Ramona? In private?"

"Stay, Whiskey," he said. "You need to know what's going on. The shooter fired those last three shots from your property." Brady pointed out the window toward the woods near my driveway. "I found shell casings along the treeline."

When Ramona gasped, I told him, "Get ready. She likes to faint."

"So do you."

"I don't do it on purpose."

Jeb asked Brady, "Did you find any other evidence?"

Brady frowned, making himself look older than his twenty-six years. "Roscoe couldn't follow a scent."

"What do you mean?" Jeb said.

"Roscoe did what he does when he gets confused. He ran around in circles like there was no trail at all."

"How can that be?" Susan interjected. "Every human leaves a scent."

"That's usually true," Brady said.

"When is it not true?" demanded Ramona.

"Well, I heard about a case once where a killer confused police dogs by spraying himself and the whole area with deer urine. Wait. Or was it rabbit blood? Or maybe dog saliva?"

"You don't know?" Ramona asked.

"I don't pay much attention. I only work here part-time."

"Brady studies art history online," I explained. "And takes care of two kids at home. His wife just had a baby."

On cue, Brady whipped out a wallet-sized photo. After we admired the human blob that was his newborn daughter, he said, "I also freelance for Peg Goh at Generation Tattoo. I do about half the tats in Magnet Springs."

A reduced demand for gourmet coffee and fancy sandwiches had motivated our mayor to open a tattoo parlor behind her restaurant. The gimmick? Designer tats for out-of-towners, although so far all of Peg's clients had been local.

Susan cleared her throat, reminding us why Brady was in my living room.

"Somebody shot at Ramona and me," she said. "First, when we were a few miles up the road, and then again when we got here. Do you think it's the same person?"

"Let's hope so," Brady says. "Or else you have a lot of enemies."

"What I mean is, do you think it's possible for one person to move that fast?"

"You did. Presumably the shooter was traveling in a car, like you were."

Brady proceeded to interview Susan and Ramona while the rest of us listened. Susan offered prompt responses until Brady broached the topic of personal enemies. That one seemed to stump her.

"Come on," I said impatiently. "We can always tell when people don't like us."

"A lot of people don't like Whiskey," Chester said. "But she means well."

"Everyone loves Susan," Ramona gushed. "How could they not?"

I believed that every *man* could love Susan, or at least lust after her. The pretty Junior Leaguer looked like a marriage-buster to me.

If so, her enemy would be female. Yet I couldn't imagine a wronged wife using a long-range rifle. Poisoning Susan's coffee at the country club? Stabbing her to death in a moment of madness? Oh sure. But stalking her along a country road through a rifle's telescopic sight? Uh-uh.

Then there was Brady's theory about sprinkling animal fluids to cover one's tracks. No woman would do that. At least no woman whose husband I'd contemplate stealing.

"I hate to speak ill of a fellow breeder," said Ramona. "But I will if Susan won't. There's a certain member of the Afghan hound community who's very hostile toward her."

"About what?" Brady prompted, pencil poised above his pocket-sized spiral notebook.

Susan sighed. "We had a disagreement concerning stud service."

"Stud service?"

"For my bitch. The breeder required a stud fee up front as opposed to the pick of the litter later," Susan explained. "His terms guaranteed a pregnancy, or the next semen would be free."

"Something went wrong?"

"My bitch never got pregnant. And the breeder never made it right."

"You mean ... there was no further semen?" Brady said.

"Yes. And I never got my money back."

Brady used the eraser end of his pencil to scratch his forehead. "Then you were the wronged party. Right? Why should the guy with the stud be hostile toward you?"

Susan and Ramona exchanged knowing glances.

Thoughtfully Susan moistened her lips. "While mounting my bitch, his stud had a stroke. Poor Maximus died two days later."

"Your dog killed another dog *with sex*?" I blurted. "That sounds like something Abra would do!"

My canine roommate had cuddled up to Officer Roscoe, her tousled blonde head resting coquettishly on his left front paw as her right front paw stroked his inner thigh. Roscoe quivered slightly but remained focused on the investigation—and the far wall.

"Let me get this straight," Brady said to Susan. "Are you saying the other breeder held you responsible for killing his dog?"

"Not legally, no. But ethically and emotionally, yes, I'm afraid so. That was four years ago. Mitchell Slater still hates me."

"And she didn't get her money back," Ramona reminded Brady. "Although pregnancy was guaranteed. Or the next semen was free."

Brady frowned. "But the dog died. How could there be more semen?"

"Mitchell had a freezerful!" Ramona said. "I think he's still selling it. Susan should have pursued legal action, or at least a National Afghan Hound Association sanction, but she's too kind."

I tried not to imagine how one ended up with a freezer full of dog semen.

Writing in his notebook, Brady said, "How do you know Slater hates you, Mrs. Davies?"

"Why, by the way he behaves at events," Ramona replied. Apparently, she had appointed herself Susan's official spokesperson. "He gossips about her dogs and shuns her when they meet in public. The man is cruel. And very petty."

She added, "Susan is too modest and forgiving to tell you this, so I will: she paid a *five-thousand-dollar* stud fee up front. You see, Maximus was an international champion. His puppies would have been worth every penny. The outcome was worse than you know. Not only did Susan fail to get puppies from the deal, but her beloved Saloma was permanently traumatized! After Maximus convulsed, the poor bitch went into shock. She has never been mounted since."

I fought the urge to fly across the room and clap both hands over Chester's ears. Fortunately Jeb handled the crisis.

"Hey, Chester, how about coming with me to the kitchen?" he said. "We'll put on a pot of something."

"Sure," Chester said. "But this is Whiskey's house, so it'll have to be something instant."

"She can't cook, either?" Susan sounded happy again.

"Whiskey doesn't even go to the grocery store," Chester said. "Unless I remind her."

Ramona clicked her tongue in clear disapproval.

SIX

SUSAN AND RAMONA DIDN'T hang around long enough for me to demonstrate any additional infirmities. Ramona snapped photos of Abra while Susan wrote out directions to the exhibit hall in Nappanee. They departed in the bullet-marred Audi after Ramona had said good-bye to everyone but me. Brady planned to follow them to the scene of the first shooting as soon as he checked with his boss.

"Is Jenx going to involve the sheriff's department?" I asked him.

Everyone in Magnet Springs knew that Jenx resented the way county and state law enforcement sniggered at her department. Still, she called them in whenever a case required more police power than she could muster locally.

"Both shootings occurred within our jurisdiction," Brady said. "We'll reserve the right to call for back-up 'til after I surveil the first scene."

"Maybe this time Roscoe will pick up a scent," I said.

"I doubt it. Looks to me like we got a shooter with a careful plan. Or a baffling body odor."

He whistled for Officer Roscoe to accompany him. I thought I saw a flash of regret in Roscoe's brown eyes as he stepped stiffly away from Abra's illicit touch.

"Your dog gets to his dog the same way you get to me," Jeb whispered in my ear.

We were in the foyer, Jeb's lean body pressed against my back, his arms locked around my waist. I hushed him and scanned for Chester.

"He's in the kitchen with the dogs," Jeb whispered. "I don't know how he did it, but he found the ingredients to make mac 'n' cheese."

"Incredible," I murmured, more in response to Jeb's ear-nuzzling than to Chester's cooking, although how anyone could create a meal in my under-stocked kitchen was a miracle.

"Sorry to interrupt." Chester's high-pitched voice stopped us en route to the boudoir.

"You're not interrupting us, buddy," Jeb said, stepping back from my body as if sprung.

"I was just wondering how many there will be for dinner this evening. Not counting the dogs."

Jeb said he was hungry, and I admitted I was, too. As usual, I couldn't remember eating much of anything for lunch, and I always skipped breakfast. Moments later, we were treated to a version of mac 'n' cheese worthy of the term "delicacy." Chester had opened a drawer in my fridge that I'd forgotten existed; in it he'd found a couple gift packages of brie and gouda from some Christmas past. A search of my pantry had yielded evaporated milk and whole-grain pasta, surely purchased by Deely. Chester knew just what to do to make culinary magic.

"You should be a chef someday," I remarked, giving in to the urge to lick the last smears of rich cheese from the serving spoon.

"I'd rather cook for friends and pursue a different profession," Chester said.

"Such as what?" asked Jeb.

"I'm considering a career in canine legal defense."

I nearly choked. "Is there such a field?"

Chester nodded vigorously, the glow from my overhead light fixture bouncing off his wire-framed glasses.

"Lucky for you, there is. You might need it if Abra gets in trouble again."

"Don't you mean *when* Abra gets in trouble again?" Jeb said.

"Abra's a repeat offender," Chester agreed. "The nearest canine defense attorney is in Chicago. Fortunately, he's licensed in four states. Including Michigan."

If Abra's past antics predicted her future, one of these days her luck with the courts would run out. So far, every judgment had come down mostly in the dog's favor—and hence my own. But if she ever got into deep legal doo-doo, I intended to take the Fleggers position that my dog was her own person, and she needed her own attorney. Although I'd probably have to foot the damned bill, at least I could separate myself and my business from her canine crimes.

"There are feline defense attorneys, too," Chester said.

Jeb grinned. "I can't picture a cat needing a lawyer."

"That's because you've never met a Devon rex," Chester said.

I agreed, recalling the demon feline named Yoda who had terrorized Vestige six months earlier while Jeb was on tour. That cat had been caught in Fleggers' wide-scale neutering net and then sent—through a bureaucratic snafu—to a holding center at *my* house. The big-eared, curly-haired creature had seemed to fly.

"Whatever happened to Yoda?" I asked Chester.

"Faye Raffle adopted him."

Chester was referring to my former office intern, the most promising future sales agent I'd ever met. Faye had decided to go off to college now and pursue a real estate career later. With the economy the way it was, who could blame her?

"It's good to know Yoda's gone from Magnet Springs," I sighed.

"I doubt Faye took him with her when she went away to school," Chester said. "Yoda's probably here with her parents."

I reminded him that Faye's parents were newspaper correspondents who traveled at least half the time. They were hardly the type to adopt a cat, let alone one as demanding as Yoda.

Chester said, "I'll send out a few inquiries."

"Please don't," I said. "If that cat is still in town, I'd rather not know about it."

After dinner, Jeb and I offered to load the dishwasher. Chester had already done more than his share of domestic duties, especially since he was the guest. Then he reminded me why he was here: he had lost his key and nobody answered the door at his house. That sounded like a fair excuse for him to spend the night. And for Jeb to go home. As excited as I had been by Jeb's ear nibbles an hour earlier, I knew I should sleep alone. I desperately needed some perspective on our relationship. If we never spent time apart, how could I tell whether we were good together?

At around 7:30 Brady phoned to report that he'd found nothing in the vicinity of the first shooting. Not even shell casings.

"I couldn't tell where the shooter was standing," he admitted. "The target was a moving car, and I don't know how to calculate that stuff."

"I thought Jenx sent you to a seminar on bullet trajectory," I said.

"That was the plan," Brady said, "then my son got the mumps, and I had to stay home."

"Can't Jenx figure bullet trajectories?"

"Nope. She got a D in trig. She said you did, too."

"True. But I became a Realtor. To do my job, all I need is a pocket calculator."

I suggested that it was time to call in the county sheriff, whether Jenx wanted to or not. Brady disagreed.

"All Susan needs for her insurance claim is a police report, and I provided that. Unless something else happens, we're putting this one to bed."

Speaking of bed, Jeb reluctantly went home around nine, promising to dream about me all night long. And to drive me to work in the morning.

Chester would sleep in the guest room with Prince Harry and Velcro. Knowing their "issues," I insisted that he take the dogs out *twice* before bedtime. Then he fetched a step-stool from my garage to place next to the bed. Prince Harry needed no assistance; however, the stool solved Velcro's separation anxiety and protected his fragile joints from the necessity to jump.

Abra may have been a recidivist felon, but she was far easier on the nerves than that teacup dog. I didn't even mind giving her a bedroom all her own. If I wasn't going to sleep with a man, I certainly didn't want to share my sheets with a big shaggy dog.

The dark house was profoundly silent, save the squeaks from my mattress as I tossed and turned. For the first time in months, I found myself battling insomnia. And losing. The more I rearranged myself in my king-sized bed, the more I realized that I missed having Jeb in it. Was this proof that I needed him in my life? Should we live together full-time?

I finally surrendered my determination not to check my bedside clock and gazed in horror at the blue digits screaming 3:44. Had I slept at all? Maybe warm milk would help. If I had any. In a few hours I was due at work, where nothing much would be happening. Then Abra the Bad Example and I were off for a full weekend of Afghans and Amish.

While nuking a mug of the evaporated milk left over from Chester's gourmet mac 'n' cheese, I felt a presence behind me. Whirling around—which is easy in cotton socks on a tile floor—I confronted Chester, wrapped in the hugely oversized white bathrobe I kept in the guest room.

"Why aren't you in bed?" I demanded. And then I remembered what really mattered. "Where's Velcro?"

I simultaneously scanned the floor for stray poop and steeled my nerves for a strident chorus of yips.

Chester silenced me with a finger to his lips. "Velcro's sound asleep, which isn't easy when you're up banging around."

"You're up, too," I whispered back.

"Yes, but I know how to move with stealth." He flourished a sheaf of computer printouts. "I had a dream about the dog show you're going to. So I checked it out online."

"A dream? Please don't tell me you're psychic," I said. "This town doesn't need one more person with telepathy."

"Not a psychic dream. A regular dream. Then I woke up and Googled Mitchell Slater."

"Who?"

By now I was sitting at the kitchen table, slurping my hot evaporated milk. It tasted smooth enough to knock me right out.

Chester said, "The breeder whose stud had a stroke while mounting Susan's bitch!"

That snapped me wide awake. "What about him?"

"He might be the shooter, and he's coming to Amish country."

Chester pulled out a chair, sat down across from me, and spread his pages on the table so that I could read them. They outlined the schedule of events at the Midwest Afghan Hound Specialty. Using a highlighter, Chester had marked Mitchell Slater's name wherever it appeared. Apparently the man headed several committees.

"He'll be in Nappanee, Whiskey."

"So?"

To make his point without shouting, Chester stood on his chair. "Slater might be the shooter! If he is, Susan could wind up dead!"

"His stud died four years ago," I said. "If he'd wanted to kill Susan, I think he would have done it by now. We have no proof he's the one who fired those shots!"

"If he's not the shooter, then Susan has a bigger problem," Chester said darkly. "An enemy she doesn't know."

"Or won't admit she knows," I said.

"She needs a bodyguard," Chester declared, "and so do you if you plan to be near her."

"I'll be with Abra. She scares the crap out of people."

"Only people who don't know Afghan hounds," Chester said.

I understood his point. People who didn't know the breed didn't know how to handle Abra's speed and springiness. She had disarmed more than one would-be assailant. But we were headed for an event where people knew all about Afghan hounds.

"If Susan doesn't hire MacArthur this weekend, then you should," Chester said.

"He's your driver," I said. "Isn't he supposed to drive you places?"

"This weekend I can ride my bike. Besides, Velcro and Prince Harry need a workout."

SEVEN

I CHALLENGE ANYONE TO have a four a.m. conversation about shooters and bodyguards and then fall asleep. By the time Chester and I headed back to our respective bedrooms, I'd sacrificed whatever soporific benefits were possible from a cup of hot evaporated milk.

I must have dozed off at some point, though, because I woke to the sun slanting through my blinds and Jeb insistently tooting the horn on his new BMW. I don't care how classy the car is; a horn is a horn is a horn when it interrupts your beauty sleep. I threw on my robe, stumbled down the stairs, flung open the front door and shouted at him to hang on a freaking minute while I got myself together. He took that as an invitation to come in for coffee. Go figure.

I jumped in and out of the shower, ran a rubber brush through my recalcitrant curls, yanked on a couple deliberately understated beige separates, and dashed downstairs. Chester, clad in a starched white chef's apron, was serving Jeb breakfast. A hot breakfast.

"Where did you find the ingredients to make waffles?" I asked. "Not to mention that apron. And isn't today a school day?"

I cared about the kid's education. But I cared more about the fact that there were hot waffles in my kitchen. They smelled like honey and malt.

"I called MacArthur, and he delivered what I needed from the Castle," Chester replied. He removed a perfect golden waffle from a gleaming griddle that hadn't come from my kitchen. "As for school, this is an in-service day, teachers only. That means I'm free till Monday to be Jeb's personal chef."

Jeb licked his chops. The diminutive chef indicated my place at the table.

"You'll be in Amish country with Abra," he said. "So I'll hang with Jeb. I'm going to try out a couple new entrées—including Steak Chester, a variation on Steak Diane."

"If you're good, Whiskey," Jeb said, "maybe Chester will give you the recipe."

That sent Chester into a spasm of laughter. Presumably because he'd never seen me so much as turn on my stove. He topped my waffle with imported Swedish syrup made from lingonberries, which I had never heard of.

"Where did you learn to cook like this?" I said.

"Cassina keeps hiring and firing chefs," he said. "I learn what I can from each of them."

After a second lighter-than-air waffle—and a third cup of Peruvian organic coffee, hand-ground by Chester—I reluctantly let Jeb drive me to work. What for, I had no idea. I walked in the door of Mattimoe Realty, buzzed and stuffed from my unexpected breakfast, to find the phones silent and my office manager sobbing.

While that wasn't typical Friday morning behavior, it wasn't unheard of, either. Tina Breen was quite possibly the most emotional person on the planet. I stared at her leaking bloodshot eyes, her runny nose, and her desk covered with sticky, balled-up tissues. Before I could ask what had set her off, she bawled, "My life's a bigger disaster than your business!"

Although I thought that unlikely, the possibility gave me hope. Whenever I'm discouraged, I like to recall one of my mother's favorite sayings: "There's always somebody worse off than you are." This morning that somebody seemed to be Tina.

So I pulled up a chair and sat facing her in the lobby. We used to have a receptionist on duty out here, but I'd laid her off months ago. Assigning the depressed and volatile office manager to double as greeter may not have been my brightest move. But we rarely had walk-in business.

I offered my best impression of a patient person. "What's wrong, Tina?"

"Ask me what hasn't gone wrong! That would be simpler!"

She snuffled loudly and wiped her red nose on the already streaked cuff of her wrinkled blouse. Tina must have run out of tissues some time ago. I fished in my purse for a fresh supply.

"Tim has been unemployed for *five months*!" she wailed. "And Winston and Neville were diagnosed with ADHD. Do you know what it's like to have toddlers with ADHD?"

"Well, no," I answered honestly. "Unless it's like having Abra…"

"My husband is out of work, my kids are driving me out of my mind, and your business is going down the tubes!"

I tried to remember how shrinks on TV do it. "Let's forget about my business for a minute and focus on *you*."

"But your business is my biggest problem! If you go under, we'll have no income! We'll lose our home and our health insurance and our car! What would we do?"

What would *I* do if my business went under? As adept at sustaining denial as I was at brokering real estate, I hadn't yet let myself face that hard question. And I didn't feel like dealing with it this morning.

I handed over to Tina all the linty tissues that had gathered at the bottom of my purse and hoped most of them were clean. Forcing a smile, I said, "Tell you what. Why don't you take the rest of the day off? Go home and play with your boys. I can handle things here."

Tina reacted as if I'd slapped her.

"Oh no you don't! You're trying to prove you can get along without me, aren't you? The next thing you know, you'll let me goooooohhhhh!"

Her passionate protest dissolved into a series of choked sobs. I waited for her to catch her breath and use half the tissues I'd provided. Finally, between ragged hiccups, she whispered, "I'd rather be here than home, anyway. The boys make me nervous, and Tim gets me so depressed. This is the happiest place I know."

Now that was tragic.

I returned the lobby chair to its original position, just in case anybody happened to come in and needed to wait for an agent. Then, for old times' sake, I asked Tina if I had any messages. To my astonishment, I did. She handed me a pink note stained with tears and something sticky. On it she had scrawled: Call Jenx!!!! Not exactly the message of my dreams, but proof that our phones could still ring. I retreated to my office, closed the door, and collapsed into my big leather swivel chair. For the hell of it—and to kill some time—I spun around and around. Till I remembered the rich waffles. Then I waited for the nausea to subside and dialed our chief of police.

"Yo, Whiskey," Jenx said, apparently recognizing my number on her caller ID. "More shootings at your place?"

"I would have called if there were," I said.

When she pointed out that I was calling, I pointed out that she had called me first.

I pictured Jenx's compact frame settled in her own desk chair, non-regulation steel-toe boots propped on her desk between canyons of manila folders. Jenx didn't file reports; she stacked them as high as the laws of physics allowed.

"I assume Brady told you he couldn't find squat at the scene of the first shooting," she said.

"He did. Maybe you should call the sheriff and ask for a crime scene investigation unit."

"Maybe you should mind your own business."

I told her I would if I had any. That must have been her cue to give me some.

"As of today, your hiatus from volunteer deputy duties is over," she announced. "I need your help with this case."

Volunteer deputies—a misnomer, really, since every one of us was drafted—made up the criminal investigation teams in our town. Chester was the best Jenx had. True, he was too young to drive, but he had a full-time driver. He also had Prince Harry, who showed potential for retrieving clues. I, on the other hand, could drive, but my dog was a liability. Usually she was in league with the crooks we were chasing.

"You need my help?" I echoed. "I flunked senior physics, and I barely passed trig. We copied each other's homework, remember? No way I can figure out where those shots were fired from."

"I'm talking about keeping an eye on Susan Davies and her friend," Jenx said. "At the dog show."

"That's in Indiana," I said. "A little outside your jurisdiction."

"Since when does that stop us? You know you love to snoop."

She had a point. That was part of my attraction to real estate: having a license to get inside other people's homes. But this was a dog show. In Amish country. Chester had said it could be dangerous; I was more worried it would be deadly dull. Having a job to do might give me a sense of purpose and also help pass the time. My eyes tended to glaze over when confronted with quilts and oak furniture.

"Do you think Susan should hire a bodyguard?" I asked Jenx.

"Is Abra going to be there?"

"She's the reason I'm going."

"Then, yes, Susan needs a bodyguard."

"I meant because of the shootings!"

"If Susan can afford a bodyguard, she should hire one," Jenx said.

"Of course she can afford a bodyguard. She's married to Liam Davies."

Jenx didn't respond.

"Hello?" I said.

"I hear Liam Davies is cash-strapped." Jenx lowered her voice. "His development business is over-leveraged, and he's amassed a lot of personal debt. Susan's spending sprees haven't helped the family finances."

Headline news to me. Suddenly I wondered if Big and Little Houses on the Prairie were a pipedream.

"The Davies' financial problems are just rumors," the chief added. "So are their marital problems. But in my line of work I pay attention to gossip."

So did I. Every successful Realtor keeps an ear to the ground.

Jenx continued, "Got any idea how many Afghan hounds Susan owns?"

"Too many."

"Eight, according to my sources. And she shares six more with her co-breeder. That's a lot of dog shit."

I agreed. "Susan needs MacArthur. He's a cleaner as well as a bodyguard."

EIGHT

I ASKED JENX HOW she'd found out so much about Susan and Liam Davies.

"I'm in law enforcement," she said. "Therefore I investigate."

"How come you need Chester and me to work for free?"

"I like to delegate."

The more I pondered my trip to the Afghan hound show in Amish country, the more I dreaded it. I despised anything that came under the heading of crafts, and I did my darnedest to avoid most dogs. But given what Jenx had said about Davies' development business being maxed out, it would probably be in Mattimoe Realty's best interest for me to learn all I could about Liam and Susan.

As soon as I hung up from Jenx, I speed-dialed Odette. Since she was representing us as Realtor of record for Davies' newest project, I wanted to keep her in the loop.

"What is it, Whiskey?" Odette snapped. "I'm with a client."

"A client?" It had been too long since I'd heard that phrase.

"I'm showing a home in Pasco Point," she said. "Can this wait?"

Of course it could. Pasco Point was arguably the best four-digit zip-code suffix in Magnet Springs. Perched high on a bluff overlooking Lake Michigan, the subdivision boasted a baker's dozen multi-million-dollar estates, each with its own ostentatious name. Until Davies developed Big House on the Prairie, assuming that he eventually would, Pasco Point was where our big commissions came from.

Odette said she'd call me right back. I told her to take as much time as she needed.

Tina's dentist-drill voice immediately announced there was a call on line one. If my phone rang at all lately, it was either a wrong number or the police. I answered cautiously.

"Top o' the morning to you, Miss Whiskey! This is MacArthur."

I wondered why Tina hadn't said so. He was one of our part-time agents. The one who sounded like Sean Connery, without the lisp. To my embarrassment, I felt a small thrill at the sound of the cleaner's baritone brogue.

"Chester and I were just talking about you," I said, omitting the fact that the chief of police and I had just talked about him, too.

"Could we meet for lunch in half an hour?" MacArthur asked.

"Well ..." When I hesitated, it wasn't because my schedule was full. My stomach was. Painfully so. It felt like Chester's waffles had expanded in there.

"My treat," the cleaner added.

Nice of him to buy, especially since he had taken my disagreeable stepdaughter off my hands. In the grand scheme of things, I was sure I owed him. We agreed to meet at the counter at the Goh Cup, the coffee and sandwich shop run by Magnet Springs' mayor.

It wouldn't matter if I couldn't eat a bite; MacArthur was the kind of eye candy no woman passed up.

I buzzed Tina to ask if she had any antacids on hand. When she didn't answer, I wandered out to the lobby. No one was in sight. Depressing indeed. This should have been a busy week at Mattimoe Realty. Historically, Leo and I had made almost twenty percent of our annual sales in September. So far this month, Odette had closed three sales. Nobody else had produced squat.

Since Tina's purse was still tucked neatly under her desk, I assumed she had taken a bathroom break. I was about to return to my office when her computer pinged, signaling an incoming email message. In the vain hope that it might be a real estate inquiry, I took a peek. Alas, it was spam. The new message, from someone calling himself Rod Wunderly (oh sure!), featured this subject line: *Thrill her with your amazing manstick.* I groaned. That was the kind of email opened by only the most gullible and insecure of men.

I was about to delete it when I remembered that this was Tina's work station, not mine. Given how slow business was, taking the time to delete it would at least offer her something to do. I glanced at her inbox. To my amazement, Tina had received, read, and *not* deleted more than a dozen recent spam emails, all of which seemed, ironically, to be about enlarging an organ she didn't possess. Even if Tina was bored enough to glance at spam, I couldn't believe she'd read, let alone save, these. Tina Breen was the most prudish person I knew.

The toilet flushed, and I jumped back from her computer as if it had bitten me.

"Looking for something?" Tina asked, a little sharply, I thought.

"Actually, I was looking for you. Do you have anything for indigestion?"

Without answering, she opened her top right desk drawer, scooped out the contents, and lined them up as if for a TV infomercial. I counted six OTC brands and several prescriptions.

"Take what you need," she said. "Since I developed my ulcer, I've tried every stomach medicine known to man."

"All I want is a Rolaid. Or something." I eyed the assortment. "Which one works best?"

Tina burst into tears again. "For me, nothing works! I'm in constant misery! My doctor says it's because of the stress!"

My own stomach now hurt much worse than it had a minute earlier.

"Please, please don't fire me, Whiskey!" Tina cried, pitching herself onto her knees. "And please don't let your business go to pot!"

"To ... pot?"

"Down the drain. Kaput. Pfft."

"Okay, I won't. Please, Tina, get up off your knees. There's no reason to panic as long as Odette still works here."

"You're right." Tina wiped her face on her sleeve. Then she grabbed the edge of her desk, grunted, and pulled herself up. Suddenly she shrieked in pain.

"Now what is it?" I said.

"My back! Ohhhh. Spinal stenosis, the doctor says. Ever since your business started falling apart, I've been falling apart, too."

"I've had better days myself," I murmured, gently guiding Tina into her desk chair. "Can I get you something? Water, maybe? To replace all the fluids you've lost?"

"Just let me keep my job!"

I nodded. "My late husband built this company, Tina. No way it's going under on my watch. At least not if Odette can help it."

At that very convenient moment, Odette called back. Since I didn't want Tina to hear my concerns about Liam Davies, I raced to my office and closed the door.

"I may have found a buyer for our listing in Pasco Point," Odette began.

"Someone with solid financing?" I asked.

"Someone with cash! The rich are still rich, Whiskey. You just have to know how to find them. Fortunately, I do."

"And I'm overwhelmed with gratitude," I said. Then I told her what Jenx had told me about Liam Davies.

Odette made her dismissive raspberry sound.

"I take it you know something Jenx doesn't?" I asked.

"Can crows fly?! What did I just say about the rich? They stay that way, even when they blow their money. That's the difference between us and them: they can always get more. Don't worry about Davies' development, Whiskey. It's going to happen. Ask me how I know."

"Okay… How do you know?"

"I'm the agent of record, am I not? I *sell* real estate, I don't just list it!"

"Of course you do! And your broker appreciates that."

My office door creaked. Tina hovered in the hallway, peering inside. Apparently the door hadn't latched. Either that or she had opened it partway. I had no idea how much she'd overheard, but I knew I didn't want to explain any of it. Thinking fast, I called out, "Tina, I'm glad you're there! Come in, please."

She did.

"When MacArthur called earlier, you didn't give me his name. You just put the call through. May I ask why?"

Tina clutched her back as if mere mention of the handsome Scot gave her a spasm. And not the good kind.

"You didn't ask who it was," she whined.

"You always tell me," I countered.

Perspiration glistened on Tina's frowning forehead.

"I never know what to say when he calls. I mean, I know he works here part-time, but... is he a good guy, or is he a... *cleaner*?" She lowered her voice. "You don't know this about me, Whiskey, but before I was married, I used to read true-crime novels. I know what a cleaner does!"

"MacArthur is a bodyguard. And a driver," I said.

Tina shook her head and limped back to the lobby. My stomach was killing me. Although Chester's waffles may have started my indigestion, I blamed my office manager for most of the discomfort I felt now. Her melodrama had kicked my gastric juices into overdrive. I slipped out the back way.

Crossing the street to the Goh Cup, I dialed Jeb.

"Do you have indigestion, too?"

"I feel great," he said.

"How many waffles did you eat?" I said.

"Three. Same as you."

"I had two," I informed him. "Then I had a Tina Breen chaser."

I hung up before I belched. Arriving at the Goh Cup, I felt no better. My plan was to sip a soda while I listened to whatever it was MacArthur wanted to discuss. For one delicious moment I let myself imagine him begging me to get Avery out of his life. Maybe he'd even go down on his knees, as Tina had, to implore my assistance. I would resist the urge to tell him I had known from the start that Avery would only bring him trouble.

Then reality set in. What if MacArthur really was about to dump Avery? While I would welcome the twins back at Vestige, provided I could convince Deely to be their nanny again, I sure as hell wouldn't want Avery as my roommate. She and I got along about as well as ... well, we didn't get along at all. In fact, we'd once tried to scratch each other's eyes out. So handsome MacArthur dumping bitchy Avery could only complicate my life. And my tummy felt awful enough already.

I couldn't have predicted what was about to happen at the Goh Cup counter. MacArthur greeted me with a view of his brand-new tattoo. Yessir. His meaty upper arm featured a full-color close-up image of none other than my sour stepdaughter. The picture must have been lifted from a photo; Avery was scowling, as usual. If she wasn't, no one would recognize her.

"How life-like," I said. "Did Brady do that?"

"Yes. And Peg gave me a discount because I'm getting two," MacArthur said.

"Two tattoos?" I strained to imagine Avery with any other expression.

"I'm getting a tat of the twins on my other arm," MacArthur said.

That was big-hearted of him since Avery had never named the twins' father, and MacArthur hadn't known them very long. To me she had admitted having sex with a fellow student who was a "real loser" and with her professor, another loser, in the space of one drunken week. The professor had ruled out his paternity with a blood test; Avery claimed not to have known the other dude's name. MacArthur seemed like a huge improvement over any likely sperm donor. Even if he was a cleaner.

MacArthur's "cleaning"—as far as I knew—involved making Cassina and Rupert look like better people than they actually were. He accomplished that by doing whatever was necessary to clean up the messes they left behind.

"I'd like to volunteer my services this weekend," he announced.

"As a Realtor? Or a driver? Nobody but Odette is doing any real estate. And Abra's going with me to Nappanee, so you might not want to drive."

His blue eyes twinkled, accentuating his thick black hair. What on earth was wrong with this man that he'd permanently inked Avery's ugly mug on his flesh?

"Did Chester tell you his parents went to Brazil?" MacArthur said.

"Yes. I can't believe they went without you. Was that wise?"

MacArthur shrugged. "What happens in Rio stays in Rio. Anyway, Avery is gone, too, this weekend. I need to feel needed, Whiskey. To keep myself sharp. So I'm volunteering to be your bodyguard."

"But I'm not the one who got shot at."

"Chester thinks you're at risk by association. He asked me to protect you and the woman with the Welsh name."

"Susan Davies? Yeah, well she comes with a co-breeder who'll be the biggest bitch at the show."

"I know about her, too," said MacArthur. "What time are you and Abra leaving?"

I was about to tell him when a familiar speech impediment stopped me.

"Pweez don't pahticipate in dog expwoitation!"

NINE

DAVID NEWQUIST WAS THE best and only veterinarian in town, as well as the dogcatcher of last resort. Because I so often needed his help, I tried to be patient when he preached Fleggers philosophy. Alas, his grim manner, combined with problems pronouncing Rs and Ls, made every lecture tedious. This time I cut him short.

"How does a dog show exploit dogs?" I demanded. "Those are the most pampered pooches on the planet!"

"Exackwee," he sighed and went on with his lesson. According to the good vet, Nature never intended the kind of breeding, grooming, and show-boating required of canine competitions.

"Then you should be proud of Abra and me," I said. "She's been invited to participate as a Bad Example. I think I deserve some credit for that."

Dr. David shook his balding head as people often did when I tried to explain myself. Here's what he said, translated into normal pronunciation:

"Animal-breeding systems imposed by humans make a mockery of the Natural World. Hence, any participation in sanctioned breeding programs is a crime against Nature."

I considered that as I stifled a fresh belch, tasting Chester's waffles yet again. Apparently my neighbor had invented a breakfast you could sample all day long.

"But you treat purebred animals," I argued. "Hence, you support breeding programs, too!"

I thought that was a pretty snappy comeback till Dr. David reminded me that he had taken an oath to help all animals.

"It's not the fault of purebreds that they were created through human vanity and greed."

Dr. David wore a yellow and white striped shirt that matched the paint job on his retrofitted Animal Ambulance. His name was stitched above one pocket; above the other was his mantra:

MAGNET SPRINGS VET CLINIC
YOUR PET'S A PERSON, TOO

MacArthur spoke for the first time since Dr. David had joined us at the Goh Cup counter. He reached past me to shake the vet's hand.

"Thanks to you, Velcro has made an astonishing recovery. The wee guy's joints are stronger, and he poops and whines little more than most dogs."

Dr. David said, "Nature never intended the descendents of wolves to be the size of teacups. But I serve all creatures."

"Even designer dogs," I added, using the term I'd learned from Ramona Bowden.

The veterinarian's blue-green eyes flared. "They may be the greatest victims of all. Proof that humans persist in trying to outsmart Nature!"

The sheen of sweat on his upper lip suggested it was time to change the topic. Fortunately, Peg Goh changed it for me. Our fearless, friendly mayor appeared on the other side of the counter with a fresh pot of coffee.

"Anyone want to try today's brew? It's a Sumatran blend."

We shook our heads.

"How about a big cookie? I've got Cappuccino Chocolate Chunk and Pumpkin Butterscotch Caramel, baked here this morning."

We murmured our regrets.

Peg let the smile slide off her plump face. Setting down the coffeepot, she said, "It sure is a good thing I added that tattoo parlor in back. I'm selling less than half the caffeine and cookies I sold three months ago. But everybody loves a brand-new tattoo. Did you see MacArthur's?"

He displayed Avery's snarl to everyone in the restaurant, which amounted to Dr. David and me.

"Brady's a natural with a tattoo needle," Peg said. "I told him he should forget about online grad school and build a career right here. He'll perfect his style by the time the tourist trade picks up."

"Where are all the tourists?" I said. "This is leaf-peeping season! People love to watch trees change color, especially with blue sky and blue water in the background."

"Have you seen the price of gas lately?" Peg said. "Most people can't afford the drive. They're watching the trees on their own street."

I couldn't help but notice the new tattoo on Peg's fleshy forearm. You gotta admire a sixty-some-year-old woman willing to do whatever it takes to save her business, even if it requires redesigning her own skin.

"Is that your ... cat?" I asked, craning my neck to view the tat right-side up. Helpfully Peg rotated her arm.

"Oh my god!" I cried. "It's Yoda!"

The heart-shaped head, oversized ears, and glinting green eyes were unmistakable.

She nodded happily. "I adopted the little bugger when Faye went off to school. First purebred pet I ever had. What a charmer."

Before Dr. David could start in with another Fleggers lecture, I said, "Yoda? A charmer? He's a Devon rex! They're the flying squirrels of the feline world."

Peg chuckled. "Yes, they are. I love the way he rides around on my shoulder."

Apparently Peg was lonelier than I had realized.

Dr. David said, "All purebreds have problems. But since Fleggers snipped his manhood, Yoda has become a much better pet."

I wanted to ask whether Mother Nature had enlisted Fleggers to go around removing testicles. But before I could, the front door opened, and we all turned to see who had come for coffee.

My office manager looked, if possible, even more wild-eyed than she had when I fled her presence. Tina's frizzy hair formed a dull blonde halo around her blotched face. Despite a bad back, she managed her signature hop as she waved for my attention.

"You forgot your cell phone again!" she whined. "So I couldn't call you. Jenx needs to see you right away. Something's gone wrong at the dog show!"

"Incredible," I said. "Abra isn't even there yet."

Then I had a horrifying thought and added, "Is she?"

"I don't think so," Tina replied. "Jenx said something about another shooting."

MacArthur was on his feet before I was. He threw down enough cash to cover his sandwich and my soda three times over. Peg thanked him and wished me luck.

As we hustled toward the door, Dr. David called, "You'll see me at the dog show, too, Whiskey! Deely and I are leading a protest!"

Jenx was waiting at the Magnet Springs police station, one block away. She showed no reaction when I arrived with a bodyguard.

"The shooter is now in Nappanee," she said without preamble. "Ramona Bowden was grooming one of her dogs outside the exhibit hall when somebody took a shot at her."

"Somebody shot at Ramona?" I asked. "I thought Susan was the target."

"So did Susan," Jenx said. "She phoned me as soon as it happened. She's ready to hire a bodyguard. For herself and Ramona."

"I've already volunteered my services," MacArthur said, "to anyone who needs them."

Jenx nodded. "Ramona wasn't hurt, but she's badly shaken. So's Susan. I advised them to stay out of plain sight till they get a bodyguard."

"I'm on my way," MacArthur said.

Then he asked if I needed him to double as my driver. I wanted to say yes because having a driver is the most decadent of luxuries. But he added that he'd prefer to go separately in order to have more freedom of movement. Since I thoroughly enjoyed watching MacArthur's free movements, who was I to argue?

TEN

As we left the police station, I commented to MacArthur that our shooter was a lousy shot.

"He's tried three times and hasn't winged anybody."

"That's because he's not trying to shoot them."

"Say what?"

"He's sending a message, Whiskey."

"What kind of message?"

MacArthur paused for dramatic effect, which wasn't necessary. A man as tall and well built as he is just naturally takes center stage.

"That's what I'm going to find out," he said. "With a little help from my volunteer deputy. Chester told me you're on the case."

I knew that Jenx preferred Chester over me in matters of law enforcement. He was more eager to please and less likely to compromise a crime scene. Also, Chester could speak canine. You'd be surprised how handy a skill that is.

MacArthur urged me to leave as soon as possible, adding "Chester will have Abra ready to roll."

His thick brogue sounded so enchanting that once again I wondered why nasty Avery Mattimoe got to live with a hunk like him. I had been jealous when she hooked up with her good-looking professor, too, before I realized he was a toad disguised as a prince. Maybe, as Avery had gleefully pointed out, I was doomed to lust after all her boyfriends.

Or, happier thought, maybe she was doomed to lose them all. The first one had walked out the day he discovered the twins weren't his. I wondered what it would take to drive MacArthur from her bed. If her surly attitude, soft ass, and bad complexion didn't do it, what would?

Then I wondered why I wondered. I had a wanna-be live-in boyfriend of my own. A man I'd already married once—before I divorced him. Jeb still got my blood boiling. The chemistry between us was as combustible as ever. And he was lobbying hard to be a regular fixture in my life again.

But he hadn't yet mentioned the M word. Did I want him to? Surely I wasn't ready for that. If I were, I wouldn't long for nights spent alone and lust after muscular, deep-voiced Scots who promised to protect me.

Would I?

"Why do you have to act like that?"

Tina's familiar whine rudely interrupted my reverie. Naturally, I assumed she was snapping at me… till I spotted her husband Tim and realized he was the unfortunate object of her attention.

Walking back to my office in a daze, I had failed to notice the Breen family car, a dingy blue Chevy Malibu, parked in front of Mattimoe Realty. As he usually did when he came to retrieve Tina at the end of her shift, Tim had brought along their toddlers, Winston and Neville. But today he had apparently managed to do or say something that annoyed Tina so much she wasn't getting into the car.

"Act like what?" he retorted. "Like I'm sick of being your chauffeur and babysitter? Maybe that's because I am sick of it! I have better things to do if we're ever going to make more money than you get paid at this dump."

Winston and Neville stopped bouncing in the backseat and stared like stone statues.

Since I was on the sidewalk only a few yards away, I couldn't pretend to be invisible. So I took the opposite approach.

"Hey, Tim!" I called out cheerfully. "Long time, no see. How ya doing?"

Tina turned crimson and glanced away. Tim waited a beat and then rolled the driver's side window the rest of the way down.

"Hey, Whiskey. Tina gave me the good news about Mattimoe Realty representing the new development on Uphill Road. Congratulations."

"Thanks," I said. "But Odette's doing all the work."

He barked a laugh and said nothing more. I couldn't help but notice that he failed to make eye contact. That wasn't like Tim. Never an ambitious man, his usual manner was relaxed and friendly. The opposite of Tina's, in other words. Today, though, he radiated hostility. Was that what happened to a man too long out of work? Without acknowledging me, Tina climbed stiffly into the car. I waved at Winston and Neville, but they didn't wave back.

—

As my volunteer bodyguard had promised, Chester did indeed "have Abra ready to roll" when I arrived at Vestige. Ever dutiful, he had managed to make her look better without formally grooming her.

"She's still a mess," he assured me, "because Susan wants her that way, but I got out the worst tangles and the smelliest debris. I wouldn't want anybody to charge you with animal neglect."

Always a possibility if Fleggers showed up.

Just knowing Abra's location was a refreshing change of pace. I was so grateful to Chester that I didn't have the heart to bring up his waffles. As it was, I blamed Tina more than my breakfast for my prolonged case of the burps.

I had promised Susan I'd deliver the Bad Example in time for the Breeder Meet-and-Greet at five. That meant I needed to hit the road ASAP, just as soon as I could toss a few beige separates and personal items into my overnight bag and wrestle Abra into the car. Or ask Chester to load her for me. I opted for the latter. By the time I snapped my suitcase shut, she was in the back of my Lexus 330, looking almost demure.

"Did you ... do something to her?" I asked Chester.

"I played Jeb's *Animal Lullabies*," he said. "And told her I love her. That usually does the trick."

I made a mental note to follow Chester's model, with minor modifications. I couldn't use love talk to bribe Abra; she'd see through that in a nanosecond. But I could and should make better use of the Fleggers CD. I already knew the happy effects of Jeb's crooning; during Velcro's stay, I'd played the tunes 24/7. It was either that or listen to the shitzapoo's nonstop yaps. By now, however, I was sick to death of *Twinkle, Twinkle, Little Star*, and the like. Trust me, lullabies can make you nuts.

But I played them all the way to Nappanee. As a result, Abra traveled well. In fact, she slept the whole way. I could only hope she wasn't storing up energy for a manic performance at the show. I could only hope …

As I drove, my thoughts kept returning to Jeb. That was natural since he sang me the whole way to Amish country. Plus, he phoned me en route to wish me luck with my Bad Example. I meant it when I told him I had no idea what to expect. I'd never been to a dog show, let alone stepped into the spotlight as the "how-not-to" human. I could only hope it wouldn't feel like a three-ring circus with me in the lion's cage.

So why was I going? What were my motives?

Jeb had insisted that bonding with Susan Davies could help my real estate business. I figured that was true only if she stayed married to her builder-developer husband. And if Liam's company stayed solvent.

Why else was I going? I'd set fire to my eyelashes before I'd admit it to Jeb, but I wanted to watch Susan in action. Correction: I wanted to catch her being bad. Women know women. Or so my mother always said. I had a feeling that Susan wasn't the nice person Ramona insisted she was.

For starters, somebody had used Susan's car for target practice. I didn't believe that was because Ramona was riding in it. I believed Susan attracted trouble. She was too pretty. And she had too many dogs. There's something suspicious about a woman who can find the time to groom herself *and* eight Afghan hounds.

Of course, I now had a bonus reason for going, which I wouldn't share with Jeb, either: I'd won a one-third timeshare in a handsome Scottish bodyguard.

If the weekend went to the dogs, there would still be treats for me.

ELEVEN

What I could see of Indiana Amish country was a letdown. It looked like farmland anywhere. I'd had the same reaction years earlier when traveling in France with Leo. The cornfields surrounding Paris were identical to the ones at home.

Back when I toured with Jeb as designated wife-slash-groupie repellent, I'd visited Amish country. Jeb didn't play Nappanee, but he did have gigs in Middlebury and Shipshewana. That was during his ill-fated folk music phase when he sang earnest songs about working hard for a living that nobody wanted to hear.

On that tour, I saw lots of white houses, white fences, and very few power lines. Today I was sticking to the main roads, which probably explained why the scenery looked like textbook Middle America: farm fields alternating with gas stations, churches, and fast food restaurants. The Amish didn't live along U.S. Route 20.

Although I was disappointed by the lack of bonnets and buggies, conditions were perfect for leaf-peeping. I hated to admit it, but the trees here were as richly hued as in Magnet Springs. Sure, we offered quaint shops, superb restaurants, and a scenic shoreline. But if you couldn't afford a tank of gas and you lived in northern Indiana, you had plenty o' pretty to gaze upon.

My destination was the ominously named Barnyard Inn, a motel attached to an exhibit hall on the east edge of Nappanee. Susan had assured me that the inn was "canine-friendly." I hoped dogs were the only livestock.

The moment the motel came into view, I understood why dogs were welcome. It was a dump—starting with the sagging roadside sign, which appeared to have been maimed in a collision with an eighteen-wheeler. Plastic letters held together with duct tape perched crookedly atop a cracked cement stand. The second R in Barnyard must have been replaced in a hurry; it was backwards. Under the motel's name was somebody's idea of an enticement to stay there: FREE TV.

I pulled into the large, mostly empty gravel lot and parked in front of the glass door marked OFFICE. Since Abra, like me, needed all the beauty sleep she could get, I left the CD player running while I went inside to register.

No one was at the front desk. Nor was there one of those bells you can ring to request service. But I wasn't yet sure I wanted any. I surveyed the dimly lit lobby, or what passed for a lobby at the Barnyard Inn: humming yellow overhead lights, cheap dark paneling, and orange shag carpet. The air was a gagging mix of rug cleaner, bleach, and floral air freshener. Even in the low lighting, I could see stains on the carpet, no doubt from those welcome canine guests.

"Hello?" I inquired. There was a door behind the desk. It was mostly closed, but from the other side came the sounds of a TV game show conducted in a language that wasn't taught at my high school.

I called out again, louder. Still no response. I was thinking about getting back in my car and pretending I'd never been here when the glass door to the parking lot opened, and in walked a distinguished man about Leo's age. Or about the age Leo was when he checked out of life early: late forties. A few inches shorter than me, as many men are, this one had thick glossy hair, ramrod-straight posture, and a rather blank, but not unpleasant, face. He wore a linen sports jacket over a pale cotton shirt. His coffee-brown pants were crisply pressed, and his shoes were Italian. Frankly, he looked as out of place in this dive as I did. But for completely different reasons.

"Nobody's working today?" he asked me.

"So it seems," I replied.

Wasting no time, he leaned over the front desk and bellowed, "We need some service out here!"

Almost instantly a petite dark-skinned woman in jeans and a Purdue University sweatshirt stained with baby spit-up appeared from the room behind the desk.

"May I help you?" she said to neither of us in particular.

The gentleman deferred to me.

"I think you have a reservation for Whiskey, I mean, Whitney Mattimoe," I said, hoping she didn't. It wasn't yet too late to go home.

Impassively scanning her computer screen, she said, "I don't see it. When did you phone it in?"

"Oh, that's all right—" I began and turned toward the front door.

The man spoke up. "Mattimoe? I know that name. You're here as a guest of the Breeder Education Committee."

Busted.

He told the clerk, "Her reservation should be under the Midwest Afghan Hound Club."

She nodded. A few seconds later, I was holding a metal key attached to a red plastic tag labeled 17.

"Uh—I have a question."

The desk clerk gazed at me with narrow, expressionless eyes.

"Where are all the Amish?"

No response.

I tried again. "The horse and buggy people? I thought this was their country. I mean, I thought this was where you find them."

Without a word or the slightest change in her bored expression, the woman plucked a brochure from a display rack at one end of the counter and held it at my eye level.

AMISH COUNTRY TOURS

SEE HOW GENUINE AMISH PEOPLE LIVE AND WORK

I took it, thanking her excessively for … what? Rudely handing me a brochure? Sometimes I was way too Midwest-humble.

"There are better tours than that one," the man told me. "If you can wait a minute, I'll point you in the right direction."

Why not befriend the attractive Afghan hound man? It would be nice to know someone at the show besides Susan and Ramona. And our bodyguard.

"Next." I smiled and made room for him at the counter.

The man returned my smile, his teeth so movie-star perfect they had to be porcelain veneers.

To the clerk he said, "You have a reservation for Mitchell Slater."

So help me, I dropped my key. *This* was the possible shooter? The bitter breeder who had failed to refund Susan's stud fee after her bitch killed his dog with sex? The man with the freezerful of dog sperm?

I scooped key number 17 from the raggedy rug. It came up smelling like chemicals and... something else. I made a mental note to rub it with hand sanitizer.

As the clerk printed out his receipt, Mitchell Slater watched me blandly. I slipped the key in my pocket and parked my trembling hand there with it. If Mitchell Slater was the shooter, I was chatting up a man who, according to MacArthur, "sent a message" with gunfire. Had he shot at Ramona this very afternoon?

"You brought the Education Dog, didn't you?" he said.

"Pardon?"

"You're here because Susan Davies and her committee invited you."

"Oh. Yes. How nice of you to call Abra the Education Dog. I've been thinking of her as the Bad Example."

"There are no bad dogs," he began.

"I know," I said. "Only bad owners. I guess that makes *me* the Bad Example."

"I was going to say, there are no bad dogs, only dogs that need training."

I liked his version much better than Susan's. In fact, I liked him better than Susan. He was way too charming to wield a high-powered rifle.

We stepped from the cramped lobby into the late afternoon sunlight. The mild air held a hint of crispness. I smelled freshly turned earth.

"You can recommend a better tour?" I asked, brandishing my brochure.

"Much better." He plucked the pamphlet from my fingers and proceeded to tear it into shreds.

"You don't care for that tour, do you?" I said.

He shook his head and continued ripping, his eyes on me. Specifically, his eyes were on a part of my anatomy below my chin and above my waist. I wasn't sure if this was flattering or just plain rude.

"So which tour do you recommend?" I said.

He tossed the tiny bits of glossy paper into the air like confetti.

"My tour," he said.

"Excuse me?"

"I recommend that you let me show you Indiana Amish country. I grew up in Elkhart. Trust me, I know all the back roads."

I was willing to bet that he did. Suddenly I understood why Mitchell Slater's face seemed strangely blank: Botox. The man had surely had injections. His neck, his hairline, and his hands confirmed that he was closing in on the big Five-Oh. Yet his face had almost no lines at all. Skin as smooth as a teenager's and an attitude to match.

"Well, that's very nice of you," I babbled, "but I'm sure you'll be busy with the show."

"Not very. Most of my committee work is done, and I hire handlers to show my dogs. So all that's left is the socializing. And collecting my ribbons, of course."

"Of course. But I'm afraid I will be busy. I'm … the Bad Example, remember?"

"Let me talk to Susan about that. There's no reason she should monopolize your time."

Mitchell talk to Susan? According to Ramona, he shunned her at every event.

"So … you and Susan are … friends?" I ventured.

He barked a short laugh. I couldn't read the emotion.

"You might say that. I left my wife for her."

Before I could concoct a response to that bombshell, a firecracker exploded nearby. I jumped at the sound.

Then I shrieked like a terrified toddler. But not because of the bang.

I screamed when Mitchell Slater staggered and fell against me. I saw no blood, but I knew by the way his muscles let go that life had left his body.

TWELVE

THE REASON I DIDN'T see blood was that the bullet shattered the left side of Mitchell Slater's head. The side not facing me.

I found that out from the cops. Later.

When Slater laughed at my question about him and Susan being friends, he pivoted toward the road. And in that instant, the shooter found his mark.

It was the closest I'd ever been to a murder victim as he was murdered.

Naturally, I passed out.

When I awoke, a woman was holding something smelly much too close to my face. In my haze, I briefly thought it was the unpleasant desk clerk trying to stuff my stinky key up my nose. Then I realized that the desk clerk was standing a few feet away, holding her baby and a cell phone, and chattering in the language of that unseen TV game show. The woman next to my face was wearing a uniform.

"Welcome back," she said, capping the smelling salts.

Some welcome. I had graduated to a sitting position, but I felt woozy. And then I saw the blood: a wide red spray arced across the gravel where Mitchell and I had sagged together, one of us already history. Blood also stained my shirt and my pants.

I instantly tasted Chester's waffles again. How was that possible after so many hours?

"Breathe," the uniformed woman ordered.

Although she looked young, she sounded professional. So I complied. I also closed my eyes, which was my own idea. I heard voices murmuring, gravel crunching, car doors slamming. A dog howling. My dog.

"Can you open your eyes?" the uniformed woman said.

I knew I could, but did I want to? As if blood and death weren't awful enough, I'd also have to handle Abra. I was a big girl, though, so I took an extra-deep breath and prepared to face the world.

The officer was leaning in so close that she was the only part of the world I could see.

"We're going to help you stand up," she said.

Immediately, two beefy men hoisted me to my feet, facing away from the nasty spray on the gravel and directly toward my car. Abra bounced between the front seat and the back seat in a mad, howling dance. Proof that even Jeb's mellifluous voice had its limitations.

The Elkhart County sheriff's department had a few questions for me. Quite a few. They suggested that I take my dog out first, correctly guessing she needed to relieve herself but incorrectly guessing she also needed to see that I was all right. Abra didn't give a shit about me. She was, however, fascinated by movement, noise, and odors. As usual, she longed to be in the thick of things and resented my restraining her with a leash.

Like getting to my feet, shoving Abra back into my car required police assistance. She was adrenalized with excitement. Crime has that effect on my canine.

Once Abra was safely stowed away again, the female officer summarized what had happened after Mitchell Slater was shot: The desk clerk heard me scream and looked outside. When she saw us sprawled on the gravel surrounded by blood, she assumed we were both dying and dialed 9-1-1. I came to, responded to police questions, submitted to a brief examination, and passed out again. Slater was removed by ambulance. I couldn't remember any of it.

Now I sat in the front seat of a police cruiser answering more questions ... to the tune of Abra howling in the background again. The officer handed me a standard report form on a clipboard and told me to write out the sequence of events. My head throbbed. I was straining to focus on the report and tune out Abra's wails when Susan Davies rapped on the patrol car window. I opened the door.

"Mitchell Slater is dead," I said numbly. "Somebody shot him."

"I know. Two officers came to the exhibit hall. That's why I'm here. What can I do for you?"

Susan seemed completely composed. There was no sign in those clear blue eyes that she'd just received jolting news.

Abra issued a fresh howl, this one louder, higher, and more sustained than any that had come before. The look I gave Susan must have said it all.

"I'll take care of her," she offered. "You need to lie down."

"Actually, I need food." I knew that low blood sugar could give me a throbbing headache, and it had been a long time since I'd eaten.

"What room are you in? I'll bring you a sandwich and a Coke."

"Seventeen. But don't bring the dog."

I handed over Abra's leash, eager to watch Perfect Trainer confront the Hound from Hell. This just might be the most entertaining event of the whole weekend: watching Susan extract my canine from my car. First of all, Abra was not generally receptive to strangers. Second, she had a two-response repertoire to any open door: flying leap or complete inertia. I hoped the pretty lady had above-average upper-body strength.

Susan approached the vehicle slowly, showing the leash. Abra stopped bouncing and stared. Susan's back was to me, so I couldn't see her face, but as she neared the window, she must have said something to Abra. I watched in shock as the dog sat demurely in the front passenger seat and waited for Susan to open the door. Then Abra not only allowed the leash to be attached, but she actually heeled as the two strutted off toward the exhibit hall.

Defeated, I located the nearest cop and turned in my report.

"Are you, by any chance, one of the officers who broke the bad news to the Afghan hound crowd?" I said.

"Yes, ma'am."

"How did they take it?"

"Real hard," he said. "Mr. Slater must have had a lot of friends. I had to insist they stay in the hall while we processed the murder scene."

And yet Susan had come on over. Why? Did she consider herself above the laws that applied to others? Or was she overcome with curiosity about the murder? She certainly hadn't seemed overcome with sadness. Or shock. Maybe, as she had said, she wanted to make sure I was all right. I was here at her invitation, and I'd been mighty close to that lethal bullet.

I had one other question the cop might be able to answer. "Where are all the cars? Except for official vehicles, there's hardly anybody in this lot, and there's a dog show going on."

"The dog show folks are parked around back, closer to the exhibit hall," he explained.

After fetching my bag from my car, I started in the direction Susan and Abra had gone, counting motel room doors. The highest number on this side of the building was fifteen, so I figured my room was around the corner.

Actually, it was around the back. Next to the RV park.

That's right. A portion of the rear parking lot was reserved for vehicles large enough to transport a rock band plus entourage. Only these RVs were adorned with Afghan hound logos and kennel names: Windrush Ridge, Zahar's Legend, Royal Sands, and so forth. I hadn't had an inkling how serious some breeders were. Or how deeply invested.

Set up on the nearby grassy area were screened crates and miniature dome-tents containing dogs that looked like mine. Who knew they came in so many colors? I had always thought of Abra as a blonde, but here were several shades of blonde: cream, gold, platinum. Afghans also came in red, black, black and tan, and blue-gray—solid, striped, or streaked. Some dogs even had masks. I was gazing at a veritable kaleidoscope of Afghan hounds.

They were surprisingly quiet, considering how many of them there were. I knew this was a breed less inclined to bark than, say, terriers. But I was still impressed. Afghans are sight hounds, I mused. Maybe they just like to look at each other.

Their quiet nature was a good thing, given that my room was right next door to Doggie World. I inserted my key and turned the knob. The metal door clicked open. I inhaled a potent cocktail of Lysol, Pinesol, and Mr. Clean.

I imagined the motel slogan:

"Welcome to the Barnyard Inn, home of creatures great, small, and smelly. We do our best to disinfect."

Blood thumped through the veins in my head, making me wince with pain at each pulsation. I had seen a man die. I needed to lie down. But first I needed to shed my stained clothes. No. I needed to pitch them.

Since the room was likely to look as dismal as it smelled, I kept the draperies closed and switched on one light only for the express purpose of locating a wastebasket. I stripped to my skin and stuffed everything, underwear included, into the not-quite knee-high bin. Then I stepped into the shower and let the hot water do its magic on my tense muscles. I dried myself with the only scratchy towel I could find, pulled a cotton nightshirt from my suitcase, popped three aspirins, and headed for the lone bed. Even in the shadowy light from the single 40-watt bulb, I could see that the bed sagged and the bedspread was frayed. I yanked off the coverlet, clicked off the light, and literally fell into bed. The springs screeched in protest. I willed myself to sleep; before that could happen, however, someone rapped briskly on my door. I assumed it was Susan with my sandwich.

"Come in," I murmured, much too tired to get up.

"Door's locked," a man responded.

The deep voice sent me into an upright position.

"Who's there?"

"Perry Stiles, Mrs. Mattimoe. I'm chairman of the Midwest Afghan Hound Specialty. Just checking on you. I trust you're doing fine?"

"Well, I'm not fine, but I'm ... doing better than I was an hour ago."

"Wonderful!" he enthused. "Susan will be along in a few minutes with something for you to eat. I speak for everyone here when I say that we look forward to meeting you tomorrow. Take care now!"

"Thank you," I said uncertainly and slid back down between the sheets, my eyes shut. Before I could draw a complete breath there was another knock.

"It's me—Susan."

"I know, and the door is locked," I mumbled, flinging off the covers. I found the light switch. My head still hurt.

Holding a white paper take-out bag and a tall paper cup, Susan was framed in the fading light of day. It lent a golden glow to her whole person. I, on the other hand, felt like a shadow in search of a dark hole.

"May I come in?" Susan asked.

I was dismayed. Why must she always invite herself to my place?

"I'm really not up to entertaining."

She laughed politely. "I just need a moment with you in private."

"I'm not feeling well," I said.

"Oh? Perry Stiles said you were fine."

I groaned and stepped back to let her enter. Her room must have been identical to mine. She didn't bother to look around for a place to sit down. There wasn't one, other than the bed. Susan went straight to it and sat on the edge, holding her goodies out for me to take. I did so and placed them on top of that "free TV" I hadn't yet taken advantage of. Then I returned to the bed and got into it. If she was determined to impose on me, then dammit, I wanted her to see how big her imposition was.

"Perry canceled tonight's Meet-and-Greet," Susan began. "Out of respect for Mitchell."

I said nothing.

"But there's a Breeder Breakfast tomorrow at seven. We're serving a hot buffet at the hall. You're invited."

"I'm not a breeder." Not in any sense of the word.

"We're making an exception in your case. After all, you're here as the guest of our Breeder Education Committee."

"Speaking of which, where's my dog?"

"Don't worry. I'm taking care of Abra tonight." Susan smiled that maddeningly lovely smile of hers. "Get all the rest you need. I imagine that girl is quite a challenge for you."

"You can't begin to imagine," I replied.

"The good news is that you're going to learn some things this weekend," Susan said.

"Will Abra learn something? *That* would be good news."

"She's learning all the time, Whiskey. You just don't know it."

"Well, here's something I do know: Mitchell Slater considered you his friend. Unfortunately we only had a minute to chat about it."

The sudden turn in conversation silenced Susan. In the low light of my tawdry room, she sat very still.

I waited a moment, then added, "He said he left his wife for you."

"Mitchell left his wife for his own reasons." Susan's voice had taken on a steely tone.

"He considered you a friend," I repeated.

"No. He considered me a trophy." Susan rose abruptly. "See you in the morning."

She closed the door a little harder than necessary.

Ah. I'd managed to make a hairline crack in her fine porcelain façade.

Why had Susan felt the need to speak to me in private? Surely she could have invited me to breakfast without coming in. Apparently I had short-circuited our conversation by bringing up Mitchell Slater. What was their relationship?

Why had the shooter missed the women but killed the man? Was MacArthur right that the earlier shots were a "message"? If so, was the message a warning for Slater? What a shame that he hadn't paid attention.

Suddenly I realized something: Mitchell Slater was killed while flirting with me.

Did that make me a *femme fatale*?

THIRTEEN

As soon as Susan left, I crawled to the end of my lumpy bed and reached for the food parked on top of the TV. Hoping to distract myself while I ate, I searched for the remote control. There was none. Apparently the TV was free, but the remote was extra. So was cable. I was able to bring in a total of four channels, none of them worth watching. But that had never stopped me before. I did my best to turn my two skinny pillows into a bolster, and I unwrapped my sandwich.

It was a lukewarm overcooked burger with everything on it except cheese, bacon, and mushrooms. Unfortunately, cheese, bacon, and mushrooms are the only things I like on my burger. So I picked off the wilted lettuce, tomato, onion, and pickles; used a napkin to wipe the condiments from the bun; and scarfed the whole thing down while watching five minutes of a sleep-inducing PBS documentary. At least my Coke tasted good. With the TV still on, I dozed off.

I awoke barely in time to make it to the toilet before I heaved. And kept heaving for what seemed like an hour. This was one meal I couldn't blame on Chester.

Either my insides were seriously on the blink, or Susan had brought me a bad burger. I did my best to convince myself that she hadn't made me sick on purpose. Provided I was well enough to get to the dog show in the morning, I would inquire as to whether anyone else who'd eaten food from the concession stand got sick.

Shakily I dragged myself back to bed, grateful I had a little Coke and ice left to sip. I jumped when my cell phone rang. What time was it? Barely midnight. Still early for most folks on a Friday night. Folks having fun, that is.

Jenx said, "No need to let your chief of police know you were nearly killed. MacArthur gave me a call."

In the pandemonium following Slater's murder, I'd completely forgotten about Jenx. And MacArthur—I hadn't seen him anywhere.

"He must be keeping a low profile," I said. "More like a spy than a bodyguard."

"Whatever," Jenx said. "He knows what's going on."

"Yeah, but is he trying to keep me alive?"

"You're still ticking, aren't you?"

Jenx wanted to hear from me what had happened. After I'd told her everything, including the fact that Susan's meal had made me sick, she said, "You've had a pretty shitty day."

"Can I go home now?" I asked, hoping an authority figure would give me permission.

"You made a commitment to show your dog," Jenx said. "After you do that, you can go home."

"Abra is no show dog," I muttered.

"No shit," Jenx said. "Unless you mean 'Worst in Show.'"

She pointed out that I had additional reasons to be there, like schmoozing Susan.

"This started as a business trip," she reminded me. "So do your business! Odette says it's high time you do some PR for the company."

Was this public relations—or public humiliation? Now that I was here, surrounded by gorgeous dogs and serious dog-people, I wasn't sure how being a Bad Example could be good for my business. Would Liam Davies like Mattimoe Realty better because his wife proved I couldn't handle my dog?

I expressed my doubts to Jenx.

"Going to the show proves you care about your community," she said. "And that's gotta be good for business."

"How does going to a dog show in Indiana prove I care about Magnet Springs?"

"You're admitting that Abra is a public menace, and you're asking for help. Speaking of help, have you talked to Jeb? He's worried about you."

Just then a call from the man himself beeped in my ear. I told Jenx I'd call her back. She told me not to … unless I got in more trouble.

I greeted Jeb's incoming call by quoting Jenx: "I've had a pretty shitty day."

"So I hear. MacArthur told me you saw a man die."

"When did you talk to MacArthur?"

"I asked him to phone me if anything bad happens to you. He's called twice already. You haven't called at all."

Jeb's voice had that whispery edge I always found sexy.

"Sorry," I said. "Catching a dead body when it falls is distracting. How are you?"

"Fine, but lonely. Chester's cooking up a storm."

"I couldn't eat a bite. Did you really tell MacArthur to let you know if something bad happened to me?"

"Yup, and I expect more calls." Jeb hesitated. "You know I'd come if you asked. Any chance you're asking?"

Part of me wanted to, but instead I said, "I'm a big girl."

"Yes, you are. Keep your head down, babe."

"I'm not sure that'll help. Still, I feel good knowing you're on my team."

"You got MacArthur, Jenx, and Chester on your team, too. But I'm the one who knows how to make you feel way better than good."

He whispered a few more lines designed to get me hot and bothered. I went to sleep dreaming about his smooth hands all over my body.

I forgot to set an alarm, which turned out not to matter since Susan remembered to wake me up. At 6:15.

From the other side of my door, she called, "Good morning, Whiskey! I'm leaving a cup of hot coffee out here to help you get started. The Breeder Breakfast begins at seven. See you then!"

Despite my mother's teachings, I could not find it in my heart to say thank you. Susan seemed to do almost everything right. As a result, almost everything she did offended me.

The coffee tasted good, much better than last night's burger. Jeb had probably been right when he said Susan wasn't to blame for that. Most concession stands produce mediocre fare, at best.

I'd been looking for ways to fault Susan ever since I met her. It's satisfying to suspect an attractive woman of having hideous flaws. In this case: compulsive lying, marriage busting, and food poisoning. Two out of the three were still distinct possibilities.

I didn't know what to make of her interest in Jeb. Was she just a loyal fan? He seemed to think so, and I wanted to believe him.

What about Mitchell Slater? If he'd left his wife for Susan, she must have given him a reason. According to her, she would have been his "trophy." Whatever that meant.

Standing in the shower, letting hot liquid jets revive me, I mulled over Susan's possible reasons for insisting I come to the dog show. Was I really here because of Abra? Or did she need me for another purpose? And if so, what was it? I was hardly the best choice in personal protection, even if I did come with a professional cleaner willing to work for free.

I couldn't buy the notion that she'd invited me and Abra because she wanted to "do good works." I'd lived long enough to recognize Susan's type. Sure, she was a reputable breeder and a frequent volunteer. But I believed that her personal agenda always came first. As soon as I could figure out Susan's intentions, I would know why Abra and I were here. Then I might be able to guess what would happen next. For now, though, I was completely in the dark.

FOURTEEN

Overnight the temperature had dropped sharply, imparting a silvery finish to the still-green grass. I inhaled decidedly autumn smells: morning dew mixed with damp earth and drying leaves.

After the ordeal of the previous evening, I felt surprisingly strong and upbeat. Even my stomach seemed normal. Until I entered the exhibition hall and caught a whiff of the hot breakfast buffet.

Hello, gag reflex. Good-bye, morning calm.

I was desperately scanning the walls for a restroom sign when a smiling woman with a nametag I couldn't read and a haircut I coveted waved at me.

"Good morning! I'll bet you're here for the breakfast, aren't you?"

"That was the plan. But first I need to find a bathroom. Fast!"

Helpfully she pointed to what would have been eleven o'clock on the dial, and I galloped off. When I reached the bathroom stall, I realized that I had no cookies left to toss, just a lot of unhappy gastric juices. So I hung out for a while, breathing deeply, and eavesdropping on other people's conversations.

Susan's name came up a few times. All references were factual comments about either her Breeder Education committee or her scheduled address to the breakfast crowd. In every case, the words chosen implied emotional neutrality, proving only that the speakers were aware anyone could be lurking behind a stall door.

I emerged from my personal "recovery room" just as one woman remarked to another, "Did you get a look at that bitch Susan brought in as Bad Example? Oh my god, what a mess!"

Both women stood at the sink, brushing chin-length silky blonde hair. Our three pairs of eyes met in the mirror, and they stopped talking. But only for a second.

"She looks awful," the second woman whispered, her voice husky with disapproval. "She has no sense of shame."

"None at all," the first woman agreed. "She turns everything into a circus."

Didn't they know I could hear them?

Still grooming their tresses, they frowned at my not-quite-blow-dried curls. My hair was so thick and unruly that it broke brushes. So I finger-combed and hoped for the best.

"A little discipline wouldn't hurt," the second woman said.

"She just doesn't care," sighed the first woman.

Wanna bet? I was all set to defend my dog and myself, not necessarily in that order, when a stall door opened, and out stepped Ramona Bowden, wearing what looked like shimmery silver pajamas. The two blondes blanched.

"Hello, girls," Ramona said. "I couldn't help but overhear you. Wait until I tell Susan that you've been gossiping about her niece."

"Her *niece*?" I blurted. "I thought they were talking about me! Or my dog."

As usual, Ramona failed to acknowledge my existence, but the two blondes stared. Ramona peered down her aquiline nose at them both.

"Lauren. Lindsey. Best of luck to you. I'm quite sure you'll need it."

"We weren't talking about Susan's niece!" the woman named Lauren insisted, but Ramona had already swept her considerable bulk from the room.

"Then who were you talking about?" I asked.

"Susan's niece," the woman named Lindsey admitted.

"Susan Davies recruited her niece as a bad example ... of what?" I said.

"A handler," Lauren said. "She's a complete disgrace."

Lindsey nodded. "She didn't come up through Junior Showmanship. Like we did."

They exchanged amused glances. Both women were about thirty years old; Lauren was slightly taller and thinner, while Lindsey was prettier. They wore expensive dark suits and sensible rubber-soled shoes. They looked like athletes. Also the products of private education. I was willing to bet they had played lacrosse.

"What's Susan's niece's name?" I said and realized that I hadn't offered my own. "I'm Whiskey Mattimoe, by the way."

"We know," they said.

"You do?"

"You're the other Bad Example," Lindsey said.

"Susan's niece is Kori Davies," Lauren said. "You'll meet her at the breakfast."

"You won't be able to miss her," Lindsey said, and they both tittered.

So it was that I emerged from the ladies' room at the Midwest Afghan Hound Specialty with the "Two L's." Apparently, they had a joint reputation as top handlers. Both had shown "countless" champions at regional and national events, including the Westminster Kennel Club show. This was going to be an extremely busy weekend because they worked for lots of breeders.

Lindsey had been right when she said I wouldn't be able to miss Kori. It helped that the young woman was standing indignantly by Susan's side. But the biggest clue to Kori's identity as Bad Handler was her appearance, outrageous by even my *laissez-faire* standards: she wore a short-skirted bubble-gum pink suit and matching running shoes. Bubble-gum pink was also the color of the streaks in her spiky black hair. And her dangling earrings, which were large enough to be detected by an orbiting spy satellite.

The combined steam-table smells of eggs, sausage, and bacon almost turned me green again, but I remembered to breathe deeply and think about things other than food. That last part was easy now that I had Kori in my sights.

"Did you find the bathroom all right?"

It was the smiling woman with the perfect haircut who had showed me where to go. Now she was close enough for me to read her nametag: Brenda Spenser from Columbus. I nodded and thanked her.

"You still look pale. Did you get a bad burger from the concession stand yesterday?"

"Yes!" I said. "Did you?"

"No, but my handler did. From now on, stick to hot dogs and nachos." She winked conspiratorially. I wasn't sure how to reply, so I winked back. Then I noticed that everyone not already wearing a nametag was fetching one from a table near the buffet line.

"I need to get myself a nametag," I said.

"That's not necessary," Brenda said, still smiling. "Everybody knows you're Whiskey Mattimoe."

"Everybody?"

She nodded sympathetically. "Susan introduced us to your dog last night. Have some dry toast and tea. You'll feel much better."

I found some comfort in knowing I wasn't the only two-legged Bad Example. Oddly, I felt superior to Kori Davies, who was probably there because of nepotism. Or reverse nepotism. Watching the body language between her and Susan—thoroughly chilly—I could only assume that she was the non-blood-relative whom Susan loved to hate.

I had one of those in my stepdaughter. Yes, Kori reminded me of Avery, who for once was far, far away. I must have stared long enough for Susan to pick up my vibe. She waved and started in my direction. The instant she left Kori's side, I saw the Bad Handler whip out a pack of cigarettes and head for the exit.

"Poor Susan," Brenda said. "She's going to be stuck with that girl for the whole school year."

"Kori's still in school?" From where we stood, I had estimated her age to be close to Avery's: twenty-two.

"Community college." Brenda pronounced the term in the same tone that Ramona had used for *designer dogs*. "Unless, of course, they can find her a job, which isn't likely."

"Liam is her uncle, right? Surely he could find her a job."

Brenda looked baffled. "Where?"

"How about in his own company?"

"There are no jobs in real estate," Brenda said. She added, "There are no jobs anywhere when you have a criminal record."

"Kori did time?"

Brenda nodded, watching Susan stride toward us. "For car theft and vehicular homicide, what Susan calls a 'joy ride gone wrong.' Kori has a tendency to sabotage every advantage she has. She's made a hash of the handler training Susan gave her, which is why she's here today—"

"Whiskey, welcome to the Midwest Afghan Hound Specialty. I hope you're feeling much better this morning."

Susan spoke from at least ten feet away. So as to interrupt Brenda?

"They're opening the buffet line now," she continued. "Our guests of honor go first."

I hoped that didn't include Abra. But I was quite sure it did include Kori, who had just sneaked out for a smoke.

"Whiskey's a little off her food this morning," Brenda told Susan. "She got a bad burger yesterday, just like Matthew did."

"Oh? What a shame."

Susan didn't seem to recall that she was the one who had brought me the bad burger.

"I told Matthew to sleep in," Brenda said. "He'll need all his strength."

"I'm sure of that," Susan said.

Brenda tossed her beautifully trimmed head and excused herself.

I assumed Matthew was the handler Brenda had mentioned earlier. Why would handlers attend a breeder breakfast? The Two L's were here, and there may have been others in attendance … besides the Bad Example. I asked Susan how that worked.

"Breeders often invite their handlers to join them at the Saturday breakfast. It's a courtesy. Except, of course, in Brenda's case."

"Oh?"

"Brenda's handler is her lover. Her much younger lover. He goes where she goes. Brenda keeps him on a short leash."

Susan gave me a smile almost sweet enough to belie the cattiness in her remark. She nodded toward the buffet line, adding, "Shall we start? Oh, dear. I seem to have lost my handler."

"You let your niece handle your dogs?" I said. "I thought she was a Bad Example!"

Susan's face took on a pained expression.

"I let her handle one of my dogs, yes. She's Liam's family. You know how that goes."

"Actually, I do."

"I know you do," Susan affirmed. "Jeb has told me about Avery."

I wondered what else my guy had confided.

"Where are Kori's parents?" I said. "Why can't they help her?"

"Brenda didn't tell you that part of the story?"

I shook my head.

"Surely she told you that Kori was in prison for car theft and vehicular homicide?"

When I hesitated, Susan said, "If Brenda didn't tell you, someone else would. Kori stole a car in order to impress her parents.

She wanted them to think she was doing well when in fact she was living with a drug addict, and neither of them had jobs."

I blinked but said nothing.

"While driving the stolen car—with her parents in it—Kori ran a red light and T-boned another vehicle. Her parents were killed, and the other driver was injured. Kori wasn't hurt. At trial the judge took pity on her, pointing out that she had just turned eighteen, and her actions had cost her parents their lives. He assumed that the accident had psychologically scarred her, and she would need a chance to rebuild her life. So he gave her the lightest possible sentence."

"When was that?" I said.

"Three years ago. She went to jail for ten months. Since she got out, she's been busy blowing most of the money she inherited from her parents' estate. Kori wasn't 'scarred' by the accident. She was born that way."

"What way?"

"Not giving a shit."

Hearing blunt language from Susan's elegant lips was a shock. But more surprises were coming.

"Her father was Liam's only brother. Which makes Kori Liam's only family. Besides me," Susan said. "Like you, Whiskey, I never had kids. Liam wanted them, but I didn't. He holds that against me. I'm sure it's why he takes Kori's side over mine. I'm doing the best I can, but that girl is almost more than I can bear."

Suddenly I felt a kinship with this woman. A kinship that couldn't possibly endure. Susan would always be too pretty and too sophisticated for me to trust, let alone relate to, save for brief moments when I recognized the excruciating similarity of her life with Kori to my life with Avery.

"This is so typical of Kori," Susan said. "She knew I was about to introduce her, so she disappeared. Just to humiliate me."

"She went outside for a smoke."

I took almost as much pleasure in ratting out Kori as I would have in tattling on Avery. It was surprisingly satisfying. I even pointed out the exit she had used so that Susan could expediently find her.

They were both back within moments, Kori wearing an expression of complete indifference next to Susan's mask of repressed irritation.

"Good morning, fellow breeders!" Susan announced from the steam table. "On behalf of the Breeder Education Committee, I welcome you and your guests, and invite you to enjoy this delicious hot breakfast. It's a lovely day in Nappanee, and we have so many beautiful dogs to show. As is customary at our breeder breakfasts, I'm going to quickly introduce our guests of honor and ask them to lead the buffet line."

She paused for the obligatory smattering of applause.

"Thank you. First, I'd like you to meet Whiskey Mattimoe, who has traveled from Magnet Springs, Michigan, with her bitch Abra."

Breeders and handlers clapped enthusiastically. I could not imagine why.

"Second, I'd like to introduce to any of you who haven't already met her, our guest handler at this event: Kori Davies."

"Don't applaud, I hate bullshit," Kori interjected before anyone had time to put their hands together.

She had an astonishingly deep voice. If my eyes had been closed when she spoke, I would have pictured a college football player. Yet Kori couldn't have been taller than five-foot-five or weighed more than a hundred and twenty pounds. The distinct odor of marijuana emanated from her bubble-gum-colored attire. Apparently Kori liked a little weed before breakfast.

"Let's eat this crap and get this day from hell over with."

Kori was already heaping an obscene amount of scrambled eggs onto two Styrofoam plates as the rest of the room stared.

Who would have guessed that I, half of the Bad Example team from Michigan, would find it in my heart to pity Susan Davies? And yet, for just a moment, I did.

FIFTEEN

WATCHING KORI DAVIES SHOVEL eggs, bacon, sausage, and potatoes onto two sagging plates as I inhaled her *eau de marijuana* cologne should have rekindled my nausea. Except that Kori distracted me and my stomach with an avalanche of comments.

"How do you feel about being the other Bad Example?"

She hadn't yet looked at me.

"Well, it's a team effort. I couldn't have done it without my dog."

"I couldn't have done it without a lot of people's dogs."

"Yeah?"

"Oh yeah. Susan hooked me up with her Afghan hound friends. She knew I loved dogs, so she figured I'd love handling them in the show ring. I do, kind of. But not the way Susan wants me to do it."

"Then why do it?"

When Kori shrugged, her double-wide load of food threatened to hit the floor. But she rebalanced her cargo.

"It's a chance to play with big beautiful dogs and mess with Susan's head at the same time. Why *not* do it?"

Kori's bloodshot eyes twinkled.

"Did Susan teach you to handle dogs?" I said.

"She tried, yeah, but I didn't make it easy for her. So she asked some other people to work with me. I learned the most from Matt Koniger. He's Brenda Spenser's boy-toy… this week. And I learned the least from the Two L's. They don't just show bitches, they *are* bitches. Did you have the pleasure of meeting them yet?"

I nodded.

"The real question," Kori said, "is how did *you* get on Susan's shit list?"

"I'm here as a professional courtesy. Her husband—your uncle—is doing business with my company."

Some part of my answer struck Kori as hilarious.

"Finding everything you need?"

Susan gracefully inserted herself in the buffet line between her niece and me. I assumed the question was mine to answer, but Kori intercepted it.

"*Duh.*"

She raised her mounded plates to Susan's eye level.

"You might want to go a little easy on the calories," Susan advised. "That new suit I bought you is a size four."

"Your size. Not mine. And now if you'll excuse me, I need to *feed.*"

She scooted away. Susan tossed me a pained "see-what-I-mean?" glance and added, "You should eat more than dry toast. It's going to be a long day."

I begged off. Watching Kori load her plates was almost more than my stomach could bear.

"We'll have a short program for breeders and their guests," Susan went on. "All you'll need to do is follow my lead."

As long as her lead didn't come with a collar, I could handle it. At the head table, Kori was tucking into both plates at the same time. I'd never seen anyone eat two-fisted before.

"Is that all you're having?" She eyed my nearly empty plate, her mouth full of eggs.

I nodded.

"Are you on a diet or something?"

"I've got a bad stomach."

It didn't take long for her to finish both plates. When she pushed back from the table like a satisfied lumberjack, I expected her to rock the room with a belch.

Instead she said, "How do you like the Specialty so far? 'All Afghans, All the Time.' More like, all attitude all the time."

I thought about it. "So far everybody's been nice to me. Except maybe the Two L's."

Kori snorted.

"If you don't mind my asking," I said, "what makes you a bad handler?"

"Can't you tell?"

"I haven't seen you in action."

"You've seen how I dress. A handler is supposed to be 'invisible' behind the dog. But this is who I am, and I'm not changing. I don't care about protocol or tradition or whatever they want to call it. And I don't care how many dark suits Susan buys me. She picks stuff she wants to wear, anyhow, so she can keep it."

Kori was guilty of having a whopping bad attitude, plus lousy taste in wardrobe. But those were minor offenses compared to, say, shooting a breeder. And yet Kori was attracting a whole lot more negative attention than whoever had murdered Mitchell Slater. I hadn't heard anybody even mention that.

Which raised another point: Whoever shot at Susan and Ramona hadn't come close to hitting either of them, but presumably the same person managed to kill Slater. With a single bullet.

Were Susan and Ramona a warning, a distraction, or target practice?

Kori was not-so-discreetly checking the contents of her crinkled pack of cigarettes. I wondered if any of them contained tobacco.

"I sure would like a smoke, but there's no way Susan's letting me out of her sight now." She studied me. "You snitched, didn't you?"

"Pardon?"

"You told Susan I was outside smoking."

My face got hot. "Well, I—"

"I don't care. It's more fun when she comes after me. She's always afraid that I'll embarrass her. Again."

I changed the subject. "How come nobody's talking about what happened to Mitchell Slater? I thought it would be the main topic of conversation this morning."

"You don't know dog-show people," Kori said. "The main topic of conversation is always their dogs. And if it isn't their dogs, it's themselves. Plus, Perry Stiles slid a memo under everybody's door asking them to have a moment of silence for Mitchell—on their own time. He doesn't want anything dragging down the spirit of the show."

"But a man was murdered," I said. "A breeder, no less. Also the chair of several committees."

Kori shrugged. "The show must go on."

I scanned the room. "Where is Perry Stiles? I thought he was in charge of everything."

"He is. That's why he's the one talking to the cops."

"Right now?"

She nodded. "I bet the cops think one of the breeders did it."

"Why do you say that?"

"Cops always suspect the person closest to the victim."

"True enough," I said. "But that's usually a spouse or lover or ex-lover."

"Well, it can't be Mitchell's ex-wife cuz she lives in London," Kori said.

I waited to see if she'd suggest that Susan and Mitchell had history, but she didn't. So I prompted her a little.

"Why would you think a breeder did it?"

"I don't know if a breeder did it or not," Kori said. "But I think the cops would think a breeder did it when they start checking things out."

Now that was interesting. Before I could check things out, however, Susan called the room to order. After going over some very boring doggy details, she introduced Ramona as co-chair of the Breeder Education Committee and gave her the floor.

Ramona's silvery ensemble seemed over-the-top for a breakfast meeting. Or any meeting before cocktail hour.

I asked Kori, "How does *she* get away with dressing like that?"

"She hires handlers who don't."

When the applause faded, Ramona addressed the room.

"As you all know, Susan and I have been at this for quite a few years, and we've learned a lot along the way. We're convinced that the best method for teaching new breeders and handlers how to do things right is to show them how to do things wrong. For the breeders, Susan has invited Whiskey Mattimoe with her bitch, Abra. For the handlers, we have Kori Davies. Please watch them closely and observe their many mistakes. This morning Kori will be in the show ring with one of Susan's dogs. How typically generous of Susan to make a personal sacrifice for the sake of breeder education!"

Ramona cued the audience to applaud. As they did, I reflected on her bathroom reprimand of the Two L's. Why would Susan care if Lauren and Lindsey bashed Kori? Susan had admitted to me that she couldn't stand her niece; she was publicly bashing her by presenting her as a Bad Example. Either Ramona simply liked to advocate for Susan, or she wanted to create the impression that she did. Or maybe Ramona was just a two-legged bitch.

She told her audience, "Whiskey and Abra will not, of course, be permitted in the show ring! But this afternoon Whiskey will walk Abra through the exhibit hall so that you can observe the dog's condition as well as her owner's complete lack of control. I promise, it will be an education!"

An appreciative murmur rippled across the room.

"It's customary for the event chairperson to speak at this time," Ramona said. "As you know, however, Perry Stiles is dealing with an unfortunate incident involving local law enforcement. So I will do the honors. Ladies and gentlemen, welcome to this year's Midwest Afghan Hound Specialty. Let the show begin!"

As breeders and guests applauded, I couldn't help but marvel at the phrase "unfortunate incident." I'd never heard a murder described that way.

SIXTEEN

I LEARNED THAT I would be reunited with Abra just moments before our Walk of Shame at two o'clock. According to Susan, Abra would enjoy her time till then playing with fellow Affies.

I had assumed most owners would keep their hounds away from Abra for fear that she'd contaminate them ... with either her messy coat or her messy morals.

The pettiest part of my nature wondered if Susan was somehow contriving to ensure that Abra misbehaved the moment she saw me. Who was I kidding? Abra always misbehaved. No coaching required. I shouldn't have been so suspicious. Surely most breeders and handlers were good people, even if one of them had shot Mitchell Slater.

Since I had the whole morning to kill, I considered taking the tour through Amish country advertised in the brochure that Slater had shredded. But I decided to postpone that pleasure till the next day. Kori was due in the ring, and I wanted to catch her performance.

She had promised to watch mine. Misery loves company, or at least an audience.

I wasn't truly free to do as I pleased since I had certain vague obligations as Jenx's volunteer deputy. During the Breeder Breakfast, the chief had sent two text messages. The first instructed me to "people watch." At least that was how I translated "ppl wtch." I didn't think Jenx wanted me to bring her home a souvenir purple watch. Ironically, her second message, written in plain English, confused me more: "Watch Susan and Ramona." For their protection—or mine?

The chief's instructions reminded me that I hadn't seen MacArthur since leaving Magnet Springs. I knew that the volunteer bodyguard was around here somewhere because he had told both Jenx and Jeb about Mitchell's murder. Still, seeing him with my own eyes would be a relief. I couldn't imagine how one could be an effective protector while staying completely out of sight. Then again, maybe I should have been impressed by MacArthur's ability to work undercover. Assuming, of course, that he was actually working.

As Brenda Spenser had predicted, the dry toast and hot tea settled my stomach. So I roamed the hall watching breeders and handlers primp their pooches. Being backstage at the dog show was like slipping behind the scenes at a fashion show. Not that I'd ever been to a fashion show.

Doggy divas posed passively while determined humans styled their hair—I mean fur—using essentially the same tools employed by my own stylist: detangling spray, steel combs, pin brushes, and blow-dryers. The only notable difference between my salon and this one, other than the presence of hounds, was the size of the blow-dryers. These were as big as floor lamps with the approximate force of a jet engine. An attractive young handler of the male persuasion helpfully explained why such machinery was necessary.

"With a regular blow-dryer, you can spend two or three hours just drying their coat. It's like blow-drying a sponge."

I had once tried to blow-dry Abra but gave up when my arms cramped; I'd left her to finish drying on a bed of towels. My way of grooming my hound was sending her to the doggie salon … when I managed to catch her … and when I could no longer deny that she was a hideous mess.

I watched as the handler lovingly, thoroughly combed the fur on, under, and around his dog's ears. Then he moved on to the armpits—if that's what you call them on a dog.

"No point doing that in real life," I sighed. "Their fur just gets tangled up again."

That was when he introduced me to the amazing invention known as the *snood*. It's a kind of doggie scarf, and apparently every self-respecting Afghan hound needs one. More than one. Way more.

Most of the backstage dogs who already had their hair done were wearing snoods—in every imaginable color and fabric. Vendors were selling them as fast as they could make change. Apparently the snood biz was recession-proof.

The handsome handler man pointed me toward the vendor with the most snoods to sell. I perused the contents of her many plastic bins, trying to decide between a silk leopard-print snood and an iridescent blue-green satin snood. After the vendor finished with a couple clients, she turned to me.

"You won't have nearly the problems you've got with Abra once she starts wearing these."

I was stunned. Not because she recognized me; Susan and Ramona had made sure everyone could do that. No. I was shocked by the implication that putting a snood on Abra might solve some of her issues.

"Is the snood like . . . a training device?" I queried hopefully.

Maybe the handsome handler man had been too busy to tell me how truly wondrous these things were. All the snood-wearing dogs around me were behaving beautifully. Could snoods be the secret?

The vendor said, "It keeps their ears from getting wet, soiled, or matted."

"I know that," I said impatiently. "I was hoping it would help with other things, like the way she never comes when I call her."

And then I saw the pitying look in the vendor's eyes. I'd seen that exact expression at least twenty times today. It implied that I was tragically unfit to share my life with the glorious creature known as the Afghan hound.

The vendor whispered, "After your Walk of Shame, stop by my booth. I've counseled many a novice about grooming issues. As for training issues . . . I have a son in the business, so I may be able to help you there, too."

So . . . "Walk of Shame" was more than my private label for this hellish experience. This very public hellish experience.

She accepted my cash for two snoods and slipped me her business card. Then she turned away to sell a hundred dollars' worth of snoods to the next eager client.

The vendor also sold something called a Pee-Proofing Coat. I almost bought one for Chester's dog, Prince Harry the Pee Master, thinking it was a house-breaking device. No such luck. It's a wardrobe item that permits show hounds to do their business without soiling their nether regions.

I read the vendor's card:

LIVE TO LOVE AFGHAN HOUNDS!
Snoods, Coats, Boots, Beds, Grooming Aids
Gifts for Humans, Too
Sandy Slater, Owner

Slater? As in the late Mitchell? Kori had said that his ex-wife was in London. Could this be a sister or a cousin? Or was Kori just plain wrong?

I studied Sandy Slater and saw no signs of distress. She was in her element selling snoods. Probably a coincidence that her last name was the same as the murder victim's. Still, as Jenx's volunteer deputy, I was obliged to snoop around till I found out. Digging for personal information among folks who saw me as a dog-owning disgrace might prove almost as difficult as training Abra. My volunteer deputy status was unlikely to motivate anyone; I was a hundred miles outside the jurisdiction where I had no legal clout, anyhow.

My peripheral vision picked up Kori exiting through the side door of the arena, probably to sneak a smoke before her performance. She was accompanied by a big silver-blue Afghan hound, presumably the dog Susan was willing to "sacrifice" in the ring so that others could learn from Kori's mistakes. If there was time before they made their entrance, Kori might be willing to answer a question or two about Mitchell Slater. Especially if the answers made Susan look bad. Kori might also know Sandy the vendor and others who had been friendly with the dead man.

I followed her, planning my next move. After quizzing Kori, I would interview everyone I'd met here so far: Brenda Spenser, the Two L's, and the handsome handler man, whose name I didn't know. There was no point talking to Susan again till I had enough information to formulate some new questions. And there was no point talking to Ramona, period, because she flat-out ignored me.

A canvas curtain hung next to the side exit, partially concealing a stash of folded chairs, tables, and stacked cardboard boxes. As well as a man and a woman in what appeared to my somewhat experienced eyes as a passionate clinch. They kissed and groped each other with a gusto commonly reserved for either honeymooners or adulterers. Since I immediately recognized the couple, I was able to rule out honeymooners.

Susan Davies was swapping spit with the handsome handler dude, who was young enough to be Kori's boyfriend.

SEVENTEEN

I WOULD HAVE LOVED to stand and stare at Susan and the boy-toy till one of them came up for air. What could be sweeter than letting her know that I knew she was a Bad Example, too?

That revelation wasn't completely comforting, however. I had already suspected Susan of philandering, possibly with my own formerly philandering ex-husband, who was once again my lover. Proof that she had no romantic boundaries only gave me more reason to worry about her and Jeb.

Now I wondered if Susan's invitation to this event was intended simply to humiliate me. Embarrassment, like beauty, is in the eye of the beholder. If she hoped to shame me in Jeb's eyes, she'd have to do better—or worse—than Worst in Show. He'd already seen me at the bottom of my game.

If shaming me in front of the Afghan hound crowd was her goal, what was the point? I didn't expect to do business with Brenda, Ramona, the Two L's, or anyone else in this hall. In fact, I planned to never see any of them again.

If Susan's goal was to make sure that I and, by extension, my company appeared to her husband as losers, then Odette was in a position to prevent that. Or at least reverse the impression. No doubt my star agent was selling Big Houses on the Prairie even as Susan sucked face.

Maybe Susan disliked me *and* her husband enough to want to punish us both. I shook myself like a wet dog. Why worry? Jeb wouldn't care how pathetic I looked; he (mostly) loved me for the mess I was. Liam didn't fancy Afghans, so he wouldn't be here to witness my Walk of Shame.

I hurried from the exhibit hall, determined to quickly quiz Kori about Sandy Slater. Several handlers loitered near the door, most of them savoring the smokes they weren't allowed to have inside. Kori was not among them. Figuring that even if every handler didn't know every other handler, everybody knew Kori, I was about to ask if anyone had seen her. Then I saw her. Or rather, I saw a flash of bubble-gum pink and the tail end of her big blue dog disappear around the corner of the building. So I followed.

I expected to find Kori lighting up either a cigarette or a joint. I did not expect to find Kori imitating her aunt. Yet that was the scene I stumbled into: Kori kissing a tall gorgeous man. Once again, I knew both the players. But I'd had no inkling these two were acquainted, let alone familiar enough to taste each other's tongues.

Finally I had proof that MacArthur was on site. He was also on Kori—pressing her to him with as much zeal as she was using to grab onto him. These two appeared to be even hotter for each other than Susan and the handler. Less inhibited, at any rate. I didn't know why I was so stunned to find them in a clinch. Kori reminded me of my stepdaughter, and I already knew MacArthur liked her; she was tattooed on his arm for the whole world to see. He may have been the cleaner at work, but on his own time he liked the messy life.

While I stared at the lovers, the big Afghan hound looked discreetly away. He had better manners than I did, but then he was the one with the pedigree. He issued a low growl, no doubt as a reprimand for my gaping; Kori and MacArthur sprang apart like fighters called to their corners.

"Hey, Whiskey!"

MacArthur was faster than Kori at finding another use for his tongue.

"Hey," I said. Why was I the only person blushing?

"Silverado doesn't like you," Kori said, indicating the hound, who was still growling.

"Neither does my dog. That's why I'm here. At the show, I mean. Not *here* here. I'm *here* here by complete accident. Really. I never wanted to see that."

I always babble when embarrassed. And it only embarrasses me more.

Kori said, "I thought you were trying to catch me smoking a joint. So you could rat me out to Susan. Again."

"I never meant to rat you out! I don't even like Susan!"

"Really?" Kori was wary, but I thought she might be warming to me.

"Really! You'll never guess what I just caught *her* doing."

"Making out with Matt Koniger? Yeah. I saw them when I went out the door. So did everybody else."

Susan Davies had seemed so ... Junior League. And yet she must have known that people would see her kissing the handler.

So *that* was Matt Koniger—Kori's favorite handler-mentor and Brenda Spenser's young stud. The one Susan had made the catty remark about just before breakfast. *My, my*.

"Whiskey, may I speak with you privately?" MacArthur's brogue broke through my reverie.

"Uh, sure. In a minute. First, I'd like to ask Kori a couple questions."

"I'm due in the ring." She tapped her bright pink watch.

"This will only take a few seconds," I said. "And it's not about you. Or him." I nodded toward MacArthur. "It's about Sandy Slater."

"What about her?"

"Any connection to Mitchell Slater?"

"What do you think?" Kori shot me a look that said I was a moron.

"Well, it's kind of a common name," I said defensively. "And you did tell me his ex-wife was in London."

"His latest ex-wife, yeah."

"There's more than one?"

Kori held up several fingers.

"*Four* ex-wives?" I asked.

"Amazing! You can count."

I probably deserved that. "Was Sandy the first?"

"Numero Uno. And the only one who never went away. No matter how hard Mitchell tried to push her. You already know she kept his name."

"They've been divorced a long time?"

"Long enough for Sandy to have had a kid as old as Matt!"

"That would be more than twenty years," I guessed.

"Try twenty-six. Matt's a little older than he looks."

"Is her kid around here?"

Kori snort-laughed and shook her head. Not in a way that meant "no," but in a way that meant I was a dumb-dumb.

"Matt's her kid! I thought you got that!" she said. "Matt's father, legally, was a guy named Koniger. He died when Matt was a baby. He wasn't into dogs, so none of the Afghan fanciers ever knew him. But judging from the way Matt turned out, Mr. Koniger donated his name only. No sperm."

When I didn't take the bait, Kori added, "Doesn't Matt remind you of somebody? Somebody you just met?"

As brief as my time with Mitchell Slater had been, I could see the resemblance: same eyes, same jaw line, same mouth.

Interesting. Neither Matt Koniger nor his mother was grieving today.

EIGHTEEN

While groping and kissing MacArthur, Kori had managed to never let go of Silverado's lead. She also never stopped chewing gum. I couldn't imagine deep-kissing around a rubbery wad, but maybe that was because I'd never tried it. Maybe there was an art to passing it back and forth, and that was what turned MacArthur on.

I didn't want to think about it.

Now Kori popped her gum and the leash at the same time. Silverado gave her his full and eager attention. She may have been a lousy handler in the ring and a genuine thorn in Susan's side, but she seemed earnestly connected to the stunning dog.

"Come on, boy. It's show time!" she said.

He woofed softly and wagged his curled whip of a tail.

"I'll cheer you on," I told her.

"Yeah, that'll help. The judge will be impressed that *you're* on my side."

Kori blew a kiss to MacArthur; then she and Silverado loped gracefully away.

That left me in the awkward position of making conversation with the cleaner, a man who earned his living by erasing the mistakes of others. Who erased *his* mistakes? Making out with one woman while shacking up with another seemed like kind of a whopper.

"I have one thing to say, Whiskey, and one thing only. I hope you'll give me a wee moment of your time."

His burry brogue melted my defenses. I could too easily imagine its effect on Avery and Kori... and who knows how many other women.

"What?" Try as I might to sound annoyed, the question came out innocently curious.

"Please do not try to find me while we're here at the show. I do my best work when I keep a low profile."

That was not remotely what I had expected. I said, "You think I was looking for you, and that's why—?"

"No time to chat now! You need to trust me."

Like Avery should trust him?

"But how can a bodyguard do his job if nobody sees him?" I said. "Nobody but Kori, that is..."

MacArthur brushed a lock of black hair from his forehead. "I didn't say *nobody* sees me. And now I must get back to work. We have a killer in our midst!"

"Before Mitchell Slater died, you thought we had a *messenger* in our midst."

"Indeed. And now we know what the message was."

"What was it?"

"Somebody was going to die. Somebody close to Susan Davies."

"But not Susan Davies," I said. "Does that mean she's safe?"

"It's too soon to tell. Fortunately, I'm here to protect her and those close to her."

"Especially her niece."

I couldn't resist. But my comment had no effect on MacArthur.

"I'm watching out for you, too, Whiskey."

"Really? If last night's bullet had gone six inches to the right, that would have been me face down in the parking lot!"

"But it wasn't you, was it? Because I'm on the job. And now I need to get back to it."

He started toward the cornfield behind the exhibit hall.

"Can I call you?" I said.

MacArthur raised a brawny arm in what I assumed was an affirmative gesture.

"I check voicemail three times a day."

With that he vanished among the drying cornstalks like the ghosts of young ballplayers in *Field of Dreams*.

—

When I re-entered the exhibit hall, nobody was smooching near the side entrance. In the show ring, I counted seven hounds with handlers. They had attracted at least fifty onlookers. Some sat in folding chairs; others stood around the circle. With "Bad Example" Kori in the competition, there was an added incentive for watching.

Kori's hot-pink ensemble flared like neon next to the subdued outfits of her peers. The judge, a tall stately man with thick white hair, showed no reaction to her attire. He fixed his full and concentrated attention on the hounds, as was his duty. After scrutinizing them, he flashed a few hand signals appreciated by everyone except me. Bursts of applause and a flurry of movement followed. Hounds and handlers dashed around the ring, some exiting, some staying. Apparently, the judge had narrowed the field, excusing those dogs not selected to continue.

Across the ring from me, Susan stood alone, closely watching the competition. Matt was in the ring showing a dog the same size as Silverado, but reddish colored, with a dramatic black face. The Two L's were there, too, each leading a blonde dog that reminded me of Abra, if only Abra had manners.

When Kori and Silverado got the nod to remain, I saw Susan's face fold—for just a moment. Then she perked up and applauded.

So the Bad Example was not the worst handler, after all. Or, if she was, she knew how to show Silverado well enough to keep him in the competition.

Matt and his dog also remained. So did the Two L's. I caught Matt and Kori exchanging grins. The Two L's made a deliberate show of ignoring Susan's niece.

As the action continued, I inferred what was happening: the judge was evaluating the "survivors" to determine their order of finish. Each handler showed his or her dog and then circled the ring again to a fresh round of applause. When it was Kori and Silverado's turn, the applause was sparse and forced. Except for mine. I clapped hard and added a whistle as they ran past. That earned me a distinctly dirty look from Susan.

Hey, we Bad Examples gotta stick together.

As that round turned out, I had another opportunity to hoot and holler. Silverado, handled by Kori, finished first. Next was the dog that Matt handled, followed by the dogs shown by the Two L's. Lauren and Lindsey briskly congratulated Matt and then swept past Kori as if she didn't exist. No mean feat considering the brilliant glow of her apparel and the broad "eat shit" grin on her face.

I could only wish for luck like that on my upcoming Walk of Shame.

While I wasn't looking, Susan had disappeared from her post near the ring. She couldn't have predicted that outcome, which seriously weakened her case for Kori as Bad Example. Although it may have increased the value of her dog and her breeding program, Susan doubtless would have preferred to prove Kori a total loser.

NINETEEN

"ARE YOU WHISKEY MATTIMOE?"

A lean gentleman in a navy blue blazer extended his manicured hand. I shook it, wondering if he'd missed my public pre-humiliation—I mean, introduction—or if he was simply being formal.

Then I read his nametag and knew he'd skipped the Breeder Breakfast.

"Yes! Nice to meet you in person, Perry. Good show ... so far."

The event chairperson pressed his lips into a thin smile that hinted at something beyond polite agreement.

"Thank you. That round was a tad surprising, wasn't it? Not what the Breeder Education Committee expected *at all* ..."

He let his voice trail off. Perry Stiles had a finely modulated sense of the dramatic. Detecting jubilation behind his words, I suspected that he wasn't a fan of Susan or her committee.

"Well, my Walk of Shame with Abra will prove 'em right," I said lightly.

Perry's expression sharpened. "You don't have to look bad, you know. That's not the point."

Before I could ask what the point was, his cell phone rang. Perry excused himself as he removed it from his inside jacket pocket. Glancing at the caller ID, he replaced the phone without answering it.

"You were saying," I reminded him, "that I don't have to look bad. I thought that was why Susan brought me here. To show breeders and handlers what not to do."

"Yes, but not at the expense of your self-esteem. Certainly not!"

"Abra doesn't care about my self-esteem ... and I'm not sure Susan does, either. In fact, I don't think she likes me. I'm sure Ramona doesn't."

Perry's eyes flicked around the arena. Then he stepped closer, his manner confidential.

"Susan and Ramona have done a lot for our organization. That being said, they have their detractors. Not everyone likes the way they choose to make examples of people who don't meet their standards."

"You mean, they've done this 'Bad Example' thing before?"

"Every year that they've co-chaired Breeder Education. And that's as many years as I've been part of Midwest Afghan Hounds. Of course, Ramona has been at it longer than Susan, but then she's considerably older. Ramona has been active in this group since ... well, since Hector was a pup."

When I smiled at the dated expression, he added, "You knew what I meant! My aunt used to say that."

"Mine, too."

"Wonder why I thought of it now," Perry mused.

"Maybe because we're surrounded by dogs?"

He chuckled. "Say, someone told me you're from Magnet Springs."

I nodded. "Ever been there?"

"Many times! I live in Chicago, on the Near North Side. Magnet Springs is one of my favorite summertime destinations. I love the beach, but I especially love the stores and restaurants."

"Chicago has some nice stores and restaurants, too."

"Of course. But the ones in Magnet Springs are so quaint."

That's what big-city people loved about our town: its quieter, calmer, cleaner lifestyle. Kind of like Amish country, without the horses but with electricity. Plus a beach. Magnet Springs was a popular playground for people from Chicagoland, especially rich people and gay people. I was willing to bet that Perry belonged to both categories.

"Do you usually come to Magnet Springs for the weekend or a longer stay?" I said.

"Weekends, usually, although last spring a friend and I rented a house on the beach for a week."

"Did you enjoy yourselves?"

Perry sighed. "It should have been our most relaxing vacation ever. I'd lined up someone to babysit my dogs and someone else to babysit my business—I'm a painting contractor, specializing in *faux* finishes—but at the last minute my friend couldn't find anyone to take care of his cat. So he brought it along. Big mistake. We should have cleared it with the landlord, I know, but everything was so last-minute, and anyway the cat was a breed that doesn't shed."

"Not... a Devon rex?"

"That's it! Ugly little sucker, if you ask me. But then I love Afghan hounds, so a cat with almost no hair is not going to make my heart beat faster. Anyway, the damned thing slipped out two days before we left, and we never found it. We spent every blasted minute of daylight looking up and down the beach and all around the dunes. We even posted signs and placed an ad in the local paper. No luck. My friend was devastated."

My skin prickled. "Was the cat ... by any chance ... gray?"

Perry stared. "Yes."

"And male? A rather aggressive unneutered male?"

Perry moved his hands and feet in a nervous little dance.

"Did you find Boomgarden? Is that what you're telling me?!"

"I didn't find him, no. But our local animal rescue did. Thanks to a complete misunderstanding, he ended up staying at my house for a few days—along with a herd of other stray cats. Then Fleggers neutered him and found him a home."

"Fleggers? Who's that?"

"Four Legs Good. They're a bunch of animal-rights crazies, but they saved your friend's cat. I know where he is. His name is Yoda now."

Perry literally squealed with delight. I was afraid that his next response might be to hug me. Since I intensely dislike emotional displays, I took two steps backward—right into Brenda Spenser. I didn't know it was Brenda till I turned around to apologize.

Unfortunately for her, I had stepped on—and smudged—the toe of her very fine shoe. A Manolo Blahnik, I think she called it. Anyway, she admitted that she hadn't been watching where she walked, either. She was distracted, trying to find Matt Koniger. I bit my tongue before I could say, "Have you checked behind the side door curtain?"

"I just saw him go that way. With Susan Davies," Perry said, pointing toward the notorious exit.

"He was with Susan?" Brenda looked baffled. "I thought he was going to relieve his mother at her booth."

Perry shrugged. As soon as Brenda was out of earshot, he turned to me.

"Matt specializes in a different kind of relief."

"I've seen it!" I exclaimed. "I mean, I saw him with Susan this morning. Behind the curtain ..."

"Most of us did," Perry said. "She's Matt's squeeze. And he's hers."

"You mean ... they do this kind of thing often?"

"Susan and Matt have been on-again, off-again for—oh—I'd say three or four years. We all know it, but we pretend we don't. It's more fun that way."

"I thought Matt was with Brenda."

"He is. Matt shacks up with whichever widow or divorcée will pay his way and give him the good life," Perry said. "That doesn't stop him from having fun! This year it's Brenda. Ramona made a play for him, too."

I gaped. "Ramona Bowden?"

"That's the only Ramona I know. We think Matt turned her down because of her size. He doesn't care how old they are, but he does like them thin."

"Is Ramona divorced?" I said.

"Widowed," Perry replied. "Twice. Two very nice insurance settlements."

"Susan's married," I said, thinking out loud.

That made Perry Stiles smile. "I wouldn't call what Susan and Liam have a marriage. More like an arrangement."

I didn't know which stunned me more—Perry's revelations or the casualness with which he shared them. Now I wondered why Susan tolerated Kori at all, let alone trained her to handle dogs, if she didn't care about pleasing Liam. Unless her goal was getting back at him. Maybe the whole Kori-as-Bad Example maneuver was just another way for Susan to piss off her husband.

But why was Perry, who had no investment in pleasing me, so eager to share club gossip? Was he trying to build his own ego, or did he simply love dishing dirt?

Perry's gaze moved restlessly around the room; as event chairperson, he no doubt needed to keep moving and schmoozing.

"Listen," I said. "I'll put you in touch with the person who has Yoda—I mean, Boomgarden—but first I need more info about Susan and Liam. Will you share?"

Perry's eyes danced. "Why? Planning to blackmail somebody?"

"No. But I work with Liam, and I feel like Susan's playing me."

"Of course she's playing you! That's what Susan does."

"Does Liam know Susan cheats?" I asked.

Perry chuckled. "Everybody knows."

"Does Liam care?"

"Care that she cheats, or care that everybody knows?"

"Either."

"Not much. Liam cheats, too. Between you and me, I think Susan tries to embarrass him with her affairs because he embarrasses her with his. I assume you know about his ... um ... taste?"

"I haven't met him yet. My company just signed on to rep his new real estate development."

"Ah." Perry checked to make sure no one was eavesdropping. "I'm going out on a limb here: is the person who did the deal for you with Liam an extremely attractive woman of color?"

"How do you know Odette Mutombo?"

"I don't. I know Liam Davies... well enough to know he loves exotic dark-skinned women. They're the only women he'll do business with."

"It's my company," I protested.

"At the risk of sounding crude," Perry said, "what I mean is they're the only women Liam will sleep with before he does business. And he has a reputation for doing business only with women who sleep with him."

"No way!"

I made my voice sound firm, but my head swam. Odette Mutombo was a real-estate-selling, contract-negotiating force of nature. She was also long-married to Reginald, the only psychiatrist in Magnet Springs. While I often wondered how those two busy and ambitious people made time to make their marriage work, I never doubted that they did. In cynical moments, I suspected that they got along well because they were too self-involved to demand much from each other. Yet I never for a single moment imagined that Odette would cheat on Reginald. Let alone use her considerable sex appeal to make a sale!

Odette was consistently excellent at her job for three reasons: She (1) knew all about real estate, (2) had mastered the art of the deal, and (3) worked her tight round ass off. Period.

Before I could sum that up for Perry, a breeder I recognized from the breakfast meeting intervened to request a moment of the chairperson's time. Excusing himself, Perry reminded me that we still needed to discuss Boomgarden, a.k.a. Yoda. As far as I was concerned, we still needed to discuss all kinds of things, including Liam Davies and Mitchell Slater. Perry promised to meet me near the concession stand after my Walk of Shame, which he generously referred to as my "Spotlight Moment."

I didn't know quite what to make of Perry Stiles. Clearly, he was a leader, an organizer, and a gossipmonger. Although his inference about Liam and Odette upset me, he managed to bolster my sagging self-esteem with the reminder that I didn't have to let Susan or her committee humiliate me. Hell, they hadn't got the best of Kori, had they?

I needed to correct Perry's Liam-Odette confusion before he could spread that misunderstanding like oil across water. Odette was my friend as well as my star sales agent. I had a duty to defend her.

But first I had a more pressing duty: to handle my own dog. Susan Davies waved to me from across the arena. At her side, on a leash, Abra was poised to bring me down.

TWENTY

Susan must have taken the time to reapply lipstick after her side-door kissing session. She flashed a glossy smile as I crossed the arena to reclaim my canine.

"Are you ready, Whiskey? Abra is."

My dog ignored me, as usual. Instead she fixed her soulful eyes on Susan and thumped her tail.

I eyed Abra warily. We hadn't seen each other in eighteen hours. Her coat was as tangled as it had been the day before. But something had changed. She gazed at Susan with what appeared to be profound devotion. Then I got it: Abra wasn't calm; she was waiting. Yes, that was it. The hairy beast was coiled and ready to spring into crazy mode the moment Susan handed me her lead.

"Here's what we'll do," Susan said cheerily. "Ramona will make a brief announcement. Then you'll hear a prerecorded drum roll and some marching music. That's your cue to walk clockwise all the way around the arena, starting from the side door, over there."

She pointed, but I didn't play along.

"I know where the side door is. I went out that way. Right past you."

Susan didn't blink. "Then you know exactly where to go, don't you?"

With that, she passed the leash. I held my breath as the leather loop slipped into my hand and around my wrist. Abra's head rotated in my direction; we locked eyes. I willed the Afghan hound to read my thoughts: *We will walk. Together. You will not drag me. You will not disgrace me. You will not dislocate my shoulder.*

I wasn't thinking about the march around the arena; I just wanted to make it to our starting position at the side door. Once we got that far, I would pray for the next miracle.

But something else happened first. Abra and I were turning toward the side exit when a cry went up from somewhere behind us. I heard Susan's voice shouting, "Drop! Silverado, drop! Somebody stop that dog!"

The next few moments were a mad blur of Afghan hound and human commotion. I whirled around in time to see Silverado, the big blue dog that Kori had shown. He was now bearing down on me. I don't mean that in a scary way. After all, this was the dog who had better manners than I did. Standing still, Silverado is a large, gorgeous dog, a picture postcard of male Afghan hound glory. In motion, coming straight at me, he was all churning legs and flying fur—an apparently airborne canine on a mission. And that mission, as it turned out, was making contact with Abra.

My bimbo bitch had attracted a brand-new hunk. A champion, no less. And this time, the hunk was the chaser rather than the chased. Usually Abra instigated and controlled all things sexual. She saw, she chased, she conquered. In human terms, my dog was a dominatrix. But not today. As Silverado flew at her, she dropped into a submissive posture. And I accidentally dropped the leash. I don't know what made me do it, the sight of Silverado charging or of Abra playing the coquette.

One brief instant of complete human detachment was all those two required. Abra bounced straight up as only an Afghan can, executed a spectacular mid-air twirl, and zoomed out the open side door, followed closely by her excited beau. Being an unneutered male, his excitement was obvious to all.

Susan was still calling for her boy to "drop," even as his silver self vanished from the arena. Matt Koniger bounded valiantly after the dogs. If he'd asked my advice, I could have saved him some sweat. Been there, done that, got nothing for it. Nobody, but nobody, can catch Abra and partner *in medias res.*

I realized then that Susan had switched from calling Silverado to cursing Kori. Fleetingly I wondered if the other Bad Example was once again kissing the invisible bodyguard. I hoped so for her sake. That way even if Kori got nailed by her aunt for screwing up big-time, she would have the satisfaction of a face well kissed.

Did I mention that I had lunged all the way to the floor? I was now in the undignified position of having lost not only my dog—and, by association, Susan's—but also my balance. Unlike some women—including, no doubt, Susan—I don't slide gracefully down. I topple. I tumble. I crash. From my position on one knee with the opposite foot turned sideways underneath me, there was no elegant way to get vertical.

Fortunately, a gentleman extended a hand. Perry Stiles smiled down at me. Correction: the man beamed.

"Now that's what I call a 'Spotlight Moment,'" he said as he gently returned me to full upright position.

I moaned, "That turned out way worse than I'd imagined!"

"*Au contraire.* Think about what happened here. Susan's unattended dog caused your dog to escape. I hate to speak litigiously, but let's be realistic. Should Abra fail to return, you might very well have grounds for a lawsuit."

"Abra never fails to return," I assured him.

Perry kept smiling as Susan bellowed for Kori; he seemed deviously delighted by the Breeder Educator's dismay.

"Isn't Kori the one in trouble?" I said.

"Susan will blame Kori, of course. But the buck stops with the owner. That's the law."

I gazed at the side exit.

"Why is that door ajar? I had to push it open when I went out earlier."

"Handlers prop it open to hear what's going on inside while they're outside with their dogs," Perry said. "Quite a coincidence, don't you agree?"

I nodded, although I had to ask what he meant.

"That Kori the handler is nowhere to be seen when Matt the handler turns into an action-hero."

I nodded again, but I still didn't get it... till Perry summed it up.

"Kori, bad. Matt, good. Kori is on Liam's side. Matt is on Susan's side. Somebody wanted to make sure Kori looked bad."

"You don't think Kori just screwed up?"

"Oh, she screwed up, all right. She won her round! Bad examples aren't supposed to best the competition. So Susan had to even the score. With a little help."

My head was starting to hurt. "Are you saying that Susan and Matt framed Kori by setting Silverado loose after making sure the door was open for his escape?"

Perry grinned wickedly. "Do I have to say it?"

"I thought Matt seemed kind of nice. Except for the illicit lover thing. He was friendly when I asked about grooming Afghan hounds."

"Oh, Matt's very friendly. Ask any woman here."

Ah-hah. Perry had given me an opening. Unfortunately, I lost it to the chaos following my Spotlight Moment. Someone was paging Perry, no doubt to deal with the complications of a lost champion and a missing Bad Example. Counting Kori, that was *two* missing Bad Examples. Perry excused himself to tend to business.

Meanwhile, for what I assumed was the benefit of the crowd around her, Susan continued to rant about Kori. I heard her say, "My niece is showing her true colors now. And they're not pink, they're yellow! When it's time to take responsibility, Kori is afraid to show her face!"

Susan seemed almost as theatrical as Ramona. Then it occurred to me that I hadn't seen Ramona lately. Not, in fact, since the Breeder Breakfast. Abra had left too soon to cue Ramona's opening remarks for our Walk of Shame.

Two ashen-faced breeders intercepted Perry before he could walk twenty feet. His smug expression instantly disappeared; in its place was a look of genuine horror.

TWENTY-ONE

PERRY STILES DASHED PAST me with such sudden speed that I couldn't compute what was happening. His run was accompanied by a chorus of shrieking sirens. Also shrieking Afghan hound fanciers; they scurried through the side door after him. I joined the fray.

The scene of the crime was around the corner of the building, at almost the exact spot where I'd caught Kori kissing MacArthur (and MacArthur kissing her back). But there was nothing titillating about what had gone down since.

My height permitted me to peer over the heads of shorter mortals. A small crowd had gathered around the prone form of Ramona Bowden. She looked much as she had when she'd fainted in my driveway on Thursday, save three major differences: (1) Jeb hadn't thrown himself on top of her for protection; (2) she was face down; and (3) there was a whole lot of blood.

Perry Stiles kneeled alongside the mound that was Ramona. He checked her pulse as everyone else formed a murmuring circle. I couldn't help but notice that Ramona's silvery pajama-like outfit, now splotched with red, showed no sign of a breath beneath it.

Since I don't do well in the presence of body fluids, I quickly stepped back. To be accurate, I stumbled backwards and narrowly missed the team of charging EMTs, who arrived post-haste with black bags and sundry portable equipment.

Just as I wondered who had dialed 9-1-1, my peripheral vision snagged a glimpse of the cleaner-slash-bodyguard. MacArthur wasn't lurking at the edge of the cornfield; he was standing there waving at me. Weakly I waved back. Then I realized that his gesture meant "Come over here!" So I went. Nobody in the crowd was watching anybody except Ramona.

MacArthur wouldn't let me speak till after we'd receded into the cornfield. Our progress through the drying stalks wasn't silent, but it was furtive. Despite telltale rustling, cornstalks provide good cover. The exhibit hall and the melee outside it had completely vanished from our view. Which meant nobody could see us, either.

"I've been alternating between watching you, Susan, and Ramona," MacArthur began.

"Don't forget Kori," I said. "You fit her into your schedule, too."

He smiled. "Every working man needs a break now and then."

"Where is Kori, by the way? I hope you know that the dog she was handling took off after Abra!"

"So I heard. I had just finished my latest tour of the exhibit hall—"

"You were *inside* the hall? When?"

"I tour and secure it every hour on the hour," he said.

"Then how come I've never seen you in there?"

"Because I know how to do my job. May I continue?"

I nodded.

"I slipped out the side door just before your dog and that champion. No sooner had I started my exterior tour than I heard a voice raised in anger. It was coming from the other side of the building."

"Only one voice?" I asked.

"Correct. It was Ramona's. She sounded agitated. Then she screamed. I rushed 'round the corner and found her lying there—just as I heard the uproar from inside the building."

"You mean, when Silverado went after Abra."

"Presumably."

"Did you call 9-1-1?" I said.

"Yes. I would have administered CPR, but it was not appropriate."

"Because Ramona's … dead?"

"No," he replied. "Because she was breathing just fine … although somebody shot her."

"Why would Ramona have been shouting at the shooter?"

"I didn't say she was. If you looked closely, you would have seen her mobile on the ground."

"Her cell phone?"

"Yes. I believe Ramona was arguing with someone on her mobile when she was shot. The two incidents may or may not be related. I checked her phone," he added, "and reported the latest numbers to Jenx."

"Will Ramona live?"

"I've never known anyone to die from a bullet wound to the arse."

"But … she's nonresponsive!"

MacArthur cocked an eyebrow at me. "Is she now?"

"She didn't respond to Perry Stiles. And there's so much blood!"

"It's a flesh wound, and the woman has a lot of … flesh. That explains the blood," MacArthur said. "As for her being nonresponsive, she used to be an actress. Off-Broadway. Strictly heavy drama."

Jenx herself called before I could ask MacArthur what he'd told the chief. She was in the process of identifying the other party in Ramona's latest conversation. The former actress had dialed a cell phone in the 630 area code. That covered northwestern Cook County, Illinois—including Itasca, where Susan and Liam lived.

"It doesn't mean the person Ramona talked with lives there," Jenx reminded me. "It just means the phone was registered there. And it's a cell phone, so he—or she—could have been anywhere. Even at the dog show. We won't know till we run down the records."

The Magnet Springs Police Department didn't have a forensics team. Or any technology worth mentioning. I was about to ask Jenx how she planned to acquire cell phone records since the latest shooting wasn't even in her jurisdiction.

"Brady's cousin Lonnie is going to hack into the other cell phone account," the chief announced happily.

I didn't bother to comment on the obvious, that hacking was illegal. But I did call the chief's attention to the fact that Lonnie was incarcerated.

"That's the beauty of it!" she exclaimed. "He's been good since he's been inside, so he's a low-security inmate—with web access. And he's already in the slammer, so there's no risk and no down side!"

"Except to you," I pointed out. "If he got caught, you could be charged as an accomplice."

"Not a chance," Jenx said. "He won't get caught cuz he's good, and the phone companies aren't smart. Besides which, he's Brady's cousin, and family is family. They don't rat each other out. Lonnie won't mess with me, either. I helped get him the lightest possible sentence for grand theft auto. The kid's messed up, but he's loyal as a dog." She paused. "Loyal as most dogs. I hear yours ran away again."

"Yes, but this time it wasn't really her fault."

Jenx harrumphed. "I don't like the direction this thing is taking. Too many flying bullets. We already have one corpse and one casualty. Not to mention two missing dogs."

"We always have missing dogs," I sighed.

"And you attract dead bodies."

"What do you suggest?"

"Get the hell out of there!" Jenx said. "You've been humiliated, so you're morally free to leave."

"Except now I have to find Abra."

TWENTY-TWO

Wailing sirens on my end made it impossible to hear what Jenx said next. I assumed that the EMTs had loaded Ramona aboard the ambulance and were heading to the nearest hospital. Probably in Elkhart.

By the time I could hear again, Jenx had disconnected. MacArthur was still with me, his considerable bulk squeezed sideways between tidy rows of yellowing cornstalks. He hadn't yet answered my question about Kori. So I asked him again where she had gone.

"She had an emergency," he said.

"What kind of 'emergency'?"

Given what I knew about Susan's niece, I could imagine a wide range of crises, from scoring dope to stealing cars.

"Kori had to counsel her sponsoree."

"I beg your pardon?"

"She's a sponsor in a step-program. The woman she sponsors was 'right on the edge,' so Kori gave her a reason to live."

"Kori ... advises people ... how to fix their lives?" I couldn't buy it.

MacArthur nodded. "She's good. I heard her on the phone. Then she went off somewhere to talk in private."

What kind of step-program would designate Kori as an advisor? Was there a self-help group for irresponsible women inclined to crash cars? And, if so, had Kori graduated?

Did MacArthur actually believe that story or expect me to? I wondered if the cleaner was determined to cover for Kori, even to the extent of bamboozling me. Was she that good a kisser?

Then I had a troubling thought: Kori currently lived with Susan and Liam. In Itasca. If she had a cell phone, it might have a 630 area code.

But why would Ramona call Kori? And even if she did, was the call relevant? I strained to imagine how Ramona's phone conversation could be connected to her getting shot in the tush.

"MacArthur, you said you were inside the exhibit hall just before Silverado got loose. Did you see what happened?"

"Sorry, no. I do have a theory, however."

I parted a couple cornstalks in order to lean closer. He cleared his throat.

"I believe Susan set it up. After Kori's unexpected win in the show ring, Susan wanted to save face by making Kori look bad."

"But why sacrifice her own championship dog?" I objected.

"You're assuming Susan doesn't know where her dog went."

"Her dog is with my dog! And my dog is notorious for leading other dogs astray."

"Here's the thing," MacArthur said. "Unlike you, Susan would want her dog back. Silverado is well trained and worth considerable money. I suspect that he had an objective."

"We all saw his 'objective'! He wanted Abra!"

"I mean, Silverado may have been coached to run somewhere specific. Think about it, Whiskey. In the commotion surrounding Ramona, nobody followed the dogs."

"Matt did—" I began. And then I got it. "Matt is on Susan's side. Nobody's on Kori's side."

MacArthur said, "It's a theory."

"Back up. I need to know how you met Kori."

He smiled innocently. "I'm here to guard you and Susan—and those close to you and Susan. Kori is Susan's niece, so I'm guarding her. And now, if you'll excuse me, duty calls."

Kori was about as close to Susan as Avery was to me. But MacArthur might have missed that irony. Not because he was dim, but because he was a man. He turned away, crashing noisily through the corn. Was he heading back the way we'd come? I didn't think so, but I'd already lost track.

Fortunately I didn't get lost, and I didn't follow MacArthur, either. For once in my life, I trusted my own instincts. I started back the way I thought I'd come and soon heard a voice raised in anger. I stopped to listen and instantly recognized the voice as Susan Davies'.

"What do you mean, it was an 'e-mer-gen-cy'?" She separated the syllables as if translating from a foreign language. "I'm not interested in your excuses!"

There was no other voice. And nothing more from Susan. I was still too deep in the corn to see beyond the stalks in front of me.

Had I overheard the tail end of a one-sided phone conversation? Was she yelling at Kori or belittling someone else? I waited a few moments for her to either speak again or be gone. Then I emerged from the field.

Blood soaked the grass where Ramona Bowden had fallen. Although I tried not to see the dark red stain, I couldn't ignore it. My stomach clenched and gurgled in response. Everyone, including Susan, had departed. Would Perry Stiles insist that the show must go on?

I needed to speak with him about several issues, starting with the little matter of returning Yoda, a.k.a. Boomgarden, to his rightful owner. That would break Peg Goh's heart. Now that the damned Devon rex was tattooed on her arm, she'd have a permanent reminder of the pet she'd only briefly been allowed to love. I hoped that Perry would find a way to make her sacrifice bearable. Selfishly, I also hoped he'd tell me who among those present might have had a motive to kill Mitchell Slater and injure Ramona Bowden.

Before my Walk of Shame was aborted, Perry had suggested we meet at the concession stand. He might be there now since it was the most likely gathering place for agitated attendees. I, for one, was in urgent need of refreshment, both to keep up my strength and to shut up my growling tummy.

With a dog missing and a breeder wounded, the event chairperson had to feel like the kid with his finger in the leaking dike. Pretty much how I felt at that moment. Or at any moment when Abra was out of control.

Rounding the building on my way to the side entrance, I nearly collided with my former nanny, Deely Smarr. Trained by the Coast

Guard in damage control, that was precisely what she was doing now. For the other side. First and foremost, Deely was a Flegger. She was also in love with Dr. David, so her role here was to disrupt the dog show. Posted at the propped-open side door, Deely used a megaphone to blast an *antispeciesist* message into the exhibit hall.

"What if human beauty pageants were like dog shows? Think about it! The judges could check out *any part of your anatomy*. And they would make you jog around the ring, *naked*! You would have to prove you had the 'right' heritage to be considered beautiful. Could *any* of you be 'best in show'?"

Deely had a point. An obscure and irrelevant point as far as this crowd was concerned. She was still holding the megaphone to her lips when I tapped her shoulder and suggested she step away from the door before someone called Security. Someone like Perry Stiles.

Then I felt a tap on my shoulder. I spun around to face Kori Davies. She looked past me at Deely.

"You got *cojones*, sister! I like your style."

"Thank you, ma'am," replied Deely.

Hastily I made the introductions. "Kori, this is Deely Smarr, former Coast Guard nanny and founding Flegger. Deely, this is Kori Davies. She's ... um—"

"I'm a Bad Example," Kori said. "But I have way more fun than those tight-asses."

She indicated the people in the arena ... who were moving rapidly toward us. Like a lynch mob.

"Silverado ran away," I told Kori. "With Abra."

"Yeah. I heard."

Kori blew a whopping big pink bubble. Angry Afghan hound fanciers, led by Perry Stiles, were closing in on us; I could almost see the whites of their eyes. Standing between Deely the protester and Kori the rogue handler suddenly seemed like a bad idea.

Deely spoke into her megaphone again: "We come in peace, but we stand in opposition! We see you for who you are: two-legged animals enslaving four-legged animals! Repent now! Set your fellow creatures free!"

"You don't really mean that, do you?" I whispered. "If they set the dogs free, they'd be strays."

"Not 'strays,'" Deely corrected me. "*Independents*. Animals in possession of their full rights and privileges."

"Yeah, well, Abra and her brand-new beau are 'independents' already. They set themselves free."

"I know," Deely said. "Dr. David and I saw them run by while we were setting up."

Before I could ask which way they had gone, Kori tugged on Deely's arm.

"Perry Stiles is gonna throw your ass in the slammer!"

"Not if I can help it, ma'am. I'm wearing running shoes."

"Me, too," Kori said. "Let's get the hell out of here!"

I waved at Perry, and then I ran, too.

TWENTY-THREE

Over my shoulder, I shouted to Perry Stiles, "Meet you at the concession stand!"

I didn't know if he heard me. Kori and Deely had set quite a pace. I was pushing hard to catch up. They had shot off toward the front of the exhibit hall, in the opposite direction one would take to reach the spot where Ramona was shot. The exhibit hall faced the RV lot and the back of the Barnyard Inn. Although the Midwest Afghan Hound Specialty was under way, a few off-duty show dogs were parked in outdoor crates near cottage-sized vehicles. They howled as we hove into view. Poor beasts. If they were anything like Abra, and somewhere under those perfect glossy coats they had to be, they just wanted to join in the run.

Deely and Kori reached the lot well before I did. Although I wanted to blame my lagging speed on my footwear, I recognized the real culprit: hunger. I'd hardly eaten since leaving Magnet Springs.

Who was I kidding? The true villain was age. Hunger was just an accomplice. Running behind Kori and Deely, who were in their early twenties, I felt more decrepit than my mother. Pumping my thirty-four-year-old legs as hard as I could didn't promise speed. It promised sore muscles and a stinging dose of reality. I wasn't young anymore. I was sliding toward middle age.

By the time I reached Deely and Kori, they'd already gotten their wind back—if they'd ever lost it. Deely was introducing Kori to Dr. David, who stood on a makeshift stage surrounded by Fleggers. I knew they were all Fleggers because everybody wore bright yellow shirts with black block letters that proclaimed

YOUR DOGS DESERVE DIGNITY.
WHY MAKE THEM COMPETE IN AN EVENT YOU COULDN'T WIN?
BAN CANINE BEAUTY PAGEANTS!

I jogged up to the edge of the stage and promptly doubled over, gasping for breath.

"Hewwo, Whiskey," said Dr. David with his signature speech impediment. Allow me to translate the rest of his remarks: "Told you we'd be here! Sorry to hear about Abra running away. Again. Wish we could help."

"Oh, please help!" I panted. "Please, please help!"

Around Magnet Springs, Dr. David—in his Animal Ambulance—was the dogcatcher of last resort. I tried not to count the number of times he'd assisted me in looking for Abra.

The good vet leaned down from the stage.

"I don't think you understand. Deely and I are here in an official capacity. We can't retrieve the very dogs we admonish owners to set free!"

"Oh shit."

This time finding Abra was going to be entirely up to me. And I didn't know the territory.

"But we can tell you which way the dogs went," Deely said helpfully.

She pointed toward the Barnyard Inn. We were looking at the back of the building, the section that housed my room. The motel faced Route 20.

"Did they cross the highway or follow it?" I asked without enthusiasm.

"Neither," Deely said. "They're in room 18."

"What?"

"Yes, ma'am. Abra was chasing the big silvery dog, running loops around the RV lot—"

"*Abra* was chasing Silverado?" I interrupted. "When I last saw them, *he* was chasing her!"

"Not by the time they got here," Deely said.

"That's right," Dr. David confirmed. "By then Abra had assumed her usual role as sexual aggressor."

He pronounced it "sexuah aggwessah." That made it sound even worse.

"The male dog—I think you called him Silverado?—left the RV lot and ran to the motel," Deely continued. "Abra followed him in hot pursuit."

No doubt.

"When Silverado scratched at the door of room 18," Deely said, "somebody let them in."

"Not room 18," Kori said. "That can't be right."

"Yes, ma'am, I'm sure it is. Dr. David and I were both witnesses."

The good vet nodded. So did the entire chorus of Fleggers arranged on the stage.

"Why couldn't it be room 18?" I asked Kori.

"Because that's my room. And I'm out here. *Duh*."

"Somebody was in there ten minutes ago, ma'am," said Deely. "We all saw it."

Dr. David and his yellow-shirted compatriots agreed.

"The bitch set me up," Kori muttered.

I assumed we weren't talking about Abra anymore. Just to be certain, I asked.

"Who do you think I mean?" Kori snapped. "My favorite auntie! Susan wants to make damn sure everybody knows I'm a Bad Example. She's getting back at me for winning that round!"

"Why would having Silverado in your room be wrong?" I said.

"Susan wants to make it look like I'm trying to steal him! First, I set him free. And then I hid him in my room. But she did it herself!"

"I don't see how," I said. "Even if Susan set him free, she couldn't have been in your room to let him in. There was no time—"

"She got somebody to do it for her! Susan has ways of making people do whatever she wants."

Kori narrowed her eyes and blew a bubble half the size of her head. I stepped back in case it exploded. No need. Kori deftly deflated it with her metal tongue stud and rolled the whole wad back into her mouth.

"The plan, if there was one, has a downside," I pointed out. "They got Abra, too. And that bitch is no bargain."

Kori asked Deely and Dr. David if the person who opened the door was a man or a woman. Neither could say, so they consulted their team of Fleggers. No one had actually seen the whole human.

Kori spat her gum on the ground. I assumed that meant she was annoyed, so I changed the subject.

"Hey, I'm next door to you. In room 17."

"No shit. Your puking kept me up half the night."

I was about to apologize because that's what Midwesterners with low self-esteem do. There was no time, however. At that moment every head in the vicinity—including those on the Fleggers' stage and those inside the RV park dog crates—turned toward the roar in the sky.

The sound stirred memories: I'd once ridden in a helicopter and endured the deafening whine of the engine, plus the *whup-whup* of the blades. As the craft drew closer, everyone who could covered their ears. The dogs had to settle for howling.

At first I thought it was a cop helicopter, zooming in to investigate Ramona's shooting. After all, this was the third round of gunfire at the Barnyard Inn—and the second round aimed at Ramona—in less than twenty-four hours. Somebody was obliged to check it out.

It wasn't the police, however. After the craft landed neatly in the parking lot, the second person out the door was Odette Mutombo. She followed a man who jumped athletically from the helicopter and then offered his hand to help her down. Wearing what I recognized as her favorite Armani suit, Odette gracefully disembarked.

The man wore a flack jacket, jeans, and boots; his still-thick hair was an equal blend of brown and silver. I couldn't help but notice he stood so close to Odette that their shoulders touched. She threw back her ebony head and laughed. Then he slid an arm around her waist, and they started toward us.

I was about to meet Liam Davies. At last.

Perry simply couldn't have been right about Liam and Odette. I'd known Odette for years, and I refused to believe she would betray her husband. Not even for the biggest commission check of her life.

And yet . . . watching her with Liam stirred an old, happy memory. The only man who'd ever made me laugh like that while doing business was my late husband Leo. And when we weren't working, we were having great sex.

TWENTY-FOUR

"We were en route to Chicago to meet with Liam's architect. The pilot got a radio message from Jenx that Ramona had been shot, so Liam decided to swing by the dog show to make sure Susan was all right."

That was Odette's story, and I had no doubt she would stick to it. My star salesperson had just introduced me to the man who might make both of us considerably richer. Provided that his plans for Big and Little Houses on the Prairie got off the ground as smoothly as his chopper.

Liam Davies was not a tall man. Nor was he what I could call handsome. But he had a quality worth way more than good looks alone: charisma. I suspected that Liam had started out in sales and worked up to much bigger things. Like convincing investors to loan him scads of cash with the promise of delivering office buildings, shopping malls, and subdivisions.

Now Odette stood on his right side, and Kori stood on his left. Neither acknowledged the other, but both seemed pleased to have at least some of the Great Man's attention. And to have one of his arms around each of their waists.

"How's my favorite niece?" Liam asked Kori.

"I won my round, but I lost the dog."

I had to admire how succinctly she summed that up.

"Don't worry. We'll get you another," Uncle Liam said.

"It was Susan's dog," Kori said.

For just an instant I thought he was going to pat her on the head. Instead Liam turned to me.

"Your sales agent is brilliant! She has a contact list that could rival Donald Trump's!"

Everybody in west Michigan knew that Odette was the best schmoozer on this side of the lake. So I merely nodded.

"I'm going to introduce O. to my Chicago contacts," the developer said.

"'O.'?" I repeated. "Odette lets you call her 'O.'?"

"Doesn't everyone call her that?"

"Not if they want to keep their teeth."

"Whiskey is funny," Odette told Liam. "You'll get used to it."

"She's not that funny," Kori said.

I stared at O.'s perfectly marcelled waves. How the hell had they remained unruffled by the chopper's tornadic blades? Come to think of it, shouldn't Liam's short hair also be mussed? I was pretty sure mine was a mare's nest, and I hadn't been that close to the copter. Maybe O. and L. were already sharing hair gel.

"And now if you'll excuse me," Liam said, "I need to find my wife. Could you direct me—?"

The eavesdropping members of Team Fleggers pointed as one to the exhibit hall.

"Thank you," Liam said, acknowledging the group onstage. "I like your shirts. Never been a dog-show enthusiast myself."

"Me, neither," Kori announced. "Susan made me do it."

We all watched as she and her uncle jogged together toward the arena. Then I arched my eyebrows at "O." and waited for the rest of her story. She arched hers back at me but said nothing. We went on like that for a minute or so. I could feel the Fleggers' collectively curious gaze.

"Can we step away from the nut jobs?" Odette asked. "Or did Dr. David draft you, too?"

"Nope. I'm still a free agent."

I gestured toward the motel, thinking we might adjourn to my room.

"Definitely not," Odette said. "I refuse to set foot in any establishment known as the Barnyard Inn. Isn't there a Starbucks around here?"

"We're in Amish country," I said. "The best we can hope for is a cheese bar."

"Where *are* the Amish?" Odette asked. "I didn't see any as we flew in."

"I've been wondering that, too, ever since I got here! The closest I've been to anything Amish is holding one of their brochures."

"It's a scam," Odette intoned. "There are no real Amish anymore. Only actors."

"I don't think that's true . . . "

But suddenly I wondered if it might be.

"We could take my car," I suggested. "Drive around a little. See if we can find us some Amish. Some real Amish."

"What about Abra? Did you lose her again?"

"Only for a few minutes this time. She's in room 18 with her new boyfriend. Don't ask."

Odette declined my Amish search invitation. She expected to be airborne again soon.

Trying to sound neutral, I said, "What's up with you two?"

"We're getting the word out on Big and Little Houses. Working night and day."

"Mostly nights?"

"Whatever it takes to get the job done," Odette replied blandly. "Liam is tireless."

Before I could insert my foot all the way into my mouth, my cell phone rang. The tune of the ring told me it was my ex-husband. Odette knew it, too.

"Tell Jeb I said hello. Also, tell him to take better care of you. You don't look good."

"Always nice to be jacked *down*." I fumbled for my phone.

"Whiskey, I'm going to sell every last home in that subdivision," Odette said. "Don't ask me how. Don't ask me when. And for god's sake don't accuse me of anything. Just because you can't trust your man doesn't mean you can't trust other men. Now go get sleep or food or sex. Whatever it takes to make you human again!"

She stalked off, and I opened my phone in time to catch Jeb.

"Hey," I said.

He wanted to know about the latest shooting. Both Jenx and MacArthur had already called him.

"What I really want to know is why *you* didn't call me," he said.

Jeb didn't sound like his laid-back self. He sounded either hurt or annoyed. Maybe both. I tried to explain that there was too much going on, what with Abra departing and Fleggers arriving.

"Abra runs away every chance she gets," he said. "And you knew Dr. David and Deely were coming. Those aren't excuses, Whiskey. You should have called me."

"Yeah? Well, maybe I needed you to call me. So I could be sure you care. Sometimes I'm not sure you do."

"You're not sure I care?"

"Sometimes, no, I'm not. Sometimes you seem more interested in other people."

"What other people?"

"Like the person who invited me here. You told me I should go to the show. You said it might help my business if I did. And I believed you. But now I think you just wanted to please Susan Davies!"

The silence on the other end of the phone was thunderous.

"Hello?" I said finally.

"I'm speechless," Jeb said. "If you believe what you just said . . . well, I have nothing to say."

"Convince me not to believe it!" I cried.

Then my stomach made a sound like a dying sperm whale—loud enough, I was sure, for every dog in the RV park to hear it. I expected a chorus of sympathetic howls.

"What's the matter?" Jeb said.

"I don't feel good. Odette said I look terrible. Oh, I forgot to tell you, she's here. With Liam. They came by helicopter."

"Liam showed up? Then he's gotta be worried about Susan. So I have a right to be worried about you," Jeb said. "In addition to being pissed at you. What do you want me to do? Should I come get you?"

"I can't leave! Abra's missing!"

Then I remembered that she wasn't. Anymore. We just had to get her and Silverado out of room 18. I hastily explained that to Jeb.

"Anyway, I have my car here," I added. "As soon as I can load Abra up, I'm heading for home. I should be there in time for dinner."

My stomach roiled again, and I wondered when or if it would be safe for me to actually eat.

"I don't know about food," I said, "but we can talk. Do you want to talk?"

"We need to talk," Jeb said firmly. "You got some crazy ideas in that head of yours."

Just then I noticed Matt Koniger. He was about fifty yards away, striding toward the exhibit hall, with a dog. One dog. Silverado.

"Excuse me," I told Jeb. "I'm gonna have to call you right back."

Of course there were other blue-gray hounds at the show. But Matt had been on a mission to retrieve that one. Plus Abra. I wondered how he'd managed to remove Susan's dog from Kori's motel room without Kori's key. She had been with me, and then she'd gone off with her uncle. What I really needed to know was what had happened to Abra.

"Didn't anyone tell you?" he said.

I shook my head.

"The door to room 18 was ajar. I found Silverado on the bed watching TV, but Abra was gone."

What little strength I had left leaked from my muscles like water from a shattered vase. Matt reached out a hand to steady me.

"Easy," he said. "You need something to eat. Let's go to the concession stand. My treat."

"No burgers," I murmured.

"No way," he agreed. "I recommend hot dogs or nachos."

I wasn't sure my stomach could handle either.

Inside the arena the competition had resumed. Perry Stiles must have decided that the show should go on.

A second show was in progress. In the concession area, Susan and Liam were having a conversation with Kori and Odette. I wasn't sure what I'd expected in that department, but it wasn't a four-way chat. The group had taken over a table in the concession area, where Silverado, Matt, and I were pointed now. I couldn't wait to see how Susan would express her gratitude to Matt for returning the lost dog. Most likely, she'd save some of her enthusiasm for their next trip to the side door.

Perry Stiles waved to me. He was in the concession area, too—standing at the condiments table, garnishing a wiener.

I thanked Matt for the offer to buy lunch, but said I'd cover my own. He promised to let me know if he heard anything about Abra, but his focus was now entirely on Susan. Did that make him his father's son?

"Good job getting the show going again," I told Perry. "And before you ask—the answer is 'Hell, no!' I have no affiliation whatsoever with those animal-rights maniacs. Except that some of them are my friends."

I flashed him my most earnest smile. The one I use whenever I have to explain myself to the IRS. Or to my mother.

Perry looked beyond me to the table where the Davies clan sat, accompanied by Odette. Susan was fussing over Matt and Silverado.

"You're witnessing a historic event of questionable taste," Perry whispered. "Susan, her husband, his lover, and her boy-toy. Plus the poor niece, stuck in the middle—with the dog."

"I just have one question," I said. "Is Matt as shallow as I think he is?"

"How shallow do you think he is?"

"Well, I met Mitchell Slater, and I don't think the apple fell far from the tree..."

Perry said, "So, you know that story! Who told?"

"The niece in the middle."

"Good for Kori! You got to love that girl's pluck, if not her wardrobe. Yes, Mitchell was a vain one, and Matt is more or less the same—minus the mean streak."

"Mitchell was nasty?"

"Ask his first wife. For that matter, ask any woman he loved and shoved aside."

"Including Susan?"

Perry looked startled. "Susan dumped Mitchell. I think she's the only one who pulled that off. If you ask me, she toyed with him just to get close to Matt. Or maybe, knowing Susan, all she really wanted was the dog."

"What dog?"

"The niece didn't tell you that story? Silverado was Mitchell's gift to Susan."

"I thought Susan dumped him—right after he left his wife for her. Then he cheated Susan out of her stud fee."

"Mitchell would have left his wife, anyway," Perry said. "He left them all. The man preferred conquests to connubial bliss. As for the stud fee, Susan didn't get cheated. Mitchell saved enough sperm to make lots of puppies. Silverado was one, and Susan got him—*plus* the full refund of her stud fee. Ramona knows that."

"Why would she and Susan lie?"

"Why do they do anything? For starters, Susan's a manipulative bitch, and Ramona's a drama queen. The latter will make a full recovery, by the way. She took the bullet in her well-padded ass, a glancing wound only."

I refrained from revealing what I knew about Ramona's acting career, courtesy of MacArthur.

Perry continued, "Ramona likes to make Susan look better than Susan is. Ramona probably thinks that makes her look better, too, by association. They're friends and co-breeders, after all. As for her lies about Slater, well, Ramona had issues of her own with that bad boy."

"What—?"

But I was interrupted. By a chili dog and a book. To be precise, I was interrupted by Odette Mutombo, who stood before me bearing gifts.

"Excuse me," she said to Perry. "Whiskey, you need to eat."

"Do I also need to read?"

"Yes. I bought this for you from that vendor over there."

She pointed to a smiling red-haired woman sitting near the concession stand, behind a table piled high with books.

"That's the author," Odette said, pointing to the woman's photo inside the book.

"Thanks... but I really don't have time to read."

"I think you should make time."

Odette tapped the cover, which featured a cartoon-like rendering of a running Afghan hound.

"It's a mystery about a dog like yours. That woman over there has written a whole series of them. Perhaps if you read the books, you would learn something."

I doubted it, but I took the book just the same, tucking it into my bag. I took the chili dog, too, with more enthusiasm. When I bit into it, I was almost overcome with hunger.

"I can't believe how good this tastes," I said, my mouth full. Then I remembered my manners, or some of them, and started to introduce Odette to Perry.

She cut me off. "Please. Let me do the talking."

Letting Odette do the talking had made me a lot of money. Which reminded me that she had stepped away from our current client. I checked the Davies table; it was now vacant. Where had the husband, his wife, her lover, her dog, and his niece disappeared to?

"Excuse me…"

I turned in response to a flat female voice. The Two L's were behind me flanked by a pair of blonde dogs who looked like them. I assumed I was blocking their path to the condiments. So I moved. But that wasn't what they wanted.

"You do know your bitch is missing, don't you?" said the L named Lindsey.

"You mean Abra?" I asked. As opposed to, say, Susan.

The Two L's nodded.

"Yes, I know she's missing. I'm going to look for her just as soon as I finish this."

When I held up what was left of my chili dog, some of the greasy garnish plopped onto Lindsey's shoe.

"Then you're aware that Abra is gone?" Lauren asked.

Did they think I was dense? Or did they suspect me of trying to lose her on purpose? Sure, the temptation had crossed my mind. But this was a very inconvenient place to lose Abra. Fleggers were everywhere, probably cheering her on.

"We're asking," Lindsey said as she wiped her shoe, "because we just saw her. And we thought you might like to know where."

"Where?"

"In the back of a wagon. With a herd of long-haired goats."

TWENTY-FIVE

Odette was the first to respond to the Two L's' stunning announcement.

"Well, somebody thinks Abra is valuable. As valuable as a goat!"

"No," Lindsey said. "Somebody thinks she *is* a goat. They don't know they've got an Af on board."

"We're talking about an Amish teenager," Lauren said. "Do you know about them?"

I didn't know about goats or Amish teenagers, and I said so.

"The goats are probably irrelevant," Perry interjected, "except for locating your bitch. Amish teenagers, now that's a topic worthy of discussion."

"I don't want a discussion!" I cried. "I want my dog back!"

"Since when?" Odette said.

Perry plunged ahead. "On the Amish country tour, you learn that Amish teens get a few years to act out and test the limits.

Then, when they're eighteen, they have to declare whether they're going to be Amish or not."

Lauren said, "This teen was definitely testing the limits. He was drunk."

"He was weaving all over Route 20," Lindsey confirmed. "We were walking our dogs around the front of the motel when he drove by."

"In a wagon," Lauren said, "pulled by two horses. He stopped to talk with a couple kids in a buggy going the other way. One of the goats nudged open the latch on the back of the wagon, and all the goats jumped out!"

"Don't tell me," I moaned. "And then Abra jumped in."

"Not right away," Lauren said. "She came running from the direction of the motel. When she saw the goats, she chased them. All over the highway."

"She stopped traffic," Lindsey added. "It took all three teenagers to round up the goats. Then Abra jumped into the wagon when nobody was looking."

"*You* were looking!" I said. "Why didn't you say something?"

Odette answered for them. "When that bitch gets going, it's like watching a train wreck."

"Which way did the goats go?" Perry asked.

"Toward Nappanee," said Lindsey. "The kid is probably driving them to his family's farm. And that could be anywhere around here."

She was right. Suddenly I regretted wolfing down the chili dog. But not nearly as much as I regretted coming to this event. I turned to Perry.

"Any suggestions?"

"Well, I'd recommend going into town. Based on what I learned during the Amish country tour, everybody knows everybody for miles around. Find out who deals in long-haired goats."

"And who has a rogue Amish teen," Odette said.

"Oh, they all have one of those," Perry said.

I moaned again, as much from my bellyache as from my brand-new headache over Abra. The Two L's made their excuses and turned their dogs toward the ring.

"The judge is about to decide 'best in show,'" Perry informed me.

"One quick question," I said. "You were going to tell me about Ramona's issues with Mitchell Slater ...?"

"Only that she threw herself at him and was summarily rejected. Ramona doesn't like it when she doesn't get her way."

"Who does?" I said.

Perry glanced about. "Not Susan, as you already know. Whatever you do, don't miss the next round. Kori expects to be back in the ring with Silverado. But I imagine that Susan has other ideas."

After he excused himself, Odette made a suggestion.

"I've thought of a way to simplify your search for Abra."

"How about amnesia? If I forget I have a dog, I can go home. It doesn't get any simpler than that."

"I was thinking of your ex-husband. Jeb could come in very handy about now."

"These dogs are calm," I said. "They don't need *Animal Lullabies*."

"I was thinking of a search party. Jeb could be here to help organize one in thirty minutes or less."

"It takes three times that long to get here from Magnet Springs!"

"By car, yes. But I'm going to ask Liam to *fly* him here. He has a second helicopter at the construction site and a pilot on call. If Jeb's ready, so is his ride!"

I said, "Liam would do that for me?"

"No," Odette said. "But he'll do it for me."

My eyes locked on hers.

Coolly she said, "Liam will do it for me because I'm going to make him lots of money. And I'll make money faster if you're working with me instead of running around Indiana looking for goats and teenagers!"

She had a point.

"Where is Liam?" I said.

"Sorting out something with Susan and Kori. Not my business." Odette yawned. "You call Jeb, and I'll call Liam."

We speed-dialed simultaneously. Jeb was expecting me to call him back, anyway, just not about this. He listened without comment to my brief account of Abra, the Amish, and the long-haired goats. When I said that Odette could get him a helicopter ride here right away, he asked what I wanted him to bring.

"Besides a camera," he said. "I gotta bring my camera."

"You want pictures of Amish country?"

"I want pictures of you and Abra at a dog show. Or nobody's going to believe it."

"We're here as Bad Examples," I reminded him.

"I only hope they put it on a trophy."

Odette, who had finished her call, reached for my phone. "Let me talk to Jeb."

She told him where to go and when to be there. I was sure he would obey; Odette had that effect on people. It explained why she sold almost every property she showed.

To me she said, "You need to make an effort to find Abra."

"I always do!"

"Let me finish. *Make an effort* so that no one can accuse you of animal neglect. Or whatever the term is for repeatedly letting your dog run away. Between the breeders and Fleggers, this is a high-profile event."

"I know, I know. But this time Dr. David can't help me. He's here in an official capacity, advocating 'canine freedom.' And the breeders don't seem to like me. Plus they're kind of busy with the show."

"Exactly why I'm bringing in Liam's other helicopter—and Jeb!" Odette said. "Whether you find Abra or not is irrelevant. Just make it look like you're looking and then get the hell out of Amish country. We have Big and Little Houses to sell!"

TWENTY-SIX

Liam Davies was our ticket to ride the real estate market all the way up again. He was also Jeb's ticket to ride in a helicopter from Magnet Springs to Amish country to help me find Abra. Odette was right, however; my real objective was real estate. I needed to get back to business.

"What's this rumor I heard about somebody claiming Yoda?" Odette said.

I summarized Perry's story about Boomgarden escaping from his rented cabin on the beach.

Odette asked, "Does Peg Goh know she's got to give up the cat she tattooed on her arm?"

"Not yet."

That was when I realized I should probably be the one to tell her. Or at least alert her to the fact that someone named Perry Stiles would soon be calling.

"You might as well get that nasty job out of the way," Odette said.

I'd had plenty of experience delivering unpleasant news by telephone but never on the subject of cats. Although this wouldn't be fun, fortunately for me Peg was one of the most stable people in town. Sure, she'd be disappointed, but I expected her to take it in stride.

I was wrong.

When I called her at the Goh Cup, Peg launched her part of the conversation with a litany of Yoda's latest "hilarious" antics, most of which sounded just plain appalling to me.

"You know what he especially loves to do?" Peg enthused. "Ride around on my shoulder—like a parrot!"

I saw no charm in that. But I seized upon her remark as a clever transition.

"That does sound like something a parrot would do. Maybe that's what your next pet should be, Peg. A parrot!"

Silence greeted my suggestion. Apparently, I was going to have to make myself clearer.

"Peg, I'm at this dog show in Indiana, and I met this guy—"

"You did? But I thought you and Jeb were back together. He's on his way to help you right now, you know. Oh, Whiskey, how could you go and fall for somebody else?"

"I didn't 'fall for' anybody!"

I glanced at Odette for guidance, but she merely gave me the "wrap-it-up-fast" sign.

"Trust me, Peg," I continued, "I'm not this other guy's type. The thing is, well, we got to talking … about Magnet Springs. It turns out he was there last spring, in a cabin on the beach—"

"And he visited the Goh Cup? Is that what you're calling to tell me? I bet he liked the big cookies! Most men do. Let me guess which flavor he liked best..."

I took a breath and plunged ahead.

"I'm sorry, Peg, but that's not what I'm trying to tell you. What I'm trying to tell you is that this guy—his name is Perry Stiles—was there with his cat—his friend's cat, actually—and the cat got lost, and the cat is Yoda! That's right, Peg, the cat you tattooed on your arm is somebody else's cat, and that somebody else wants his cat back. His real name is Boomgarden, by the way. The cat, not the somebody else. I'm sure this is shocking, and I'm really sorry it happened, but I'm just trying to do the right thing by giving you a heads up."

Her reply: silence as deep as the snow on Mount Everest and as long as a bored yawn from Odette.

"Peg? Did you hear me?"

More silence. And then, just as I was about to check our connection, she wailed.

"But I love my cat! Yoda is my family—the only thing in my life that gives me joy! You don't think I *love* slinging coffee and cookies, do you? Let alone selling tattoos! And as for being mayor of this little town, what's to love? It's high risk, low income. I don't have to tell you what happened to the last guy in that job!"

She was referring to the fact that I had discovered the previous mayor's dead body. Before I could think of a soothing reply, or any reply at all for that matter, Odette grabbed my phone.

"Peg, this is Odette. What Whiskey's trying to say is that the cat's got to go. Back to its owner. ASAP. But there's an upside: the owner's got cash, so he'll make it worth your while. You can bank on it!"

She closed the connection and returned my phone.

"You can't promise her cash!" I sputtered.

"Of course, I can."

She nodded toward Perry Stiles, who had paused on his way to the show ring to chat with a handler.

"Any guy who'd rent a cabin on the beach with another guy is not only gay but rich. He will pay a reward for the return of the cat."

"But the cat is Yoda," I protested.

"There's no accounting for taste," Odette said. "But there *is* accounting."

"I'll go talk to him," I said.

"No. *I'll* go talk to him. We want to get as much money as possible for Peg."

I nodded humbly. Nobody did deals as well as Odette.

"But first I've got to ask you a question," she said.

"Shoot."

"From what I hear, there's been more than enough of that. Is there always this much drama at a dog show?"

"Well, this is my first. But I'm pretty sure most dog shows don't involve gunfire."

"Aside from gunfire," Odette said, "why the petty personal squabbles? I hear one every time I turn my head. Who cares who handles whose dog?"

"Are you talking about Susan's dog, for example? The one Matt brought over to the Davies' table?"

"Matt, the young hottie," Odette confirmed.

I didn't add that he was Susan's young hottie. It wasn't the right moment to tell Odette that Liam's wife was as notorious for cheating as ... well, as Liam was. I didn't know how much Odette knew. Or how much she wanted to let me know she knew.

"Silverado is headed for the finals," Odette remarked without interest. "Susan wants Matt to handle him. But Liam and his niece think the niece should handle him. Frankly, who the hell cares? And now, if you'll excuse me, I'll go get Peg's money."

TWENTY-SEVEN

"I'm sorry to hear about your bitch."

Sandy Slater had entered the concession area, apparently on break from selling snoods.

"You mean Abra?" I asked, just to be sure we weren't talking about someone else.

She nodded sympathetically. "I heard that she ran away with some goats. I'll pray for you both. If she comes back this weekend, stop by my booth for a complimentary snood of your choosing. The rose sateen snoods are especially popular today."

When she pulled one out of a pocket to show me, a breeder eating nachos nearby said, "I want that one, Sandy! Save it for me."

The woman was a snood-selling machine. I thanked her and turned to go. Then I realized that Sandy should have answers to my remaining questions about Mitchell Slater. The only real question was whether she'd cooperate.

"I'll buy you anything but a burger," I offered and explained that the burgers were bad. Or had been yesterday.

Sandy hesitated. "It's not the food," she said. "I shouldn't fraternize with Bad Examples. I don't mind selling you snoods, of course, but hanging out with you could hurt my business. In case you haven't noticed, this crowd is snooty."

"Snooty about snoods?" I couldn't resist.

"Snooty about you. They don't like you. Or your bitch."

"I've noticed. At least Perry Stiles is nice."

When Sandy frowned, I realized that, unlike her late first husband, she looked her age. Whereas Mitchell Slater had been tanned, teeth-bleached, and Botoxed, Sandy was the absolute absence of vanity. She wore no make-up, had coffee-stained teeth, and sported every single wrinkle she'd earned. Lots of gray hairs, too.

"Perry Stiles is a snake," she hissed.

"He said nice things about you," I lied.

"I doubt it. He didn't like Mitchell, either. And I'm sure he gossips about my son, Matthew."

"With regard to what?" I tried to sound naïve.

"You're not as dumb as you look," Sandy snapped.

"How kind of you."

"All I'm saying is you can't trust Perry to tell you the truth. About anybody. He especially disliked Mitchell."

"Why?"

"Why do you think?"

"Maybe I am as dumb as I look."

Sandy glanced around and then stepped closer. "Mitchell was gay."

"What?!!"

Nothing she could have said would have stunned me more. Or been less believable.

"He was married four times!" I said.

"Gay men marry women."

"*Four times*," I repeated.

"Why do you think all those marriages failed?" she asked.

"Because he was a ladies' man. Anyway, why would Perry Stiles dislike Mitchell because he was gay? Perry is obviously gay."

"Obviously," Sandy agreed. "Two reasons: First, Mitchell never came out. Perry doesn't like men who live in the closet. Second, Mitchell wasn't attracted to Perry. And Perry never forgave him for that."

I couldn't buy Sandy's story. Mitchell Slater had struck me as one hundred percent straight—granted that I hadn't known him for long. Could my gaydar have been that far out of whack? Why would Sandy, who had been married to Mitchell, lie about his sexual preference? There was only one likely answer: revenge.

Mitchell had repeatedly spurned her, after all. And then there was the reality of Matt Koniger, whom Mitchell had never publicly acknowledged as his son. The gay rumor was probably Sandy's way of punishing Mitchell. But why include Perry in that plan? Unless Sandy had an axe to grind with Perry, too …

I didn't know Sandy well enough to politely inquire about the legitimacy of her son. So I stated what I'd heard and waited for her response.

"Rumor has it that Mitchell was Matt's father."

Her reply was a predictably icy stare. After a long silence, during which I vainly tried to think of ways to change the subject, Sandy said, "Let me guess. Perry told you that."

"I can't remember exactly, but, uh, yes, it might have been Perry," I mumbled. "I haven't had time to talk to a lot of other people …"

"Other people wouldn't have told you that," she said archly.

I assumed she meant because other people had discretion.

"It's just one more example of Perry's viciousness," she said.

"You mean, Matt isn't Mitchell's son?"

"For god's sake, no! His father was my second husband. Everybody knows that!"

I didn't take the time to censor my next remark. Always a bad idea.

"Then how do you explain the fact that Matt looks just like Mitchell?"

Sandy's thin, lined face flushed the rosy color of her best-selling snood.

"Can I help it if I have consistent taste in men? I like them blonde, handsome, and straight. My second husband had a lot in common with my first."

I apologized, but she stalked off before I could finish. I assumed the complimentary snood offer was now null and void.

A voice announced that the judging of Best in Show would begin momentarily. I was confused. When Susan invited Abra and me, she had said that the event ran all weekend long. Yet here we were, mid-afternoon on Saturday, ready to give out the Grand Prize? What was left to compete for tomorrow?

I spotted Brenda Spenser, also on her way to the ring, and asked.

Ms. Perfect Haircut seemed surprised to see me. Or maybe her Botox treatment blunted what was really a look of alarm. She probably feared I might tromp on her Manolo Blahnik again. To reassure her, I took a giant step back.

"The Midwest Afghan Hound Specialty concludes with this round," she explained pleasantly. "But shows go on all weekend.

Tomorrow several area clubs will hold their specialties here—groups from Indianapolis, Toledo, Fort Wayne. Many of our handlers will work those events, too. And some of the dogs you saw today will compete again tomorrow. It depends on which clubs the breeders belong to."

Brenda excused herself, smiling so sweetly that I felt quite at home. Maybe I'd been wrong—and Sandy had been just plain mean—in assuming that the breeders didn't like me. True, I didn't have a clue how dog shows worked. And my Bad Example bitch had run off with a herd of goats. But that didn't necessarily make me an outcast.

Odette headed toward me, hips wagging. She waved her latest designer bag in the universal sign for "I got money!"

"Peg will be feeling no pain," she announced.

"Peg's losing her cat," I said. "And she's stuck with that awful tattoo."

"Peg's gaining a thousand bucks! Perry's friend misses that little monster. I've already phoned Liam's second pilot, the one who's bringing Jeb. He'll take a slight detour to pick up Yoda, too."

Odette glanced at her Rolex, a diamond-encrusted model, which I happened to know she had purchased with her latest commission check.

"Liam and I are off to meet with his Chicago people. The next time we speak, Whiskey, I want to hear that you've finished looking for Abra, whether you've found her or not!"

Odette was the only employee I made a habit of taking orders from. Doing so generally proved profitable.

Now I surveyed the scene around the show ring. Sandy had timed her lunch break well. No one would be buying snoods during the final round of judging. Other vendors had left their booths, too, including the red-haired author of Afghan hound mysteries. Still smiling, the novelist stood with the rest of the crowd. When her eyes briefly met mine, I wondered if she could tell from a distance that I wasn't a reader.

Spectators had flocked to the ring; at some points they stood two and three people deep. The tall, distinguished judge was in place, like an elder statesman about to preside over matters of national import. I guessed that we were waiting for him to summon the hounds and their handlers. Searching the sidelines for a glimpse of Silverado, I wondered who would be on the other end of his leash.

"I don't have a hound in this round, but I do have a handler."

Brenda Spenser had joined me ringside. She winked as if sharing a private joke, which I didn't get… until the hounds arrived. Stepping lively, Silverado was the third dog to enter the ring, with Matt holding his lead.

I should have known. From our first phone conversation—the one that landed me here—Susan had struck me as a woman who got what she wanted when she wanted it. And she wanted Matt to handle her dog.

As the judge reviewed the finalists, Brenda kept up a chatty commentary about who owned whom, who bred whom, and who won what when. I wanted to pretend to care. Really I did. But the best I could manage was a few vague grunts while my mind wandered as waywardly as my dog.

What had been Liam's real reason for detouring here en route to Chicago? Was he trying to prove that he loved his wife, or that he had a sexy new business partner? Or did he just enjoy impressing the hoi polloi with the fact that he was rich enough to travel by helicopter?

How much did Liam know about Susan's kissy-face relationship with Matt? According to Perry, everybody knew about both spouses' infidelities. The real question was did anybody, Liam and Susan included, care?

I now suspected that the Davies duo were simply exhibitionists. Tiresome ones at that. Everybody they invited into their lives was there for one purpose only: to give them attention.

Like Liam, Kori must have moved on. I couldn't see Susan, either. But she had to be there somewhere, applauding her dog and her handler, if not also her tidy triumph over Liam and his niece. Frankly, I doubted that Liam cared all that much who handled which dog. He had made it amply clear that he didn't like dog shows.

Studying Matt standing next to Silverado, I had to agree with Brenda that they looked like winners. In his dark gray suit with his perfect posture and athletic sprint, Matt served only to enhance the sleek dog's graceful performance.

Brenda was blathering on, no doubt for my enlightenment, about the relationship between handler and hound.

"The handler is there, but not there," she explained. "Like strings on a marionette. The audience can see the strings, but we try not to because they're not part of the show."

I was impressed that anyone as handsome as Matt could blend into the background. And yet he ensured that every moment was all about the dog.

Kori had proven she could get Silverado to do what he needed to do in order to win. Still, there was no denying that her hot pink suit, spiky streaked hair, and sparkly jewelry had demanded attention, too. I'd overheard the Two L's say that Kori turned the show ring into a "circus." That was hard to deny. Even I, a complete dog show novice, could see and respect the difference between a professional handler like Matt and a rebel like Kori. She stole the show; he kept the focus on the dog. At this level of competition, it mattered.

I made a comment to Brenda about Matt's skill, but my words drowned in a sea of applause. As the finalists trotted around the ring, each one had a strong and enthusiastic fan base.

Naturally, Brenda wanted Matt's canine client to win. I wondered again if she had a clue about him and Susan. Of course I cheered for Silverado, and not just because I was standing next to Brenda. Silverado was the only dog I knew personally. Plus, he had it bad for my bitch, so the poor guy deserved my support.

But I couldn't begin to guess who deserved to be Best in Show. They were all perfectly behaved and flawlessly groomed. In other words, the opposite of Abra. Besides Silverado, who was a blue, the finalists were a solid black, a black and tan, a self-masked gold, and a cream brindle domino.

When I caught myself describing them that way in my head, I gasped. I must have actually been listening to Brenda.

Coming to this show had changed me. I had accidentally learned something about Afghan hounds. I had also lost my Afghan hound, but that happened frequently.

The judge gave each finalist one more hard look. The canine contenders posed patiently. The crowd watched, transfixed.

I was sure of one thing only, that no dog was the clear crowd favorite. If we'd relied upon an applause meter for the results, we would have had a five-way tie. Not to mention a specialty show that failed to comply with AKC regulations.

Suddenly the judge made a series of rapid-fire signals I couldn't read; dogs and handlers looped the ring on their last circuit as the crowd hooted. When Brenda shrieked with joy, I assumed that Matt and Silverado had done well. But before I could ask, and before the dogs reached their ranked positions, the entire exhibit hall was plunged into blackness.

TWENTY-EIGHT

I HEARD BRENDA GASP and say, "Oh, my!"

A male voice shouted, "Nobody move! Stay exactly where you are. I repeat: *Nobody move*! The back-up generators should kick on momentarily."

"I hope so," Brenda said. "Matt and Silverado deserve their moment of glory!"

"They won?" I whispered into the darkness.

"Best in show!" Brenda confirmed.

The arena, which a moment earlier had echoed with applause, was now a pitch-black den of whispers. Since the building lacked windows, no light at all filtered into the space. If someone could just open that infamous side door, I thought, it might admit a little illumination. Scuffling sounds—scrapes and grunts—emanated from the ring. I assumed that the dogs were restless.

"I said, nobody move!" the male voice repeated, sounding annoyed enough to be almost menacing.

A chorus of alarmed and alarming barks filled the air, followed by a human cry. Suddenly, that side door opened just wide enough and long enough to reveal the silhouette of a large man. Then the door closed, and the arena sank back into darkness.

Something had changed. The barking intensified; the human cry became a hysterical sob.

"What on earth—" Brenda began.

And then the generators kicked on, igniting low-level perimeter lighting. Although the show ring remained in deep shadow, a distressing tableau emerged: handlers struggled to control their leaping, lunging dogs, and a man appeared slumped near the edge of the circle. At first I thought it was the judge and wondered if he'd had a heart attack. Then I identified his tall, lean dog-less figure among the vertical shadows. So who was down? And if it was a handler, where was the unattached hound? A man inside the circle shouted, "Somebody dial 9-1-1!"

The regular lights banged back up. Brenda screamed.

The very still body in the ring belonged to Matt Koniger. Perry crouched next to him just as, an hour earlier, he had crouched next to Ramona. This time, though, I feared that the victim had suffered more than a rump wound. Matt wasn't an actor—unless you counted gigolo in that category. He had struck me as a virile young man not inclined to exaggerate an injury. From where I stood, he appeared unconscious.

"Oh my god, oh my god, oh my god," Brenda chanted, shaking her finely manicured hands as if to restore circulation.

Suddenly she bolted toward the ring, if in fact "bolting" is possible in Manolo Blahniks. Without thinking, I followed her. Neither of us reached our destination.

Wild-eyed and livid, Sandy Slater inserted herself between us and the show ring. Fixing her mad rage on Brenda, she screamed, "You wanted my son dead! Everybody here knows that!"

Brenda froze, but did not reply.

"Wrong," I said. "Everybody here knows he's her boy-toy."

I glanced sideways at very pale Brenda. "Sorry to be so blunt," I said.

Then, back to Sandy. "Why would she want him *dead*?"

"Because he's blackmailing her, that's why!"

That was when the ever-pleasant Brenda Spenser revealed her inner bitch. In a single smooth move, she slipped off one of her prized Manolo Blahniks and pounded Sandy's face with it. Fortunately for Sandy, Brenda employed the pointy heel as handle, rather than as a stabbing device. Yet I had no doubt that the finely crafted leather sole could sting, particularly when applied with manic vigor.

"Down, girls, down!" boomed an authoritative male voice.

As I stood helplessly by, the dog-show judge broke up the cat fight. He seized Brenda's right arm, effectively stopping her in mid-swing, at the same instant that Perry pulled Sandy beyond striking distance. The intervention happened so fast that I barely had time to savor the irony: Sandy was dragged to safety by the very man she'd accused of sand-bagging her late ex-husband and her son.

"How's Matt? What happened?" I shouted over Sandy and Brenda's spewed epithets.

"EMTs are on their way," the judge said.

But Perry locked eyes with me, and in them I read what I knew to be the real answer: Matt was beyond human help.

As the judge restrained a squirming Brenda, and Perry did the same with a kicking Sandy, Susan darted past us all, bound straight for Matt. Perry called after her to wait; she didn't listen. Handlers and breeders closed in around her, blocking both Susan and Matt from my view.

Looking stern, Perry said something to Sandy, who shook him off. Then she stepped away to compose herself by drawing several sharp breaths. When she turned back, her face was as hard as a statue's.

Meanwhile, the judge was holding Brenda's arm like collateral and whispering to her. The scene reminded me of a parent trying to calm a tantrum-prone child. Brenda's eyes seemed to lose their focus. She swayed like a dizzy drunk before folding herself against the judge.

My eyes followed Sandy as she lurched toward the ring. The snood business may have been good this weekend, but her personal life had gone hideously wrong. I expected the small crowd gathered around Susan and Matt to spring open as his mother approached. Instead, they visibly tightened ranks.

Why? To protect Sandy from the sight of her dead son? Or to protect Susan from Sandy? Maybe insiders feared that Sandy, in her moment of grief, would blame Susan for choosing Matt as handler. Or maybe they knew that Sandy had other issues with Susan, beginning with "A" for adultery.

Then again, hot-tempered Sandy could have had issues with lots of folks. If this was a woman who'd never given up loving, or at least lurking around, her first husband, she might be the kind of gal who nursed every grievance.

Several people moved in to comfort—or stop—Sandy, and soon I couldn't see her at all.

Watching the handlers lead their dogs from the ring, I realized that Matt was not the only casualty of this round. Silverado, best in show, was gone. I hadn't seen him when the lights first came up, and I couldn't see him now. The dog had vanished.

Had Susan even noticed? When Silverado charged out the side door earlier in the day, she had freaked. But that had no doubt been to highlight Kori's incompetence. As Perry had suggested, the gaffe was surely a setup intended to make Liam's niece look bad.

This scene differed in every detail. First and foremost, it appeared to be murder. Susan would look shallow indeed if she showed as much concern for a missing hound as for a mortally wounded handler.

I couldn't imagine who or what had taken Matt down. It was unthinkable that one of his fellow competitors would kill him at close range. There was not only the logistical problem of shooting, stabbing, or bludgeoning to death a man running in the dark; there was also that longstanding AKC tradition of sportsmanship. At least inside the ring.

Yet the handler of the best dog in show was down, presumably dead or dying. And the winning dog was gone. Sirens grew louder as, once again, emergency vehicles converged on the Barnyard Inn.

The Two L's stood nearby, identically pale and drawn. Although they paid no attention to me, I heard Lauren tell Lindsey, "Thank god Susan never hires us."

Whoever took the dog had probably killed Matt. But what came first: the plan to steal the dog, or the plan to kill Matt? In other words, which was the primary crime? I was sure, without quite knowing why, that one was the motive and the other a consequence. Or a side effect.

EMTs dashed into the ring, dissolving the clot of bystanders. I glimpsed Matt—still in the same sprawled position—with Susan kneeling to his right and Sandy standing to his left.

What had happened here? I replayed my mental snapshot of the side door opening to reveal a large man in silhouette. There was no dog in that picture. Unless… the man had been carrying the dog. Mature male Afghan hounds like Silverado weigh about seventy pounds. The man in my memory was large enough to carry such a load. Who could he be, and why would he kill Matt? Or maybe his goal was to take the dog, and Matt's death was collateral damage. Had Matt made the fatal mistake of trying to save Silverado?

TWENTY-NINE

THERE WAS NO POINT watching the EMTs. I was quite sure that this time they wouldn't be able to work their medical magic. And I desperately needed a breath of fresh air. My sour stomach had returned with a vengeance that I couldn't blame on the concession stand.

Across the ring, I spotted the red-haired writer furiously jotting notes on a pad. Either she doubled as a local newspaper reporter, or she was harvesting material for a future novel. Odette had said she wrote humorous mysteries. How the hell do you make murder amusing?

I chose to exit via the side door, not only because it was closer, but also because I was curious about the man whom I'd glimpsed using it. Would I find any trace of him? Or Silverado?

What I did find when I pushed open the heavy metal door was my undercover bodyguard. Down on all fours.

"Did you lose a contact lens?" I said.

With surprising agility, he sprang upright.

"No. But I found this."

I didn't at first understand the significance of what he showed me. Or even recognize what it was. MacArthur waited as I studied the tiny item resting in the broad palm of his hand.

"It's a bristle from a pin brush, isn't it?" I said. "The kind a groomer uses."

"Or a handler," MacArthur said.

"You know about Matt?" I asked. When he nodded, I said, "We should have assigned you to him and his dad instead of to Susan, Ramona, and me."

Then I considered that Ramona had been shot, too, and Susan had lost her prize pooch. All in all, MacArthur was making a hash of his job this weekend, even if he was doing it for free. Maybe he was distracted.

"Seen Kori lately?" I asked.

"She's in her room, packing to leave," he replied.

"And you know that because … ?"

"Deely and Dr. David said so. Fleggers are protesting in the parking lot. They said Kori stopped to make a donation before going to her room."

I told MacArthur what I'd seen inside the exhibit hall from the moment the lights banged down. When I got to the part about seeing a large man silhouetted in the doorway, I stopped.

"When were you last inside?"

"About thirty minutes ago," he said. "I watched Liam Davies confer with his wife in a storage area next to the concession stand. They both became a bit agitated, so I stayed close by. Then she went her way, and he went his. I followed him and Odette out to the helicopter and saw them leave. So I missed the final round."

MacArthur's size made him a perfect match, at least in silhouette, to the man I'd seen. Why would he lie? Unless he was trying to protect someone. But his job was to protect Susan, Ramona, and me.

"I saw a man leave through the side door. And now Silverado is gone." I pointed to the pin brush bristle still resting in MacArthur's palm. "Do you think *that* means anything?"

"It means something. The question is *what*. Most likely, at this spot, one of three things happened: someone was grooming a dog, *or* a dog shook off a bristle caught in his coat, *or* a human shook off a bristle caught in his or her clothes. I've been studying this area closely, and I'm certain that bristle wasn't here an hour ago."

I wanted to believe everything MacArthur said. After all, when he wasn't being a bodyguard or cleaner, he supposedly worked for me. Or he would work for me once the real estate market rebounded. Meanwhile, he lived with my surly stepdaughter and her adorable twins. Although I could understand him cheating on Avery, I was concerned about the ramifications for my grandbabies. Would they soon be back at Vestige with me? Catching MacArthur kissing Kori made me question his fidelity. Seeing people die, and a canine champion go missing, made me question his skills.

"Incoming!" MacArthur shouted over the roar of another approaching helicopter.

"It's Jeb this time!" I said. "Coming to help me find Abra!"

MacArthur nodded before I finished as if he knew more than I did. He motioned for us to go meet the chopper. Jogging behind him, I wondered how much he really knew about Silverado, Matt, Mitchell Slater, and Ramona. MacArthur's fundamentally mysterious nature made him either a sexy bad boy or a scary bad boy.

By now Fleggers had expanded their protest from the makeshift stage to a circuit of the entire parking lot. Some carried signs. Others marched and shouted. The theme was more or less consistent although the chants varied: "Dogs deserve a full life, too!" "Let your dog be as free as you and me!" "Animals are natural beauties! Boycott dog shows now!"

For just an instant I wondered if Silverado had succumbed to this propaganda and excused himself from the ring. Who was I kidding? He was a good dog; Abra was the rebel hellion.

The protesters scattered as the second helicopter descended thunderously into the parking lot. MacArthur pointed to Dr. David and then jogged off in that direction; I assumed he was going to ask the good vet if he'd seen anything helpful.

When the helicopter door opened, the first person out was not my ex-husband but my next-door neighbor Chester, who ducked dramatically as he debarked. That amused me. At four feet tall, Chester was hardly endangered by the churning blades. Then I saw the real reason for his hunched posture: the poor child was toting both a duffel bag and a large plastic case.

Involuntarily my heart lifted when I spotted Jeb. He still moved in the loose, youthful way of that boy I'd fallen in love with back in high school. He had less hair now, but not from this distance. From here, he might as well have been seventeen again because that was how young and hopeful he made me feel. Time to remind myself of our long, bumpy history: heartbreak, disappointment, divorce. How could I possibly be tempted again? And yet I was...

Foolishly, I had hoped that a few days' separation might frost my desire, but now I knew the opposite was true. I'd been away from Jeb for only a day and a half, and I wanted him more than ever. Flying in like a hero made him as provocative as a man in uniform. Not that I had a thing for soldiers, but part of me longed to be rescued. Who was I kidding? I needed to be rescued. The Barnyard Inn was turning into a boneyard.

As my libido soared, I gave silent thanks that Abra wasn't around to distract us. If we pretended I'd never had a dog, then of course I hadn't lost one. We could drive straight to a cheap, dark motel devoted to one-night stands and totally opposed to pets.

Then I remembered that we had Chester. He would insist on looking for Abra. No doubt that was why he was here—besides playing porter. Jeb was hauling luggage, too. Way more than a camera case and an overnight bag. Why had they brought so much baggage? And how had they found time to pack?

Jeb set one suitcase down long enough to wave. I returned the cheery salutation. But his aim wasn't right; he was looking beyond me. To my dismay, Susan Davies was moving purposefully in Jeb's direction.

Chester came straight to me, however.

"Hey, Whiskey!" he panted. "Here I am!"

"Indeed you are," I said. "And I can't help but wonder why."

He dropped the duffel bag and then carefully set down the plastic carrier before pointing to the tin badge pinned to his navy blue school blazer. It was the chintzy, cereal-box-grade badge that Jenx gave every part-time volunteer deputy. Since being mistaken for a clown, I refused to wear mine.

"Jeb called Jenx, and she enlisted my assistance. I speak canine, you know."

Yoda's gray heart-shaped face and oversized ears appeared in the mesh opening of the plastic carrier. True to form, the ugly cat hissed at me.

"Long time no see, Yoda," I said. "But not long enough."

"He's traumatized by his separation from Peg," Chester said. "Also, cats don't like helicopters."

"You speak feline, too?"

"Yes, but not as fluently as I speak canine. I've had less practice with this species."

When the cat hissed again, I said, "Is he telling you he hates being in a cage?"

"No. He hates you."

Speaking of enemies, what the hell was Susan up to? She just happened to be hugging my ex-husband. The man who had flown here expressly to help me.

"I'll be right back," I told Chester.

Yoda yowled. I did not request a translation.

"Hello, Jeb!"

My tone was more business-like than affectionate. In salute, he raised a hand currently wrapped around Susan. She turned her head in my direction.

"Oh, Whiskey, Jeb is so good."

"How would you know that?"

She paused to wipe what would have been a tear from her cheek. If she wasn't faking it.

"Jeb called me to say he was flying to Nappanee. So I asked him to load my luggage."

"*Your* luggage?" I said. "Don't you have luggage here?"

"Yes, but with everything that's happening, I… may not go straight home. And I always keep a few bags packed, just in case."

I wondered if "everything that's happening" referred to the murders or to her fights with Liam.

"Jeb made sure all three of my bags got on the chopper," Susan said. "He counted them himself."

I said, "His mother would be proud."

"And just now, when I told him about the shooting," Susan sniffed, "he knew exactly the right thing to say."

"Which shooting?" After the attack on Matt, I wondered why Susan would be crying about Mitchell Slater or Ramona.

"The EMTs said Matt was shot at close range," Susan said. "The gun had a silencer. Silverado might have been shot, too. When the forensics team gets here, they'll test the blood on the floor to see…" she choked, "if it's all human."

Sobbing, she buried her beautiful face in my lover's shoulder. Jeb did not push her away. Instead he shot me a look with that basic male message: "Hey, what can I do?"

THIRTY

"JEB IS HERE TO help *me*," I told Susan when my ex-husband didn't. "Together we're going to find Abra. Or at least look for her."

"And I'll help!" Chester tapped his volunteer deputy badge. "I speak canine, so Chief Jenkins sent me to assist local law enforcement. As a consultant."

I tried to imagine any police department other than Magnet Springs relying on a precocious eight-year-old to solve crimes, especially an eight-year-old who looked six and claimed to speak canine. But, hey, maybe Nappanee's finest were more open-minded than most.

As if reading my thoughts, Chester added, "I'll probably keep my investigation on the down-low until I have solid evidence."

"Good plan," I said.

Just then Yoda yowled, and Susan frowned at the cat carrier. "Why would you bring a cat to a dog show?"

On Chester's behalf, I explained that Perry's friend had lost a cat while vacationing in Magnet Springs, and I happened to know that the cat had been found. Hence Yoda, a.k.a. Boomgarden.

"We're returning him," Chester said.

Susan squinted at Yoda's face in the mesh opening. "I've seen that cat."

"Really?" I asked. "Do you know Perry's friend?"

"That cat belonged to Mitchell Slater."

"I don't think so. He belongs to the man Perry vacationed with."

Susan shot me a "How dense are you?" look and replied very slowly, "I said, that cat belonged to Mitchell Slater. He and Perry had a little fling."

Was Sandy Slater right about Mitchell being gay? She'd insisted that Perry dissed Mitchell because Mitchell had rejected him. I still couldn't believe it.

"Mitchell Slater told me he left his last wife for *you*," I reminded Susan.

Suddenly I realized that we had ventured into mature, if not illicit, subject matter in front of a young child. Granted, Chester was the child of a pop music superstar renowned for her own highly questionable behavior. But I wanted to set a good example.

"Chester," I said in my best schoolteacher voice. "Why don't you take Yoda into the exhibit hall and ask someone to direct you to Perry Stiles?"

"Okay," he said, picking up the carrier. "But don't worry about me. There's nothing I haven't heard before."

The way he said it, I felt almost inadequate. As soon as he was out of earshot, I asked Susan, "Are you denying that you had an affair with Mitchell Slater?"

She had stepped back from Jeb and recovered her complete composure. I saw no trace of those crocodile tears.

"I'm denying that it's any of your business!"

With a toss of her lustrous hair, she told Jeb, "Please take my bags to room 11."

Then she followed Chester into the exhibit hall.

When Jeb stooped to scoop up her bags, I had a coughing fit. He put the bags down. Conveniently, MacArthur jogged into view. He and Jeb shook hands.

I said, "MacArthur, I know you're a cleaner, a Realtor, and a volunteer bodyguard. But would you mind taking Susan's bags to—"

"I know where her room is." MacArthur swept the bags off the pavement. He told Jeb, "We need to formulate a strategy for maximum efficiency. Meet you inside, at the concession stand, in five."

"What about me and my strategy?" I said.

"Carry on," MacArthur said.

"Carry on . . . with what? I don't have a strategy. I have a missing dog!"

"Then we'll make a place for you in our strategy," MacArthur said. "And together we'll find your dog."

"We only have to *try* to find her," I assured him.

He jogged off with the luggage as if it weighed nothing at all.

I waited for Jeb to finally greet me in an appropriate manner. By now, my initially warm—if not steamy—response to his arrival had cooled. It was well on its way to downright frosty.

Jeb correctly read my emotional temperature.

"Hey," he said, making no move.

"Hey, yourself."

We locked eyes as if daring each other to reach out and touch. Neither of us stirred.

"Feel better?" he said finally.

"Compared to what?"

"Last night. I thought you were sick."

"Right." I made him wait. "I was sick this morning, too. But now I just have indigestion. All the time."

Too much information. If Jeb hadn't killed the romantic mood with his attitude toward Susan, I had slain it with gastric references.

"Sorry to hear that," he said.

"Are you?"

"Sure, I am. I like a girl with a healthy appetite."

"For what?"

Jeb smiled carefully. I smiled carefully back.

"What's going on with you and Susan?" I said, trying to sound neutral.

Okay, maybe there was a slight tone. A slightly hostile tone.

Jeb's smile flickered out like a dead flashlight. "What the hell are you talking about?"

"Hewwo, Jeb!"

We were saved from a fight by none other than Dr. David and Deely. They had put down their protest signs and were waving at my ex-husband.

"Hey, David! Hey, Deely!" Jeb said. "How's the animal rights biz?"

After they'd exchanged pleasantries, Dr. David announced that he was sorry to hear about the latest shooting.

"Proof of man's violent ways," he said in his own unique speech pattern. "And why Fleggers protects and preserves the rights of innocent creatures. Fortunately, Silverado saved himself."

"What do you mean?" I said.

"We saw him leave."

"Leave? How?"

"In the back of a Ford pickup, ma'am," Deely replied.

Dr. David supplied the details. "There was apparently human intervention, but the dog left via his own free will. We witnessed him leaping into the truck bed, unleashed and unassisted."

"Did you see the human?" Jeb asked.

Dr. David shook his head. "We heard barking and looked over in time to see a dog fitting Silverado's description sail into the back of the truck. The driver was already in the cab. He sped out of here, tires squealing."

"How did you know about Silverado?" I said.

"MacArthur came over to talk to us when the helicopter landed," Deely explained. "He described the missing dog, and we told him what we saw. We'll tell the police, too. When they get here."

"Where exactly was this Ford pickup, and what color was it?" I said.

Deely pointed to the corner of the Barnyard Inn, not far from room 17. Kori's room. "It was silver, ma'am. Kind of like the dog. Sorry I couldn't see the license plate."

"You think a man was driving?" I asked.

Deely looked to Dr. David for his input. Neither one could be sure.

"We heard a man's voice coming from the truck," the vet declared. "He shouted, 'In, boy!' and the dog jumped aboard."

"In case you're keeping score," I said, "we now have two missing dogs—one well-trained, and one hardly trained at all. Seen Kori Davies lately?"

I was thinking about her man-like voice.

Deely said, "She stopped to talk to us just before the first helicopter left."

"That's right," Dr. David recalled. "She was on her way back to her room to pack. She said she was through with dog shows. Forever."

"She wished us luck with our mission," Deely said. "And made a generous donation."

"Every protest secures another victory," Dr. David declared. "In her case, a complete conversion, from animal handler to animal advocate."

I was sure Kori had done it just to piss off Susan. Or to give herself an alibi.

"Did you tell MacArthur you saw Kori?" I said.

"Yes, ma'am," Deely said. "But he didn't seem interested."

I suspected that Kori interested MacArthur very much, and not just for her kisses. He would make the same connections I did: The truck was parked by Kori's room and driven by someone with a manly voice. Dr. David and Deely last saw Kori before the first helicopter left. She wanted them to remember seeing her, so she made a donation. In the confusion of the chopper's departure, Kori might have left her room and helped someone steal Silverado. True, I hadn't seen her in the exhibit hall, and she was too compactly built to be mistaken for the man I'd glimpsed in silhouette. But that didn't exempt her from a role in the dog's disappearance.

I had never believed MacArthur's story about Kori excusing herself to advise her twelve-step group sponsoree. Why would he lie or be receptive to her lies except for the only and obvious reason that men get stupid around women: s-e-x.

Kori would never hurt a dog, so that was not a worry. If she took Silverado, either she had found a better home for him, or she planned to keep him herself. But how would she earn a living without Uncle Liam's support?

Something else didn't fit. Kori had claimed to like Matt best among all the handlers. On that point she had seemed sincere. Why would she participate in a crime that resulted in his death? Was that part an accident? Or had Kori's partner in this venture kept the real agenda a secret?

THIRTY-ONE

Dr. David and Deely had something going on that Jeb and I didn't: a damned good time. Although they officially opposed almost everything happening at the Barnyard Inn, they did so with joy and affection. I saw them exchange cutely covert kisses before rejoining their Flegger ranks. Jeb and I hadn't touched since he'd landed.

Just in case the chill between us was even remotely my fault, I decided to melt it. I reached for Jeb's hand as we approached the exhibit hall main entrance. Unfortunately, at the very second I would have made skin-on-skin contact, the double glass doors flew open and out dashed a red-faced Chester, swinging the plastic cat carrier. I couldn't help but notice that its grated gate was flapping wide open. And Chester was flanked by two bounding hounds.

"Whoa, buddy!" Jeb said, positioning himself to catch my small neighbor.

There's no way to catch flying Afghan hounds. But I did track which way they went. Straight into the cornfield.

"What's going on?" I said.

"Yoda—I mean Boomgarden!" Chester panted. "When Perry Stiles took him out of the carrier to verify his identity, Boomgarden got startled by a hound! He clawed Perry, who dropped him on the dog's head. The dog reared up and bolted around the arena like a wild horse. Every Afghan hound that wasn't secured joined in. There are at least five dogs running loose inside. And two more outside!"

He'd no sooner spoken than the Two L's burst out of the arena dangling dog-less leashes and looking angrier than any bluebloods I'd ever seen.

"They went that-a-way!" I said, pointing helpfully toward the cornfield.

They bounded off without bothering to say thanks. I wondered how the hell they thought they could catch hounds inside those tall walls.

"The place has gone crazy," Chester said, glancing back at the arena.

"Courtesy of Yoda," I said. "Before that cat arrived, every dog here was the perfect anti-Abra!"

"That is correct," Susan Davies announced.

She had followed the Two L's out the front door and now stood glowering at me. She was also towering over me—a feat made possible only because I was crouching next to Chester.

"Whiskey, the time has come for me, as Chair of the Breeder Education Committee, to invite you to leave."

When I straightened to my full height, I saw that Susan had brought reinforcements. Behind her, melodramatically leaning on what appeared to be an ivory cane but was probably a plastic theatrical prop, stood Ramona.

"You've been more than accommodating in providing us with bad examples," Ramona said. "In fact, you've managed to inspire utter chaos. Please leave immediately. And take your trouble-making little friend with you."

Melodramatically, she pointed her cane at Chester.

"Thank you so much," I said, "for finally acknowledging my existence! Because now—Chester, please cover your ears—you've made it possible for me to say what I've wanted to say since the moment we met: Fuck off!"

Before Ramona or Susan could respond, MacArthur emerged from the arena with four wild-eyed Afghan hounds on leashes.

"I'm pleased to return your dogs," he thundered. "Ramona, kindly take Laughing Moon's Son of Flavio and Ego Narcissus. Susan, here are your bitches, Debbani's Whiter Shade of Pale and Taji Crystal Chandelier. They sorely lack training with felines. May I suggest that next year your own hounds should be your Bad Examples."

MacArthur loomed ominously large. The only reason I didn't tremble was that he was on my side. Ramona and Susan flinched as they accepted their AWOL Afghans. We watched them retreat stiffly toward the Barnyard Inn.

Then Chester leapt up and high-fived the cleaner. I joined in.

"Good news," MacArthur announced. "Perry Stiles convinced Boomgarden to come down from the display curtain. They're making nice with each other now."

To Jeb he said, "We can review our strategy options over a cuppa. You can eat if you want. Stay away from the burgers, though."

I cleared my throat. "Um, what about *my* strategy? After all, Abra is *my* Bad Example."

Annoyance flickered in the cleaner's eyes, but he recovered quickly.

"Of course, Whiskey! We'll come up with something you can handle while Jeb and I track the killer."

"I thought Jeb was here to help me pretend to be looking for Abra."

Because that sounded awful, and Chester was listening, I added, "During those rare moments when I'm not looking for her by myself. High and low."

"Indeed," MacArthur agreed amiably. "We'll begin by reviewing our strategies, starting with my own wee list."

From the hip pocket of his jeans, MacArthur withdrew a piece of yellow paper folded to the size of a postage stamp. He opened it deliberately, coughed softly, and read, "Power."

After a beat I said, "What?"

Chester frantically waved his right hand, an "A" student competing for the teacher's attention. When MacArthur called on him, he said, "When we know who caused the power outage, we'll be close to knowing who killed Matt the handler and took Silverado the dog!"

"Excellent!" MacArthur declared.

"That's not fair," I said. "Chester wasn't even here when it happened. He got that answer from somebody inside!"

The eight-year-old adjusted his deputy badge and stood as tall as possible. "Whoever perpetrated this double crime is somebody close to the victims. Somebody participating in the show."

"You always hurt the ones you love," Jeb chimed in, gazing at me.

"Or hate," I said.

We were about to adjourn to the concession area for the remainder of our strategy session when we heard what sounded like cries of frustration and calls for help. Female voices were coming from the cornfield. MacArthur, followed by Jeb and Chester, sprinted toward the wall of stalks.

"It's only the Two L's!" I reminded them, implying that the lost souls weren't worthy of rescue.

"Keep shouting! We'll talk you in!" MacArthur informed the stranded handlers.

"I'm over here!" Lauren or Lindsey cried out.

"And I'm here! Right here!" the other L shouted.

A dog or two barked, also. The women had found their hounds but lost each other, as well as their way back. MacArthur, Jeb, and Chester enthusiastically called them in as I leaned against the building and observed. It made for a fascinating study in male ego-fluffing. Even one as young as Chester swelled with importance and pride at the prospect of rescuing damsels in distress.

I reflected on my own brushes with danger and wanted to call out to the Two L's that I'd stared down the barrel of a gun. They were scared of corn rows! Proof that upper-class chicks are wimps.

When the Two L's emerged from the field, their ash blonde hair and dark suits were dusted with yellow-brown flakes and tendrils. So were their hounds.

"It's a jungle in there!" Lauren said.

Ever the job-conscious handler, she whipped out a pin brush and immediately set to work on her bitch. Lindsey did likewise. The guys waited for acknowledgment of their manly achievement. As if being loud and obnoxious wasn't something boys enjoyed, anyway. But the Two L's were too refined to thank the little people, and I'm not referring only to Chester.

Seeing the handlers expertly wield those brushes brought a question to mind.

"Excuse me," I said, approaching Lindsey. "I'm wondering if you can tell me which is more common: for one of those pin bristles to stick in a hound's coat after grooming or to the groomer's own clothes?"

"No professional would leave debris in her hound's coat. Nor would she fail to brush off her own clothing before entering the ring."

"Of course," I said, backpedaling. "But how about someone who wasn't a professional? Could they make a mistake like that?"

"Kori Davies does it all the time," Lauren sniped. "She's a loser."

"She won her round this morning," I pointed out.

"Even a broken clock is right twice a day," said Lindsey.

Both handlers turned their attention back to their hounds. I could tell that the guys and I had blinked out of their consciousness like stars in the dawn sky. But MacArthur's somber face told me he got the point: If the pin brush bristle he'd found by the side door was a clue at all, it wouldn't lead us to a canine professional. More like a hired gun. Or Kori.

THIRTY-TWO

WHILE WE WERE OCCUPIED with the Two L's, a swarm of patrol cars arrived at the Barnyard Inn. Two murders in two days had to be bad for Amish country tourism.

According to the food concessionaire, the first officers on the scene had ordered a lockdown of the exhibit hall only to discover that a third of the show's participants had already scattered. Detectives and forensics team members were doing the best they could to analyze a "compromised" crime scene.

"At least Afghan hounds are quiet," the concessionaire remarked. "If this had happened last week, during the Bassett hound specialty, you wouldn't be able to hear yourself think."

I nodded. Except we all knew this would never happen around Basset hounds.

Over cola and nachos for Chester, Jeb, and MacArthur—and ginger ale for me—MacArthur laid out his strategy. He and Jeb would track down every breeder or handler "of interest," and ask where he or she had been, and whom he or she had seen, around the time of all three shootings: Mitchell's, Ramona's, and Matt's.

I pointed out the flaw in that plan: "Some breeders or handlers—like, oh, say, Kori, for instance—are already gone."

MacArthur said, "Nobody saw Kori go. I'm sending Jeb to her room."

At least he was willing to solicit a second opinion instead of asking us to rely solely on his. Let's say Kori was still there. Even if she was a superb kisser, I knew Jeb wouldn't fall under her spell. He liked his women slender and feminine. Like Susan.

Which reminded me… "Who's going to interview the Breeder Education Committee? And it can't be Jeb."

As I glared at my ex, both MacArthur and Chester volunteered for the job.

"Back to the power issue," MacArthur said. "The electrical outage, that is. Here's how I plan to investigate." He pointed to the female sheriff's deputy I had met last night, now getting a complimentary cup of coffee from the concession stand. "Whiskey, go ask her what happened."

So I did. And it was almost that simple, although the cop seemed slightly wary. Maybe because of my questions, maybe because I'd been near two different men who were shot to death. After asking me a few dozen questions of her own, the deputy told me what she knew about the power outage.

"Somebody pulled the plug."

I waited for the rest of the story, but that was essentially it.

"This place must have been wired by somebody's nephew," the deputy said. "It's not even close to being up to code. Anybody who could follow a line could find their way to the circuit box and cut the power with a couple flicks of their wrist. I'm going to bust the building inspector."

She was sufficiently P.O.'d at that township official to show me the inferior setup. Even I, whose knowledge of electricity was limited to flipping a wall switch, could see that this didn't look right. A mare's nest of heavy black cables fed into stacks of industrial-sized power strips under an outdated circuit box.

"So the only thing someone had to know was the location of the power source," I mused.

The deputy nodded. "And to do that, all he'd have to do is follow the black cables."

She was right. I'd been so preoccupied with hounds and shootings that I hadn't noticed the obvious electrical lines crisscrossing the arena floor. The only area free of floor cables was the show ring.

—

Back at the concession stand, there was no sign of either Jeb or MacArthur. Chester was still there, deep in conversation with the middle-aged female food vendor, who had joined him at our table. That is, Chester was talking to her when he wasn't licking a perilously tall soft ice cream cone.

"Look, Whiskey. I got a quadruple dip. On the house!"

I thanked the vendor for her generosity and asked Chester to follow me. He withdrew a folded bill from his inside blazer pocket and pressed it into the vendor's palm, a gesture better suited to the senior member of a men's club than a third-grader. The vendor glanced at the bill, gasped, and tried to return it. But Chester waved her away.

"You can afford to pay for your cone," I told him a little peevishly.

"I know." He slurped melted ice cream from the back of his hand. "But I'd rather let people give me things when they want to and then over-tip them to the point where they practically faint."

He looked very pleased with himself. And his ice cream.

"Just out of curiosity, Chester, how much did you tip that lady?"

"If you have to ask, you can't afford it, Whiskey."

We both knew I couldn't afford it, so I let the topic drop. I wanted to know what had happened to the rest of our team. Chester explained that Jeb and MacArthur had drawn up a list of "persons of interest," split it down the middle, and gone off to find those folks.

"MacArthur will interview Ramona and Susan," Chester reassured me.

"Thank you."

"And Jeb will interview Kori," he added.

Chester should have been much too young to understand those issues, but life with Cassina was an education in domestic drama.

"What do you know about Kori?" I said.

"Only that you don't like her, and you don't like the way MacArthur likes her, but you don't think Jeb will like her, so that's okay."

He'd pretty much summed it up. What I didn't want him to know, however, was that even if Kori wasn't a killer or a dognapper, she might be a homewrecker. And the home she might wreck was at the other end of the Castle from where Chester slept. Never mind that MacArthur had Avery's ugly mug inked on his arm. Tattoos do not an enduring relationship guarantee. Just ask Peg Goh.

"What are we supposed to do now?" I said.

Wherever we went, Chester would need a shower first. His cone had melted all over his sleeve and was now dripping onto his Italian leather shoes.

He licked the ice cream off his Patek-Philippe watch and announced, "The chopper pilot is expecting us."

"For what?"

"An aerial tour of Amish country. Jeb and MacArthur think that's the most efficient approach to finding Abra. So up, up, and away!"

During my previous helicopter experience, I'd accidentally stolen the pilot's flotation device. Since we weren't flying over water today, at least no water larger than a small inland lake, our pilot didn't have flotation issues. His name was Brad, and his only concerns were that we buckled up so we wouldn't fall out, and we wore headsets so we could hear each other en route.

MacArthur had instructed Brad to take us where we wanted to go. I explained that our goal was to find a blonde bimbo Afghan hound last seen in the company of an Amish teenager and his long-haired goats.

Brad paused his preparations for take-off.

"Was the Amish kid drunk?" he asked.

"How did you guess?"

"When I flew in, I saw an eastbound wagon weaving all over Route 20. It was carrying livestock."

Chester bounced in his seat. "Take us to the drunk Amish kid!"

THIRTY-THREE

EVEN WITH A HELICOPTER on our side, I couldn't believe finding Abra could be as easy as Pilot Brad made it sound. I wanted to believe it, but experience had taught me otherwise.

Chester, on the other hand, declared that we were "overdue for a lucky break." I couldn't argue with that logic. I was more than ready to lift off from the Barnyard Inn, scene of murder, mayhem, and way too many Afghan hounds.

Rising straight into the sky is an experience like no other. Helicopters offer a surprisingly smooth, if vertigo-inducing, ascent. Given the recent state of my stomach, I wanted to squeeze my eyes shut during take-off and keep them that way for most of the ride. But Chester kept shouting into my headset, "Look at that, Whiskey! Look at that!"

Since we were on the trail of my lost dog, I felt obliged to comply.

On my first chopper ride last winter, I had been searching for Chester. Happily, the little guy was now safe and secure next to me, loving every moment of our adventure. A helicopter tour feels like an amusement park ride… except that you're actually traveling. Skimming treetops and buildings gives you both the big picture *and* the small picture simultaneously. Although I wasn't sure it was the best way to experience Amish country, it seemed the most likely route to Abra.

Since we were in the middle of nowhere interesting, I'd expected the scenery to be one boring farmer's field after another, broken up by look-alike houses and barns. I was wrong. With the late afternoon sun at our backs and U.S. Route 20 under our feet, we were treated to meadows of green, gold, and coffee-brown rolling away to our right and left. And the trees! Clots of vivid color greeted us wherever a patch of woods remained. This was leaf-peeping in a close-up, high-up rush. Chester squealed with delight.

I had to remind myself of our reason for being airborne: tracking the traffic along Route 20 for signs of a weaving Amish wagon.

"This is where I saw the wagon on our way in," Brad announced. "That was thirty-five minutes ago. He could have turned off anywhere east of here, so start scanning the side roads."

"Roger dodger!" Chester replied.

Brad took us up another hundred feet for a more sweeping panorama.

"Most of the Amish live south of Route 20," he said, "so our driver probably turned right."

My eyes were peeled for a horse-drawn farmer's wagon. But what I spotted first was a silver pickup truck with something bluish-gray in the back. The truck was heading to our left, north, on a curving paved road. I shouted to Brad to take the chopper down for a closer look.

"I don't see a wagon," the pilot said.

"Oh, we've got way more trouble than that," Chester told him.

Brad followed instructions and brought us down dizzyingly close to the moving truck. Until the cargo came into focus, I held my breath in suspense.

"Looks like a big plastic bag of trash," Brad said. "Is that what you're looking for?"

"Nope," I said. "We're looking for big wayward dogs and killers."

"I didn't copy that last word."

"Just as well," Chester sighed.

So up and back around to Route 20 we flew. Now I found myself distracted by every single silver pickup truck I saw. And they were not uncommon. But none had anything in the back that might have been Silverado.

After flying in silence for several minutes, Brad said, "I gotta tell you, I don't think it's likely that wagon went this far east. We need to focus where the Amish farms are."

Chester and I agreed. One right turn improved the scenery immensely. Gone was that gray ribbon of concrete connecting cities from east to west. In its place was an undulating landscape crisscrossed with gravel roads and dotted by neat square buildings. Brad made ever wider and higher circles. After ten minutes of seeing nothing but bucolic splendor, punctuated by the occasional lone buggy, I gave silent thanks that I wasn't paying for this ride. At least not straight from my pocket. I had no doubt that Liam Davies would expect—and receive—extraordinary service in exchange for this gift.

"What's that?" Chester asked.

I followed the imaginary line from his pointing finger, and so did Brad.

"Looks like goats to me," the pilot said.

I squinted into the distance at a fenced pasture containing a few dozen animals that looked, from here, decidedly less elegant than horses and skinnier than cows. But I couldn't be sure how tall they were.

"I'm not up to speed on barnyard critters," I admitted. "What could they be, besides cows?"

"Goats," Brad repeated. "We're going in!"

That was my first clue that he was weary of our wild goose—I mean goat—chase. Brad did the helicopter pilot equivalent of stomping on the gas as he took us down. Although I knew less than nothing about physics, I'd once heard a test pilot on TV describe "atmospheric pressure" on re-entry. This felt like that. Panicked, I glanced at Chester, who grinned like he was being tickled. It must be a guy thing.

Although, theoretically, you can land a helicopter almost anywhere, Brad was concerned about setting his craft down.

"Nobody's expecting us," he pointed out. "So if we land on their land, we're trespassing. If we land in the road, we block traffic."

Ultimately, our pilot selected a spot on a dirt lane about a quarter-mile from the goat paddock. And, yes, we verified that they were goats before we landed although we couldn't get close enough to be sure they had long hair. I was reasonably certain that none of them was Abra, not because I could see the critters clearly but because I could see the fence. No way that thing could contain my bitch. Unless she liked the goats well enough to hang with them.

Stirring up dust may have been preferable to spewing gravel. However, it was hard to see anything until a few seconds after the blades had stopped. Brad would stay with the craft, of course. Chester and I needed to get our bearings. Now that we were back on planet Earth, everything was jumbled. The pilot helpfully pointed us toward the goat paddock. It was up a low hill and down the other side.

"If we're not back in, say, an hour, call the cops," I told him. "Better yet, call my cop."

I wrote down Jenx's name and number.

Brad seemed amused. "Do you expect to be attacked by Amish?"

"I expect to have to chase my dog."

Since neither Chester nor I was dressed for a cross-country hike, I hoped we wouldn't encounter anything truly rural, like mice or ticks. Or cow patties. After a short walk down the dirt lane, we faced our first field. From the air, it had seemed innocent enough. Close up, it proved to be a cornfield. We both knew what had just happened to the Two L's. Without exchanging a word, Chester placed his small hand in mine. We steeled ourselves for adventure, and passed through the first wall of corn.

"If we follow this row, we should be all right," Chester reassured me. "It runs right up the hill and over to the pasture."

There was only one problem. Make that two problems. First, the Amish didn't plow and plant with powerful automated equipment. Second, their land wasn't flat as a dance floor. As a result, we soon discovered that our chosen row wiggled and weaved like that drunken teen driving the family wagon.

"Which direction are we going now?" I asked Chester after what seemed like an eternity but proved to be eight minutes.

He squinted at the sky. I assumed he was calculating angle of the sun or whatever it is Cub Scouts learn to do in case they forget their compass.

"I don't know which way we're headed, but I think it's going to rain."

Perfect. If that happened, we'd not only be stranded in the corn, we'd also be soaked to the skin. To comfort myself, I checked my cell phone battery. I still had two bars. If only I'd remembered to ask the pilot for his number. Chester hadn't gotten it, either.

"I'm sorry, Whiskey," he said. "But I thought you'd handle something."

Fair enough. At least I had Jeb's number. And MacArthur's. One of them could probably reach Brad. The best I could do was stay calm and trust Chester.

"You still think we're going toward the goats, don't you?" I asked him.

"I think by now we may have made a cumulative right-angle turn," he said. "But we can't see far in front of us, so for all I know, this path may self-correct."

I might have whimpered a little because Chester added, "Cheer up, Whiskey. If our row doesn't end at the pasture, it will end at a road. We can't be stuck in the corn forever."

I swore to never, ever pay a dime to enter a corn maze, one of those autumn tourist attractions contrived to make city people think they're lost. This field was terrifying enough, exactly as man and plow had made it. It was more terrifying than a maze because there was no promise from the farmer that he'd get you out before sundown.

Suddenly I was thirsty. Very thirsty. And my feet hurt. So did my head.

"Think about something else!" Chester commanded when I complained.

His pale hair and navy blue blazer were flecked with dried corn leaves. That meant I was disheveled, too. More disheveled than usual. I tried to flick a bug or something from my eye. But it wouldn't go away, so I rubbed it. That only made it worse.

"Ouch! Now I can't see."

We stopped walking. I bent over so that Doctor Chester could check my right eye.

"Hmmm," he said. His tone suggested that I needed surgery. Or at least a second opinion.

"What?" I demanded.

"You rubbed it too hard. I think you've given yourself a corneal abrasion."

"Great, just great!" I cried hysterically. "A corneal abrasion in the corn! What next?!"

"By now you should know better than to ask that question," he said.

As if cued, the sky—denim blue until just moments ago—opened up, pelting us with raindrops the size of my sore eye.

I think I may have screamed. Patiently Chester reminded me that if we stopped where we stood we would get wet, and we would get nowhere. Placing one hand in his hand and my other hand on his shoulder, I let him lead me through that hell of rain and corn.

Damn Amish country, I thought.

Until a sweet little voice said, "How come you're playing in our field?"

Parting the dried stalks like curtains were two children from another century.

THIRTY-FOUR

THEY WEREN'T TIME TRAVELERS, of course. They were Amish. And they were adorable. A boy and girl not much taller than Chester. The boy even looked like Chester, without his glasses and fifty-dollar haircut.

The girl wore a black bonnet and a dark blue *Little House on the Prairie* style dress. The boy wore a straw hat, green shirt, and overalls.

"It's raining," the little girl said as if city slickers like us couldn't tell. "What's wrong with your eye?"

Before I could answer, Chester explained that I had got something in it and then rubbed it.

"She should know better," the girl said.

Chester agreed. Then he made the introductions. The children were alarmed when they heard my name.

"It's just a nickname," I explained.

"Why?" The girl was suspicious.

"Because my real name is Whitney, and I don't seem like a Whitney."

"Because you like whiskey," the boy concluded.

"No! As a matter of fact, I *don't* like whiskey."

"And whiskey doesn't like her," Chester chuckled.

The joke bombed. But Rachel and Jacob shook his hand, anyway. When I extended mine, they tucked theirs in their pockets. I'm quite sure they would have backed away if there had been room in our corn row.

At least the rain was letting up. And the natives knew the lay of the land.

"This is our farm," Rachel said. "Our house is that way."

She pointed in the direction from which they'd come.

"Great," I said. "Where are your goats?"

Jacob said, "Why do you want to know?"

"Because I'm looking for my lost doggie, and I think she ran away with your goats."

"Our goats didn't run away," Jacob said. "We have new goats."

"Yes! And if you look real close, you might see that one of your new goats is a doggie."

I smiled as warmly as I knew how. Maybe I showed too many teeth. Or too much gum. Or maybe I was just too tall. Something about my approach wasn't working. Jacob and Rachel shrank back like I was everything English they'd ever been warned against.

"It happened like this," Chester interjected and proceeded to tell the tale of Abra jumping on the wagon with the goats, omitting only the part about the teenage driver being drunk.

Jacob and Rachel conferred quietly. After a moment, Jacob said, "Our cousin Nathaniel was driving that wagon. He's in a lot of trouble."

I nodded sympathetically. "Most people who get involved with my doggie are."

"Nathaniel's in trouble because he's like you," Rachel said. "He likes whiskey!"

"I don't like whiskey. I am Whiskey."

For some reason, that made her cry.

"If you want to see our goats, come this way," Jacob said, one arm around his sniffling sister.

"I'd rather see your cousin. He might save us some time."

"Naughty Nathaniel," Rachel said. "He's being punished."

I wondered how that worked in Amish country. I mean, if you don't have a car, TV, cell phone, or iPod, what can your parents take away?

Jacob supplied the answer: "Nathaniel can't go to town for a whole month. And Uncle Noah's making him rake the manure out of the goat pasture. That's where we'll find him."

That wouldn't be good for my shoes. But maybe the field would be clean by the time we got there. At any rate, it was our best shot at tracking Abra. We were probably closer to her now than we'd been since she took off.

The rain had completely stopped, but my right eye throbbed fiercely. I kept my hand cupped over it. Either my reptilian brain was telling me to protect it, or my vanity was telling me to hide it.

The Amish kids sure knew how to navigate a cornfield. We trod purposefully behind them. Jacob waved to us to follow as he cut kitty-corner across a couple dozen rows. The next thing I knew, we had emerged into open air within a few feet of a white rail fence.

"Is that the goat paddock?"

I couldn't see a single goat.

"They're at the other end. Come on!"

The Amish kids were already scrambling over the fence. Even with short legs and a long skirt, Rachel managed to scale it before I could figure out how to begin. I gave silent thanks that the only audience for my performance was three kids, two of whom already disliked me.

"She's a little out of shape," Chester told Jacob and Rachel.

"On account of the whiskey?" Rachel whispered.

The long trek across the goat pasture did not improve my mood. If, as his cousins had said, Naughty Nathaniel was on punitive muck duty, then he hadn't gotten very far. Goat shit was *everywhere*. Brown pellets half the size of my thumb stuck to my shoes like, well, shit. About every fifty steps I stopped to survey the mounting debris on my soles. It was like an extra layer of insulation but not the kind anybody wants. What I couldn't understand was why nobody else was picking up half as much of it as I was. Chester pointed out that my soles weren't made of leather like his, Jacob's, and Rachel's. Mine were made of some inferior petroleum-based composite intended for exclusive use in goat-free zones.

"City slicker," one of the Amish kids murmured. Probably Rachel. She was a pretty little girl, but hostile to all things civilized.

"Look out! They're going to butt you!"

"What?"

I glanced up from the sticky sole of my shoe to see Rachel pointing toward something behind me. Before I could check it out,

I received a hard shove in the derriére. Since I was standing on one foot only, the impact sent me sprawling. I landed on my knees and elbows, which might have been mildly amusing had it not been for the goat shit and the three—count 'em, three—aggressive long-haired goats now in my face. I was down; they were up. And they were in the mood to head-butt.

Adrenalized, I reached into my bag and pulled out the closest thing to a weapon that I possessed: the Afghan hound mystery, courtesy of Odette. Without thinking, I aimed the book's solid spine at the muzzle of the nearest goat and swung with all my might. The impact sounded like a ball cracking a bat. The goat stumbled sideways, his eyes crossed. When the next goat came at me, I swung the book in a sharp uppercut. Although the sound of the connection was less satisfying, the angle of my blow lifted the goat's front feet from the ground and sent him reeling. Right behind him, the third goat left me no time to strike, so I flattened myself to the ground and let him sail over me.

Chester cheered. Cautiously I lifted my chin; the first goat was charging back this way, head down for the power-butt. I was adrenalized and inspired. Taking aim, I launched the book; it ripped through the air like the potentially lethal Frisbee that every trade paperback is. When it collided with the crown of the goat's head, he grunted like a fullback and fell.

Chester helped me to my feet. My clothing was sticky and smeared; I expected the Amish kids to snigger. They didn't, however. They merely stared. Chester whispered something about their culture opposing combat in any form. Great. Now I was all about whiskey *and* violence. Maybe Nathaniel would like me.

He did, as it turned out. Though not immediately. I met him while running away from yet a fourth angry goat. This one clutched what was left of the projectile novel in his jaws. The book looked half-eaten, and the goat looked pissed off. Why, oh why, did the hoofed demons attack only me? Although Chester was just the right size to knock down, he probably spoke goat and thus talked them out of it. I did the next best thing: I unleashed a stream of expletives that should have been clear in any language. But the damned critter kept up the chase, forcing me to run in ever wider circles toward the far end of the pasture. I caught sight of a muscular young man with a blonde bowl haircut wielding an oversized old-fashioned rake. Nathaniel for sure.

"Help!" I cried. "That goat has got me in his sights and he won't quit!"

I tried to position myself so that Nathaniel was between me and the goat, but he didn't stop raking, and the goat kept circling.

"Can you help me out here?" I panted.

Nathaniel said nothing.

"Hey, I know about your mess with the wagon," I said. "It's why I'm here. I think you saw my dog! If you help me, I'll make it worth your while!"

That got his attention. Nathaniel leaned on his giant rake and grinned. "Will you get me a six-pack of beer?"

"You bet! I got a helicopter, and it's parked right over there!" Still dodging the goat, I pointed toward the cornfield.

"Where?" Nathaniel asked.

"Ask that kid who's coming with your cousins!"

Nathaniel shaded his eyes for a better look at the three children running toward us. "Is that your son?"

"Even better. He's my bodyguard. Well, one of them. The good one."

With perfect timing, Chester shouted, "Don't hurt Whiskey! She means you no harm!"

"'Whiskey'?" Nathaniel looked confused.

"It's my name," I said.

Nathaniel winked. Then he shouted something in German that drove the goat away. Before I could ask what it meant, the children arrived.

"She says she lost her dog!" Rachel said, watching me with continued wariness.

Jacob added, "She thinks her dog jumped on your wagon."

"Is that so?" Nathaniel said.

He had classic "bad-boy" good looks: mussed hair, twinkling eyes, a crooked grin, and lazy posture. Apparently some Amish men were born to be trouble, just like my ex-husband.

I proceeded to describe Abra, and what the Two L's had seen her do. Chester chimed in now and then to keep the narrative on course.

"The bottom line," he told Nathaniel, "is that Abra runs away all the time. So she's good at it."

"I don't have your dog," Nathaniel said. "She was on my wagon, though. Till she jumped off it to chase another dog."

I groaned and smacked myself in the forehead so hard it hurt.

"Where did that happen?" Chester said.

"We were still on Route 20. A Ford pickup passed us with a big hairy dog in the back. The dog was barking at my wagon. Then all of a sudden it jumped out. I had to swerve not to hit it. The next thing I knew, another big hairy dog was leaping over my head—

and over my horses—to get to the dog on the road. I almost ran over them both."

"What color was the first big hairy dog?" I said.

"Gray. Like the truck."

"Silverado!" I cried.

Nathaniel shook his head. "The Silverado's a Chevy. This was a Ford."

"I mean the dog! Silverado is the name of the dog. He's missing, too."

"About that pay-off you promised me..." Nathaniel raised an eyebrow.

"I'm good for it, but you gotta tell me more. Where on Route 20 did this happen, and which way did they go?"

"How about you and me take a ride in your helicopter," Nathaniel said. "I'll show you where, and you'll get me what I want."

Rachel said, "You can't ride in a helicopter! You're in trouble!"

"You'll be in trouble, too, if I tell your mother you're sneaking food to the barn cats," Nathaniel said. More nastily than necessary, I thought. Rachel turned white. Then she clambered over the gate and ran for the house.

"I won't tell on you, Nathaniel," Jacob said. "No matter what you do. Neither will Rachel. She's just scared."

"I know." The older cousin lifted the boy's straw hat and ruffled his hair, but he kept his gaze on me. "Jacob, go take care of your sister. If anybody asks about me, tell them you just saw me in the goat paddock."

Jacob placed a hand on top of the gate to pull himself up.

"Wait!" Nathaniel said. "Take your little English friend along, why don't you?"

He was looking at me to grant permission, but I turned it over to Chester. "Do you want to?"

"Oh yeah! Can I?" His eyes widened behind his glasses.

"Sure. We'll be back before you know it ... assuming Nathaniel can walk me through that cornfield to the chopper."

"Why not land the chopper right here?" Chester said.

Producing his cell phone, he speed-dialed Jeb, who gave him Brad's number. Then he dialed the pilot, introduced him to Nathaniel, and let the two of them work things out.

Nathaniel couldn't have looked happier. Handing the phone back to Chester, he told me, "We'll be out of here before anybody can stop us."

My little English bodyguard waved and followed Jacob over the fence. Seconds later, I heard the whine of the approaching helicopter.

Nathaniel leaned his rake against the fence and checked over his shoulder.

"If you see my family coming, don't panic. Nobody around here has a gun."

THIRTY-FIVE

I WAS TOO WORRIED to do anything but my infamous ostrich routine. As the helicopter drew near, I shut my eyes and let somebody else make things happen. You'd be surprised how often that turns out to be the right choice.

While I wasn't looking, Brad the pilot found the paddock and neatly landed the chopper. Long-haired goats dodged every which way but at me. Nathaniel the Amish bad boy shouted that it was time to board. I didn't look back till we were airborne. From that vantage point I could see an Amish family jogging toward the paddock, with Rachel, Jacob, and Chester bringing up the rear.

Brad signaled for me to give our new guest a headset. Nathaniel held it in both hands for a long moment before slipping it on. At first, I thought he didn't know what to do with it; then I realized he was savoring the moment.

"Nathaniel's going to show us where Abra and Silverado got together," I told Brad. "Out on Route 20."

Even as I said it, I knew it sounded ridiculous. Nobody in the world cared as much as I did about tracking trouble-making dogs. Maybe it was time I stopped caring. Maybe I'd already made enough of an effort to find them. I was half-blind and covered with goat shit. I had a business to run, after all, and a screwed-up personal life to sort out.

Nathaniel seemed utterly unfazed by his aerial experience. Pointing helpfully, he showed Brad the exact spot on Route 20. Along the way, he identified every farm and road.

"I was about to turn there, on County Road 60," he said, "when the dogs jumped!"

"If only you'd seen which way they went after that," I sighed.

"I did!" Nathaniel said. "They headed back west on 20."

"Like they were returning to the dog show?" Brad asked.

"Well, they didn't do that," I said.

We flew in silence for a few moments looping pointlessly around the designated intersection. I noticed with irritation that Nathaniel's focus seemed to be elsewhere.

"That's weird," he remarked finally, gazing to his right.

"What?"

"Over there. It looks like a dog. No. Make that two dogs. Are those the same two dogs . . . ?"

Brad automatically swiveled the craft in the direction our Amish passenger was pointing. I leaned forward in concentration. And then I saw what Nathaniel saw. Loping west along Route 20 were two examples of the most graceful breed of dog ever placed on this planet. From the air, one looked blonde, the other steel-gray. Guess who was leading?

"She's at it again!" I said. "Luring another new boyfriend astray."

"Or leading him back to the dog show," Brad said. "Maybe she's some kind of hero."

"Please. You've never met my bitch."

Then Brad explained something I already knew, that he couldn't set the helicopter down on Route 20.

"Here's an option," he continued. "I can go ahead of the dogs and find a side road to land on. Then you can run after them…"

"What's the next option?"

"We can follow them, and you can direct someone on the ground to intercept them."

"Call in the cavalry, you mean?"

"Those are your options."

How I wished that Chester was here to help. The kid had a knack for canine problem-solving. I opened my cell phone, prepared to speed-dial Jeb. Then I remembered that he had arrived by chopper and did not have a car at his disposal. Sure, he could have used mine, except that I had the keys. So I phoned MacArthur.

"You've reached my voicemail. Have at it."

Indeed I did, forcibly omitting all expletives on account of our Amish guest. I tersely summed up the situation, concluding with "We're in the air following the dogs. Call me back! Fast!"

"Look at that!" Nathaniel said as I ended the call.

Below us, a big black car was making a U-turn on Route 20. As we stared, the vehicle passed our fast-moving gray and yellow targets, then pulled over onto the berm ahead of them. The rear door on the driver's side opened, and in jumped both dogs. The door closed, and nothing else happened.

Brad slowed the craft until we were literally hovering above the vehicle.

"Do you recognize the car?" he said.

"No!" I said.

"Well, whoever's driving knows they got an audience. Let's see what they do next."

"The damn dogs got into a limo," I said numbly.

"That's not a limo. That's a Cadillac," Nathaniel declared. "Probably a 2009 DTS." When Brad and I stared at him, he said, "I know cars."

"You're Amish," I said.

"I'm seventeen. I haven't decided whether I want to be Amish or not. When I get the chance, I hang around car dealerships in Elkhart. I think I might like to sell used cars someday."

"Amish teens—I've heard about that," Brad said, sounding suddenly energized. "You get to explore your choices, right?"

"Right. Our families give us a lot of freedom."

"Speaking of freedom, the dogs are driving away!" I shouted. "Follow that Cadillac!"

Calmly Brad said, "Now would be a good time to enlist your friends on the ground."

"If they'd answer their phones!" I fumed.

When I called MacArthur again, I got his voicemail again. This time I left a few choice words in my message. For emphasis. And to scare the men in the chopper. Then I tried Jeb, on the off chance that he might be with MacArthur. I got his voicemail, too. I don't remember exactly what I told him, but it wasn't pretty.

To Nathaniel, who was eavesdropping, I said, "How do you know what your limits are? Or don't you have any?"

"We're not supposed to shame our families."

"Good plan," I said. "What about your adventure with the wagon?"

"That shamed them," he admitted. "To sober me up, my uncle made me swim in the creek with my clothes on. Then he made me rake out the goat paddock."

Brad laughed into his headset. "Reminds me of myself at your age! Without the goats."

I was in the midst of male bonding.

"I'm lucky," Nathaniel told Brad. "She's going to buy me a six-pack."

"Who?"

The teen pointed at me. "She said if I helped find her dog, she'd get me something good. Maybe even something with her name on it."

"I never said I'd buy you whiskey!" I protested.

"Hold on," Brad said, glaring at me. "You promised to buy an under-age Amish kid *booze*?"

I felt like the Antichrist. Maybe according to the rules of Amish country, I was.

"Beer only, I swear! His little cousin got confused about whiskey because it's my name!"

Brad shook his head in disgust. To Nathaniel, he said, "Here's a better offer. As soon as we finish this job, I'll show you how a chopper works. That's way more fun than a six-pack!"

"How about this," Nathaniel counter-offered. "You drop me off at the Cadillac dealership in Elkhart, and I'll forget about the beer. And whiskey."

I wasn't sure if he meant the beverage or me. Then my cell phone rang; Jeb was calling.

"Where's MacArthur?" I shouted. When I couldn't hear Jeb's answer, I repeated the question. Louder. Three more times. I never did hear his answer. By then Jeb had given up.

"This isn't working," I told Brad.

"We'll track the car as far as the Barnyard Inn," he said. "Then you can jump in your own car and take it from there."

"We have to retrieve Chester!" I reminded him.

"I'll pick him up on the way back from Elkhart. I have instructions from Mr. Davies to return Chester and Jeb to Magnet Springs."

"Tonight?"

"Tomorrow morning," Brad said. "Unless they insist on going back tonight."

"Nobody's going back tonight," I growled. "Not when I have to waste all this time looking for dogs!"

I thought about Jeb, his overnight bag, and our passion, the latter of which we'd probably squandered. This time I couldn't blame Abra for everything that had gone wrong. I'd been a bitch, too.

The black Cadillac was directly under us, passing every car in its lane. As Brad observed, they had to know they had aerial company. I asked if he could swoop down and get the license plate number, but he said that wasn't possible.

"I saw somebody do it in a movie," I whined.

"Sure you did," Brad replied. "In a movie."

THIRTY-SIX

My heart sank as the black Cadillac zoomed past the Barnyard Inn, and Brad prepared to land the helicopter in the parking lot. Now it would be entirely up to me to continue the chase. In my own earthbound vehicle.

Peering out the window during our descent, I counted three police cars and nine sign-toting Fleggers still on site. Then I counted my ex-husband—as a major disappointment. He was leaning up against a familiar white Audi, chatting with a woman I had grown to intensely dislike. Although we were too far away to see the bullet holes, I was sure there were still two in Susan Davies' shiny car. And I no longer gave a shit about who had put them there.

"Thanks, anyway," I told Brad as I handed back my headset.

Nathaniel made no move to remove his. In fact, he appeared to have settled in happily for the ride to Elkhart .

"Not a problem," Brad said. "I do what Mr. Davies tells me to. Within reason."

When I stepped out of the chopper into churning air, MacArthur jogged toward me across the blacktop.

"The dogs are in a black Cadillac heading east!" I shouted. "And Chester is with the Amish."

Without replying, he grabbed me by the arm and pulled me along until we were well beyond the helicopter's wind and noise.

"Kori's gone," he said without preamble. "Jeb went to interview her, but she'd checked out."

"Yeah, yeah," I told him. "I know about her silver pickup!"

"That's not hers. Kori drives a black Lincoln, courtesy of Liam."

"From the sky, does a Lincoln look like a Cadillac?"

I filled MacArthur in on what we'd witnessed along Route 20.

"A Lincoln might look like a Caddy," he said, "to you and an Amish kid."

"The pilot was there, too! He didn't disagree."

"He doesn't get paid to."

"Well, all I know is somebody's driving Abra and Silverado down Route 20 right now! They just passed the Barnyard Inn, and I'm going to follow them!"

MacArthur reacted in a way I could not have predicted. He doubled over in laughter.

"What the hell is so funny, Mr. Never-Here-When-I-Need-You Bodyguard?!"

"What's funny, Whiskey, is that you have no training whatsoever in aggressive driving!"

He rolled a whole lot of Rs in that sentence, but I was still annoyed.

"Isn't aggressive driving something you get ticketed for?" I said.

"I'm talking about competitive and evasive techniques used by professional drivers. I took a course in Glasgow. You're coming with me!"

With that he grabbed my arm again, and we took off running toward… I didn't know where. Presumably toward MacArthur's car. Since I had never actually seen his car, I didn't have a clue what it looked like.

"What's up with Jeb and Susan?" I panted. "I thought *you* were going to question her."

"I did," MacArthur replied as we ran.

"Well, there he is, flirting with her again!"

MacArthur braked abruptly, pulling me around to face him.

"I can't keep your man on a leash, and neither can you. Take a wee spot of advice from Fleggers on this one, and *let it go*. Now, shall we find Abra?"

Off we went again, dashing past many parked cars, including Susan's. I refrained from waving at her and Jeb. Or giving them the finger.

"Where the hell are you parked?" I gasped as we left the lot behind us and continued along the side of the exhibit hall, running on grass. I knew that MacArthur had slowed his pace for me. Even so, he was twenty feet ahead.

"Over there," he said at the exact instant I spotted his vehicle.

"Oh no!" I wailed. "I don't know how to ride a motorcycle!"

"*That* is no motorcycle. That is a Harley. You don't have to know how to ride it. All you have to do is hold on. And wear this."

He tossed me a Darth Vader-type helmet, then leapt astride the machine as if mounting a stallion. How can I put this? MacArthur took what was left of my breath away.

I would have put the freaking helmet on backwards if he hadn't stopped me. After that I sat where he told me to sit and put my hands where he told me to put them: around his massive chest. Okay, so that part was pleasant enough. When MacArthur kicked the bike to life, I inhaled the last complete breath I would catch for some miles. I only wished I could have seen the expression on Jeb and Susan's faces as we roared past. Unfortunately, I was too terrified to open my eyes.

"How fast was the Caddy going?" MacArthur whispered in my ear.

That is, it sounded like he was whispering. Actually, he was speaking through the headset built into my helmet. Since I had a mouthpiece in my helmet, there was no need for me to shout. Except of course from pure terror.

"How the hell should I know how fast it was going? I was in a helicopter!"

"Allow me to rephrase the question," MacArthur said calmly. "Was the Caddy passing other cars, or were other cars passing the Caddy?"

"The Caddy was the passer!" I yelled.

Through my now slightly open "good" eye, I saw MacArthur touch his helmet. Possibly to turn down the volume dial…

"One more question," he said. "Was the driver in complete control of the car? Or did he swerve?"

"No swerving!"

MacArthur touched his helmet again. "Then we have one very cool customer."

"Or one very reckless one," I said. "Did you check Kori's driving record?"

MacArthur didn't answer. Instead, he commanded me to hold on tight. Tighter. I squeezed my eyes shut again. From the sound and the smell—and the eternity required to get around it—I gathered that we were passing an eighteen-wheeler. By the time we were back to the regular roar of the road, I had forgotten what I wanted to ask him. Hell, I had forgotten my middle name.

If there was a blood clot anywhere in my body, road vibrations had surely jarred it loose by now. Who worried about stroke or heart attack? I was way more afraid of ending up a smear on the pavement.

As we wove in and out of traffic, leaning into what felt like a series of forty-five-degree angles to pass every car and truck, I wondered if MacArthur had a death wish. More important, I wondered if I could make him understand that I didn't. No simple task when I couldn't gather enough oxygen to speak.

Suddenly I heard and felt a vehicle surging up behind us. When the driver leaned into the horn, I knew we were in trouble. The next instant we were buzzed by a silver pickup passing so close that it literally forced us off the road. The hair on my arms stood at attention.

MacArthur kindly let me scream till my throat hurt and my blood pressure slid back to normal.

"Feel better?" he inquired.

By then we were parked on the berm, holding our helmets.

"You sure can ride that thing," I conceded. "Thanks for stopping."

His black curls were matted with sweat, and rivulets of perspiration sprang from his hairline.

"I couldn't risk your life," he said. "Somebody wants us out of the way."

"Do you think they were chasing the Caddy, too?" I asked. "Or are both drivers working together?"

"My guess is they're meeting up somewhere down the road."

"Why on earth would anyone go to all that trouble to steal my Bad Example?"

"Get real, Whiskey. It's only Silverado they want. Abra is along by accident."

He had to be right. I said, "You don't think they'll just dump her, do you?"

"They could try," MacArthur said, grinning.

Abra had a long history of making human life miserable, and not just mine. Most of the criminals she had consorted with ended up wishing they'd never met her.

"What now?" I asked.

"If we were in Magnet Springs, I'd suggest contacting local law enforcement. But here they're unlikely to know the finer points of dognapping, so they'd no doubt waste our time."

My mind was on retrieving Chester and getting back to real estate where I belonged. Not that I was willing to give up on my dog, but I was more willing to get on with my life.

MacArthur said, "We need to find out from the Barnyard Inn what kind of vehicle every show participant drove. That will narrow our field of investigation."

"We're still investigating?" I let my disappointment show.

He didn't notice, though, because he was dialing his cell phone.

"Hello, Jenx!" he boomed. "Could you run a plate for me?"

MacArthur had managed to get the license number of the pickup that almost killed us. I hadn't even managed to keep my eyes open. Speaking of which, my right eye no longer felt so bad.

Nothing like a near-death experience to put minor aches and pains in perspective.

"You forgot to tell Jenx we were almost killed!" I said.

"She knows I only call her if it's a matter of life and death."

THIRTY-SEVEN

As we headed west on Route 20, I was stunned by how common big black cars are. Although I couldn't identify the make of most that rushed past us, many reminded me of the vehicle we'd seen from the air.

Back at the Barnyard Inn we parked at the end of the building, in a spot not visible from the office. I asked MacArthur how he liked his motel room.

"I didn't register," he replied. "I'm working undercover."

I wanted to know where one sleeps if one travels by Harley and doesn't rent a room, but he wasn't talking. Had MacArthur shared Kori's room, the one right next to mine? He opened the lobby door with exaggerated gallantry.

The scene was exactly as it had been twenty-four hours earlier. Since then, however, two guests had died, one had been shot at twice, and a couple dogs were missing.

The lobby smelled of curry, dog urine, and disinfectant. Although no one was at the desk, a television blared through the slightly open fake-wood door behind it. This time the foreign-language program sounded like a soap opera.

I expected MacArthur to demand service. Instead, he reached over the counter, adjusted the computer keyboard and screen, and started typing.

"You can't do that," I hissed.

But of course he could. And did. My amazement was incomplete, however, till he activated the noisy printer, which ground out four full pages, testing the limits of my frayed nerves. I was absolutely sure that the clatter would draw somebody to the desk. As the fourth page ever so slowly made its way through the machine, the phone on the desk jangled. I jumped. The TV volume dropped, and footsteps rapidly approached the door.

"MacArthur!" I cried, but he kept his eyes on the printout.

Suddenly a baby wailed, and the footsteps receded.

MacArthur ripped the last page from the printer, readjusted the monitor and keyboard, and pushed me gently toward the door. We were out of there by the end of the second ring.

"Just as I thought," he said, scanning the printout. "Nobody registered a Ford pickup."

"What does that mean?"

"Either somebody lied when they checked in, or somebody arrived here expressly to steal that dog. Or to kill Slater and Koniger."

"That's a lot of *or's*," I said.

"They're all connected. We just need to find the link."

"You can look for the link! And Abra, too. I need to collect my neighbor and go home. I should probably look for Jeb, but I don't think I'll like what I find."

My cell phone rang. Apparently it was my turn to hear from Magnet Springs' finest.

"Yo, Whiskey," Jenx said. "Still no luck finding the dogs?"

"We really only want one back," I said.

"You should talk to your ex. He's a little worried and a lot P.O.'ed. Why ya giving the guy a hard time? He's only trying to help."

"He's only trying to help Susan," I said.

"Save your insecurities for the bedroom! We got bigger things going on. The dog-show murders are on *Yahoo*! *News* already. And there's a YouTube video of Silverado and Kori, posted forty minutes ago by somebody with the handle 'luvssdogss'. You should see all the text comments. Everybody's worried about Silverado. This could be as big as Vivi the whippet!"

"Oh, come on," I said. "Vivi disappeared after winning the Westminster! Silverado's lost in Amish country."

"Where tourists flock to eat smorgasbords and ogle buggies," Jenx said. "I tell you, Amish country is what makes this story hot!"

When she asked to speak to MacArthur, I passed him the phone. He listened for a minute, grunted once, and closed the call.

"What now?" I said.

"Jenx isn't happy that you left Chester with the Amish."

"He wanted to stay! He's probably milking a cow right now and tipping the Amish for the privilege."

"No matter. Jenx wants us to fetch him."

"How are we supposed to do that? In the first place, I haven't got a clue how to get there by road! And in the second place, Brad the pilot said he'd pick up Chester! Just as soon as he returns Nathaniel from the Cadillac dealership."

"We won't be waiting for Brad and Nathaniel. Jenx says Brad was busted in Elkhart for buying Nathaniel a beer."

Either Brad was less virtuous than he had seemed, or Nathaniel was a real conniver. I voted for Nathaniel. An Amish teen who aspired to sell used cars was made of something stronger than cheese.

I'd meant what I said about having no idea how to find Chester. In the highly unlikely event that I could remember the general vicinity of our turn-off from Route 20, I had no idea which road Rachel and Jacob's house was on. Or what it looked like… other than that it was white with a big white barn and a long white fence. Like fifty other farms.

"I don't even know their last name!" I told MacArthur.

"That wouldn't help us much, anyway," he said. "Almost everybody here is a Yoder or a Miller."

Our unproductive discussion was interrupted by the arrival of Susan Davies in her Audi. After spraying me with gravel, she powered down her window and spoke directly to MacArthur.

"I'm driving Jeb to Chicago on business. Thanks for keeping me alive. No thanks for losing my winning dog. And my best handler."

What a bitch. I couldn't believe her nerve in nabbing my ex-husband, who had come to help *me*, and the comment about MacArthur losing her dog and her handler wasn't very nice, either.

Jeb leaned across Susan to speak to me.

"Wish I could help, Whiskey, but you've got MacArthur, so you'll be fine. Susan lined up a last-minute gig for me at her country club. I'm playing the brunch tomorrow. It's an Afghan hound rescue fundraiser."

I could have shouted any one of a dozen retorts that would satisfy my bruised ego now but make me cringe later. In a rare moment of maturity I simply said, "Good luck."

And I almost let it go at that. Then I considered what Jenx had said and decided I had nothing to lose but loss. I strode to the car window and leaned in above Susan's firm breasts. My face and Jeb's were inches apart.

"Did you come here to help me or to love me?" I asked him.

"I came to do both," he replied. "But you didn't want either."

"I *want* both! I want *you*."

Susan's perfume was everywhere—light and floral with a hint of ginger. Too expensive and girly for me. I was the blunt one, the clumsy one, the one who stank of goat shit. Also the one who loved Jeb.

I couldn't recall another time when I'd been so public in my display of affection. Or desperation. In the backseat Susan's two blonde show dogs panted eagerly.

"We'll talk about this later," Jeb said, his voice soft.

"Get your head out of my car, please!"

Susan revved her engine. Let me tell you, German engineering can sound ominous. I withdrew just in time; Susan peeled out of the lot, spraying me with gravel. Again.

MacArthur laid a steadying hand on my shoulder and said one word only: "Chester."

"You're right," I sighed, wrestling control of my emotions. "Screw dogs and lovers. We have a child to save."

Considering that Chester was with the Amish, I doubted he needed saving. Then I thought about Nathaniel. There were no guarantees.

THIRTY-EIGHT

"First things first," MacArthur said, helpfully distracting me with those deliciously rolled Rs. "Let's call Chester and tell him we're on our way. Maybe he can provide directions to the farm."

I nodded, speed-dialing my diminutive neighbor.

"Uh-oh. He has a new outgoing message."

I switched my phone to speaker mode.

"Greetings from Amish country! Wish you were here. In honor of my host family's religious beliefs, I'm turning off my cell for the duration of my visit. But feel free to leave a message. I'll return your call as soon as I resume my regular hedonistic lifestyle."

"Next suggestion?"

"We're going to follow your memory and my instincts," MacArthur said. "In your car."

He and I were already walking toward the back of the Barnyard Inn, where I had parked. MacArthur was again studying the printout from the front desk.

"Interesting," he murmured. "Besides Kori, three folks here drive big black cars."

"Not Susan," I quipped. "Susan drives white, like one of the good guys."

And then I did something I'd never done before. I spat in the dirt. It was satisfying… in a vicarious kind of way.

"Not Susan," MacArthur agreed. "But guess who?"

I shrugged, working up enough resentment and saliva for one more good shot.

"Perry Stiles, Ramona Bowden, and Mitchell Slater."

I gagged on my spit. "Mitchell's dead."

"Yes, but he drove a Cadillac DTS, exactly like your Amish kid identified. Maybe somebody borrowed it. Mitchell Slater won't need it anymore…"

"What does Ramona drive?" I said.

"A Caddy. Not a DTS, though. She has an older model. A Seville. One of her husbands left it to her."

"You got that off the printout?"

"I got that from my interview. I quizzed her, remember, while you were in the sky?"

"How about our own Mr. Stiles?" I asked. "What kind of black car does he drive?"

I hadn't pictured Perry as a fan of the Big Three automakers. He seemed like a Saab or Volkswagen kind of guy.

"He registered as driving a Chrysler 300," MacArthur replied. "A rental. I interviewed him, too. He said he was in Cincinnati on business last week and rented a car to drive here. A big enough car for the two dogs he traveled with."

"He lives in Chicago and paints houses in Cinci?" I asked.

"He was there to investigate the possibility of opening a *faux*-painting franchise. Or so he said."

MacArthur paused to survey the collection of cars and RVs still on site. Many were now gone. After all, the main show had concluded with a bang. And a whimper. I imagined that some folks planning to show dogs tomorrow had decided the risks were too high.

"Perry's Chrysler is still here," MacArthur said.

As he spoke, Brenda Spenser emerged from her room, staggering slightly. She carried a shoulder bag and led a gorgeous black Affie on a leash. We watched as she struggled to load her dog and her bag through the passenger door. Her coordination was definitely impaired.

"Brenda's drunk," I whispered. "Check her out on your printout. She's got a big black car!"

"A Mercedes," MacArthur confirmed. "But she's not registered, and I couldn't find her when I did the interviews."

"How could she not be registered?" I said.

"Room 19 was Matt Koniger's room," MacArthur said, checking his sheet. "He listed no car at all."

"Impossible. Everybody knows Matt didn't pay for anything, and that car has got to be Brenda's!"

MacArthur grabbed my elbow and steered me toward her.

"Tell her you're concerned for her loss, Whiskey. Then let me do the talking."

For the first time since I'd arrived at the show, Brenda didn't look pleased to see me. Although her haircut was still fabulous, she didn't smile, and her eyes seemed unfocused.

"Brenda, I'm worried about you. Are you doing all right?"

"You? Worried about me?"

Her voice had the shrill brittleness of someone angry and far from sober. Drawing close, I distinctly smelled gin on her breath. Brenda moved to the driver's side. With difficulty, she opened the door.

"Yes, I'm worried," I said. "I don't think you should drive."

"*You* don't think I should drive? Oh, that's a good one! Miss Whiskey thinks I can't handle a couple shots of Tanqueray. Well, let me ask you this: who the hell is left to drive me? In case you missed the finale, Matt is *dead*! My beautiful, beautiful man is dead!"

She froze as if hearing the news in her own voice finally made it real. Brenda wailed piteously, cupped her hands over her face, and folded like a bleacher seat, falling backwards into her car. She landed hard against the steering wheel and then slid sideways onto the seat. If she'd been sober, that would have hurt.

When MacArthur cleared his throat, I remembered my cue. It was a relief to step aside. I don't do drama well even though I do it often.

Brenda's sobs abated quickly. Either MacArthur had a miraculous effect on her, or her whole meltdown had been a charade. After he helped her stand up, the two chatted amiably, MacArthur leaning on the hood of the car, Brenda draped coquettishly against her open door. I for one wanted to applaud the Afghan hound in the backseat. Abra never would have sat still like that. She wouldn't have even stayed in the vehicle.

MacArthur gave Brenda his business card. Which one, I wondered. Cleaner? Bodyguard? Realtor? Whatever it said, she read it with interest. Then she offered him her hand to shake. After he helped her into the car and gently closed the driver's door, she put it in gear, gave him a flirtatious little wave, and peeled out of the lot, weaving all the way.

"That woman is unfit to drive," I declared. "You should have stopped her."

MacArthur was dialing his cell phone. "We'll let the highway patrol do that." Tersely he told the dispatcher that a black Mercedes, Illinois license plate 4EVRAF, was swerving on Route 20 just west of the Barnyard Inn.

"You're really good at getting those plates," I remarked.

"'Forever Af,'" he said. "That one was easy. Anyway, it's part of the job."

We both knew it had nothing to do with being a Realtor.

I asked MacArthur if in the course of his interviews he'd heard about any trouble between Matt and Brenda.

"Sandy Slater told me that Matt had 'issues' with Mrs. Spenser," he replied.

"She was keeping him, but he was having an affair with Susan," I said. "After Matt got shot, Sandy accused Brenda of wanting him dead because he was blackmailing her. You should have seen what happened next."

"Catfight?" guessed MacArthur. "Well, somebody was driving Brenda's car not long before we got here. The hood was hot."

"Could Brenda's car be the one I saw from the air? If it is, what happened to the dogs?"

Before MacArthur could offer a theory, a familiar male voice called out to us.

"Hewwo again! Did you heah about Jeb? He's going to sing and sell CDs in Chicago!"

Twenty feet away Dr. David and Deely were loading protest signs into the back of the Animal Ambulance. They looked sunburned and satisfied with their day. I paused for a major mental adjustment. There was no point letting the subject of my ex-husband and his current companion make me insane.

"Yeah, I heard."

I tried to say it like it was a good thing. Like my heart hadn't been kicked to shreds.

Although he didn't say it the way it's spelled, Dr. David enthused, "Jeb is going to sell a whole lot of *Animal Lullabies*!"

"We're proud of him, ma'am," Deely added. "Five percent of the profits from every sale go to Fleggers."

I pasted a fake smile on my face. It hurt to do that, but letting my real emotions show would have hurt more.

"Jeb is a real go-getter," I agreed. "He goes where the opportunities are. With whoever is there to drive him ..."

I probably spoke through gritted teeth. Something belied my smile because the next thing I knew, Deely was coming toward me, her head cocked in sympathy.

"You're not *jealous* of Mrs. Davies, are you, ma'am?"

"Jealous? Why on earth would I be jealous? Just because she's rich, cool, and beautiful—and I'm a Bad Example?" My laughter sounded manic even to my ears. "If she wants to spend time with my boyfriend, she's welcome to him! I divorced him once already, and I can bounce him out of my life again. Like that!"

I snapped my fingers. Then I belched. And then I started crying. Full-out messy bawling. Which I never do, even when situations are truly sad. And this situation was simply ridiculous. Between my chronic indigestion and my spiky emotions, I hardly recognized myself. I certainly didn't like what I saw.

Ever the Damage Control Specialist, Deely produced a handful of tissues. I wanted to cover my face with them. Fortunately, MacArthur and Dr. David did what men do best at a moment like that: they pretended to be busy with something else.

"Abra's gone, too," I sobbed. "She ran off with a herd of goats and ended up with Silverado ... in a big black Cadillac! What if I never see her again?"

Now everyone was staring, and I knew why. They had all been around me long enough to know that I complained nonstop about Abra. Even though I dutifully looked for her whenever she ran away, I also made it perfectly clear that it would be fine if she didn't come home. Now faced with the prospect that she might be gone for good, I was a basket case. Deely handed me another giant stack of tissues.

"Don't worry. We'll put out a Fleggers all-points bulletin for her, ma'am."

"I thought Fleggers believed that dogs should be free," I sniffled.

"We believe that dogs are entitled to a full life," Deely said. "That doesn't necessarily mean they should leave their human families. Not if the humans are enlightened."

"You think I'm enlightened?" I asked hopefully.

Deely deferred to Dr. David on that one.

He said, "We think you're moving very nicely along the learning curve."

I couldn't stop weeping. To think I'd imagined that life without Abra would be carefree. Yet here I stood, in a parking lot outside a crummy motel in Indiana Amish country, crying about my missing dog. Okay, my missing boyfriend was also a factor. But I knew where he was. And I knew he was having fun. Abra and Silverado, on the other hand, could be in serious trouble. Even if they were riding in a Cadillac.

MacArthur platonically patted me on the back. "Abra has a knack for landing on all four furry feet. Let's not give up on the old girl yet."

Dr. David concurred. "Now that our fellow protesters have gone home, Deely and I are free to be friends first and Fleggers second. On our way back to Magnet Springs, we'll watch for signs of Abra."

"And we'll ask about black Cadillacs everywhere we go," Deely promised.

I pulled myself together enough to thank them. After they drove off, waving, in the Animal Ambulance, MacArthur coughed and said—rather timidly, I thought—"Ready to go fetch Chester?"

Living with Avery had no doubt taught him respect for, if not fear of, female histrionics. He produced a neatly folded linen handkerchief from his hip pocket. I accepted it, dabbed at my eyes, and stifled another burp.

"MacArthur," I said firmly. "We will never speak of this again."

THIRTY-NINE

THE VOLUNTEER BODYGUARD DROVE my car, which suited me just fine. Although my tears had washed the remains of bug irritation from my eye, I was rattled by recent events. Having survived two murders, two canine disappearances, and desertion by Jeb, I faced a daunting new challenge: recognizing at ground level the turnoff from Route 20 to the Amish goat farm that Brad had found from the sky.

"I remember that!" I shouted, pointing to a tire store coming up on our left.

"Turn there?" MacArthur asked, flipping on the blinker.

"No. I just remember it, that's all."

He turned off the blinker.

We rode in silence for at least five more minutes as I desperately scanned the landscape.

"Everything sure looks different from down here," I remarked for the sake of making conversation. "Yessirree. This is like being on a road trip instead of, you know, a helicopter ride. Wow, what a difference."

"Close your eyes—" MacArthur said.

"How is that going to help?"

"Close your eyes and visualize what you saw from the air. Colors, shapes, sizes. What was the last thing you remember before Brad found the goat farm?"

I did as I was told and recaptured the physical sensation of leaning forward in my seat as Brad angled the chopper in widening arcs south of Route 20. I'd focused on green-gold fields and white buildings while the gray ribbon of highway receded ... I opened my eyes. MacArthur was adjusting the steering wheel and our speed to accommodate a rare bend in the road.

"This curve!" I shouted as if I were still in the chopper. "I remember this curve in the highway! I saw it from the air! We were almost directly south of here, I think!"

"I'll take the next left," my driver responded.

"Yes! That might be the road! But we landed on a dirt lane next to a cornfield. And hiked in from there."

"Let's use the front door this time, shall we?" MacArthur said.

I liked that idea. We bumped along our unnamed road past tidy rolling fields in various shades of green, copper, and brown. This late in the season, many acres had already been harvested.

"Amish homestead up ahead," MacArthur announced as we drove over a low hill. "Does this look familiar?"

"I never saw the house," I admitted. "Only corn, goats, and the back of a barn."

"We got corn and a barn," MacArthur said. "That's two out of three."

He pulled into the driveway just far enough to clear the road, adding, "We'll stay back to show respect for their ways."

Too little too late. Not only had I inflicted my loopy dog and precocious neighbor on them, but—thanks to me—their teenage nephew had flown off in a chopper and been busted for drinking beer in Elkhart. Oh, yeah, if this was the right house, I could only imagine how pleased they'd be to make my acquaintance.

I was about to close the passenger-side door behind me, when a familiar *roo-roo* reached my ears.

"Did you hear that?"

MacArthur had frozen, too.

"Definitely an Afghan hound," he confirmed. "Yours?"

And then I saw her, a flash of gold on gold. The late afternoon sun striking her back made her blonde coat glow as if lit from within. Madly she raced away from me along the edge of the cornfield on the other side of the road.

"Abra!" I shouted. "Abra! Come back here!"

Without thinking, I launched into a sprint. At first my muscles resisted, but before I'd gone twenty paces every fiber had activated. My legs and arms pumped as my feet slapped the gravel road. I kept my eyes trained on Abra.

Ahead a silver pickup truck shot out of a narrow dirt driveway, tires squealing. The truck turned toward us, fishtailing wildly.

"Abra!" I screamed, terrified that she would be struck right in front of me.

The truck lurched and then backfired.

I felt sudden intense pain, a sharp sting like fiery metal scalding flesh. With my left hand I clutched my right elbow and tried to keep running.

Another boom, another flash of pain. This time in my right shoulder. I could no longer see my dog. Or call for her.

"Whiskeeeeyyyy!" MacArthur yelled, stretching my name into a dirge.

The third and fourth booms came from behind me. My legs buckled as the truck whooshed past. The last thing I glimpsed was its windshield splintering apart.

FORTY

"WHITNEY, WAKE UP. COME on, Whitney."

A friendly voice was addressing me by a name used only by attorneys, preachers, IRS agents, and my mother. That didn't give me an incentive to reply. Opening my eyes had never been such a chore. Focusing them proved even harder.

"That-a-girl, Whitney! You're doing fine."

Something wasn't quite right. My elbow and shoulder throbbed when I moved my right arm. And the person coaxing me to wake up may have sounded like Chester, but he didn't pass inspection. First, Chester's ever-present glasses were gone. Second, his usually spiked hair appeared to be suffering from a bad case of hat head. Third, his school blazer had been replaced by overalls. And finally, Chester never called me Whitney.

"You're at the Elijah Yoder farm," he went on cheerfully. "And you're perfectly safe. Mrs. Yoder put a couple poultices on your arm, so please don't try to get up."

Leaning closer, he lowered his voice. "Whatever you do, don't make me call you Whiskey. It upsets the whole family."

Groaning, I tried to find a comfortable position. Lying on my back with my arm propped on downy pillows did not exactly feel natural.

"What happened to my arm?" I whispered and realized that my throat was parched.

Chester was ready with a ceramic mug of cool well water. He helped me into a semi-sitting position so that I could drink.

"You were shot, Whitney. Luckily, both bullets just grazed your arm—one right above your elbow and the other at your shoulder."

I drank eagerly, the water tasting better than anything I had consumed in years. Including Pinot Noir. Glancing up, I spotted a worried-looking woman somewhere between age twenty-five and forty studying me from a wooden chair in the far corner of the room. Dressed in dark clothing and wearing a small white cap, she sat with her arms crossed.

"That's Mrs. Yoder, Rachel and Jacob's mother," Chester said helpfully. "She's the one who cleaned and dressed the wounds on your arm."

"Thank you, Mrs. Yoder," I said. "Sorry to be so much trouble."

I wondered exactly how much trouble I was getting credit for. Did she know about Nathaniel? And my dog?

"You can call me Sarah," the woman said, but not in a way that made me want to take her up on the offer.

I turned to Chester. "What happened to MacArthur?"

"MacArthur's fine. He's downstairs talking to Mr. Yoder and the elders. They're trying to decide what to do about you."

"What about Abra?" I whispered. "And the silver pickup?"

"MacArthur says Abra is okay. He saw her dash into the cornfield, and he's sure she wasn't shot. As for the driver of the pickup, MacArthur couldn't get a good look because he—or she—was wearing a hood and dark glasses. They just kept driving."

"But why shoot *me*?" I asked.

"Why not? Your luck has been pretty bad lately."

"I mean, were they *trying* to shoot me? Or was Abra the target? Or MacArthur? What did they want?"

"I think you should ask MacArthur," Chester said.

With my left hand, I grabbed the strap of Chester's overalls, pulling him toward me.

"Where are your glasses, and why are you dressed like that?"

He grinned. "The Yoders let me go Amish! They loaned me Jacob's clothes and straw hat. I was helping move the goats to a different part of the pasture when that brown and white one who ate your book charged me. He knocked off my glasses, and I accidentally stepped on them."

"Your mother won't like that."

My response was automatic and completely irrelevant. Chester's mother was Cassina, the perpetually self-involved, stoned celebrity who rarely remembered she had a son, let alone what he did, or the fact that he owned two dogs.

Chester said, "It was so worth it! Wait till I tell the kids at my academy that I got to be Amish. They'd pay ten thousand dollars for a day like this!"

Here's what I knew about Chester's academy: all the kids had chauffeurs, personal assistants, and trust funds for life. Being Amish for a day would strike them as exotic.

"Fortunately, I had my Blackberry," Chester whispered after verifying that Mrs. Yoder wasn't listening. He produced his state-of-the-art cell phone from an overall pocket. "As proof that I was here, I made a video of Jacob and Rachel doing their chores, and I asked them to shoot me with the goats. Then I showed them the video of the dog show that I posted on YouTube."

That caught my full attention. "Are you ... ?" I kicked the cobwebs from my memory.

"luvssdogss?" Chester asked. "Yup, that's my *youtube* handle! You should see all the videos I've posted of Abra, Prince Harry, and Velcro!"

I sincerely hoped he hadn't posted any of me drooling in my sleep with poultices on my arm.

"Chester, who knows about my getting shot?"

"Well, MacArthur called Jeb right away. Jenx, too. She's on her way."

I took the plunge. "Is Jeb coming, too?"

"He would if he could," Chester said gently, "only he has that gig in Chicago tomorrow. He said he was sorry, but he's sure you understand."

"I understand, all right. His music—and other women—will always come first."

"The show must go on," Chester reminded me. No doubt his mother used the same excuse. "Don't feel sad, Whiskey—I mean, Whitney. MacArthur, Jenx, and I will never let you down."

I squeezed his hand and closed my eyes, willing away the tears.

Across the room, Mrs. Yoder coughed softly. I heard the fabric of her dress rustle as she stood up.

"I'll go see if the elders have finished," she said. "You need to rest, Mrs. Mattimoe."

The next voice I heard was the cleaner's. Somewhere down the hall, MacArthur thanked Mrs. Yoder for her poultices. A moment later, he was at my side.

"How does if feel to be the luckiest English in Amish country?" he said.

"You call getting shot twice 'lucky'?"

"Getting grazed is lucky indeed. Getting killed would have been unfortunate."

"Why didn't you take me to a hospital?" I said.

"If I'd done that, I would have had to report the shootings," MacArthur said. "I fired my gun, too, you know…"

I remembered hearing his weapon fire twice. "What did you hit—besides the windshield?"

"Nothing. The glass shattered, but I'm sure the driver was fine. He—or she—never lost control of the truck."

Gingerly I touched the cloth compresses on my arm. Minor wounds. My heartache over Jeb hurt more.

MacArthur went on, "I carried you to the house and asked Mrs. Yoder to make you a poultice. When I told her it would be the fastest way to get rid of you, she agreed. The elders want you out of here ASAP. We're just waiting for Jenx."

"Why is she coming?"

"First, she's been tracking this case since shots were fired at Susan's car. Second, she's your friend. Strange as it seems, she really cares about you."

Maybe it was a delayed reaction to everything that had happened. Or maybe I was simply exhausted. At any rate, I burst into tears. For the second time that day. Chester handed me a big old white cotton handkerchief.

"The Amish use these instead of tissues." The way he said it, you would have thought that cotton was a new invention. "They're economical and very absorbent. I've got another one in my pocket in case you need it."

"Clear the room, folks. It's my turn to talk to her!"

We hadn't heard Jenx coming. The compactly built Magnet Springs police chief leaned against the door frame. Although she wore her blue uniform, she'd removed her service revolver, presumably out of courtesy for our hosts.

"This is a first," she said. "A visiting Realtor gets shot down in Amish country. Can't wait to hear your side."

She shooed MacArthur and Chester from the room and closed the solid oak door. I resumed sobbing.

"You puke and you faint, but you never cry," Jenx said.

"I don't know what's wrong with me," I bawled into Chester's borrowed handkerchief. "I just feel so sad!"

Jenx said. "Good thing Jeb's not here to see you like this."

That activated a new chain of sobs.

"What's going on with you two, anyhow?" the chief said.

Jenx had drawn up the wooden chair Mrs. Yoder used and was now leaning back in it, arms crossed, head cocked.

"Why don't you ask Jeb?" I said. "He was supposed to help me find Abra, but he took off with Susan Davies. I think they're having an affair! She does that, you know, with lots of people!"

"Jeb's just being Jeb," Jenx said calmly. "And you're just being you."

"Being a volunteer deputy *for you*!"

"That's not a license to get stupid," she said.

"Can I help it if my dog's gone, my boyfriend's gone, and I got shot?"

"Your dog runs away every chance she gets. And your luck sucks, especially with men. Face it, Whiskey, you attract trouble like Odette attracts clients."

"You should investigate that bitch Susan," I told the chief. "I'll bet she killed Mitchell *and* Matt!"

"You think Susan shot at Ramona, her co-breeder, *twice*?" Jenx asked. "And then shot at you, just for fun?"

"She hates me," I said.

"Well, sure, but I don't see Susan driving that pickup. And she couldn't have shot at her own car when she was in it."

"She hired somebody! You don't know Susan. She has a way of getting people to do her bidding. I came to the damn dog show, didn't I?"

"Yeah, but you did that for mercenary reasons."

Jenx removed a notebook from her pocket and flipped through it.

"Here's what we've got so far, based on MacArthur's info and my background checks."

The chief recapped events in order, starting with Susan's report that she and Ramona were fired at as they drove to Vestige on Thursday night. Then someone shot at either Ramona, who was outside with Jeb, or at Susan's car, which was parked in my driveway. When Officer Brady Swancott asked Susan to produce a list of enemies, Ramona brought up a certain breeder.

"Susan didn't want to talk about Slater," I recalled. "According to Ramona, his dog had a stroke while having sex with Susan's dog, so Susan never got her stud fee refunded, and Slater never forgave her for killing his dog. But that's not right."

Jenx checked her notes. "How so?"

"Perry said that Susan was the only woman who ever dumped Mitchell. And Susan did get her stud fee back, FYI—*plus* a puppy: Silverado. She also got Mitchell's hottie son, Matt."

Jenx raised a finger to stop me.

"You're saying Susan used Mitchell to get the stud fee, the stud dog, and the human stud? Then why would she kill him?"

"Beats the hell out of me," I said. "But since Mitchell's dead, is there any reason Peg can't keep Yoda?"

"Perry says Mitchell wanted *him* to take care of Yoda," Jenx said. "So Perry is being responsible. He's paying Peg a thousand bucks. You know she needs the cash."

"She needs Yoda, too! He was all the family she had."

"Not anymore. Deely and Dr. David got a lead on another gray cat looking for a good home. Fleggers like Peg. They think she's enlightened. Brady can alter her tattoo."

Referring to her notebook, Jenx ticked through a long list of observations, most of them relayed by either me or MacArthur. They included the power outage at the exhibit hall, Matt's death and Silverado's disappearance, the cat fight between Brenda Spenser and Sandy Slater, and Kori's sudden absence. I told her my theory that Kori had used the distraction of the first helicopter's departure to cover her exit in the pickup. Or the Lincoln. Jenx didn't seem impressed.

"I ran the plates on the silver pickup," the chief said. "It's not registered to Kori or her uncle. It's not even registered in Illinois."

After a long silence, I realized that Jenx was staring at me.

"What?" I said.

"What the hell kind of volunteer deputy are you? Don't you want to know who the silver pickup belongs to?"

I propped myself up as best I could. "Sure. Is it somebody I've heard of?"

"It's somebody in Magnet Springs," Jenx said.

FORTY-ONE

IMMEDIATELY I THOUGHT OF every Magnet Springer I knew who owned a truck. Most were fellow Main Street merchants. None seemed potentially violent or even conniving. Sure, we were all hard pressed to make a living these days, but nobody struck me as desperate enough to kill. Or crazy enough to kidnap an Afghan hound. Especially not if my dog was along for the ride.

At my bedside, Jenx produced a folded sling. Then she carefully removed Mrs. Yoder's poultices and slipped my right arm into its new cradle.

"You always carry medical supplies in your hip pocket?" I asked.

"Only when I come to rescue you."

As she eased me out of bed, I remarked that I'd never seen this nurturing side of her.

"And if you tell anybody," she said. "I'll kill you. I know how to do it and leave no trace."

Moving through the Yoders' home, I suddenly found myself thinking like a Realtor for the first time in days. Based on its interior details, the farmhouse appeared to have been built in the nineteen-teens. I admired the four-inch oak molding, the brass door hardware, the old plank floors, and the high ceilings.

MacArthur and Chester were waiting for us in the kitchen. Chester had dressed again in his school blazer and chinos, but his hair was still flat from its time under a straw hat. Jacob and Rachel were there, too; the little girl clung to Mrs. Yoder's skirt, apparently for protection. Next to the freestanding kitchen sink, which was powered, I noticed, by an old-fashioned hand pump, stood a severe-looking bearded man I took to be Mr. Yoder.

"Your home is beautiful," I said, beaming at him and his wife. They did not beam back. In fact, they averted their eyes. "Of course, I haven't seen the outside because I was unconscious, but the inside is very well maintained."

Nobody replied. That was my cue to do what I always do when I get nervous: I babbled.

"Even though I'm not licensed to sell real estate in Indiana, I would venture to say that, should you decide to put your farm on the market, you could probably get close to your asking price from the right buyer, even in this economy. That's often the case with unique properties. I don't know how many acres or outbuildings you have here, but let's focus on the house itself. Assuming you're not in a floodplain, your foundation is solid, your roof is recent, and your chimney flues can be brought up to code with heat-resistant tiles, you've got yourselves a winner! Sure, these old farmhouses typically lack closet space and have small rooms by today's standards, but your kitchen is plenty large. In fact, it feels downright spacious."

Suddenly I understood why. There were no major appliances taking up space. But did that stop me from enumerating sales features? Hell no.

"I know from drinking your delicious water that you have either a fine spring or an excellent well. Are your wiring and plumbing up to code?"

Chester cleared his throat. Right. There was no wiring in this house because there was no electricity. And how much indoor plumbing could an Amish home have? I didn't recall passing a bathroom, although they must have a chamber pot and tub stashed somewhere. Did they heat the water in the kitchen and haul it?

"Anyway, lovely room!" I gushed. "Although I recommend upgrading to granite countertops. You'll be glad you did."

Chester and Jenx dragged me toward the door.

"Thank you for your hospitality! And the poultices!" I called out.

"She's in shock from her wounds," MacArthur told the Yoders as he closed the door behind us.

Back at the Barnyard Inn, Chester helped me pack up the items I'd strewn about my room. Then he loaded my bag in the back of my car and waited while I neurotically returned to Number 17 for one last overview. The stained carpet, tattered drapes, and ragged bedspread were beyond depressing. Abra, now gone—who was my whole reason for coming—hadn't spent a single night there with me.

I emerged to find my eight-year-old neighbor chatting up the red-haired mystery author as she loaded unsold books into her minivan. Leaning against my car, I watched Chester charm her as only Chester could. There's something delightful about a boy who looks six and talks like a forty-year-old guidance counselor.

Suddenly he pointed at me, and the author smiled. Then she waved. I waved back without enthusiasm. All I wanted to do was hit the highway. The author handed a box of books to Chester. So many books that he staggered under the load. She climbed into her minivan, tooted her horn, and drove off as Chester trundled the box over to me.

"Please don't tell me you got her to *give* you those. You can afford to buy books, Chester."

"I did buy them," he huffed, signaling for me to open my hatchback. "I'm going to donate them to the Magnet Springs library."

"No wonder the author looked happy."

"Oh, that's not why she's happy," he said. "I told her you used a copy of her latest book to fend off a goat attack. She liked that idea so much she's going to put it in her next novel!"

Because of my injuries, Jenx had recommended that MacArthur drive me and Chester home in my car. So I climbed into the passenger seat and waited for the cleaner. Chester busied himself with his Blackberry in the backseat.

When MacArthur arrived, I asked how he planned to get his Harley back to Michigan. He said he had friends who would handle it. MacArthur didn't seem the type to have friends, only clients with sticky issues. I knew very little about his personal life.

Although he had kept me, Susan, and Ramona alive, I wasn't terribly impressed with his performance as bodyguard. Both Ramona and I had been shot, after all. Still, he was working for free, and I appreciated the relaxing drive home. But who was this guy, and what was his relationship with Kori? Did he simply like stealing kisses from bad girls? Or was he actively protecting a convicted felon who had run afoul of the law yet again?

Nobody said much on the ride back to Magnet Springs. The evening was classic Midwest autumn: a sky sliding from azure to slate blue as the day's vibrant colors relaxed into gray, the air chilled down, and the night breeze turned still. Through my slightly open window, I caught the scent of distant wood smoke and the tang of apples rotting on the ground. We were traveling through Indiana, but it smelled like home.

That night, back at Vestige, I dreamed of the dog show. Abra—handled by Kori—burst into the ring while the judge was making his "Best of Show" decision. The crowd went wild, giving Kori and Abra a standing ovation, complete with whistles and hoots. The judge stopped what he was doing and signaled the spectators to settle down. Then he requested a microphone and made an announcement: "I couldn't live with myself if I didn't acknowledge the unique achievements of this hound and her handler. Therefore, it gives me great pleasure to recognize both Abra the Afghan hound and Kori Davies as Worst in Show!"

The judge presented them with an oversized gold trophy. Kori performed an erotic dance accompanied by Abra's piercing howls and leaps. I wept with pride.

I awoke confused in the early darkness of Sunday morning. The dream seemed almost plausible. Shaking my head, I giggled a little. Suddenly I felt a stab of sadness. Abra was still missing.

Then I rushed to the bathroom and threw up.

What the hell was wrong with me? I wanted to blame my nausea on the stress and bad diet of recent days. A vague fear gnawed at my consciousness. As usual I repressed it, took a long shower, and got on with business. I was relieved to discover that my arm hardly hurt at all.

Traditionally, Sunday is a work day for Realtors. A mighty important work day if you have open houses. Or if you're an agent in a popular tourist location like Magnet Springs. Alas, the current down market had turned Sunday into a Realtor's day of rest.

I needed a challenge. Something to occupy my mind and stretch my body. I wasn't about to let little things like a gunshot wound, stomach trouble, or an economic depression slow me down. So, dressed in my most comfortable and ugly sweats, I headed straight to the office to catch up on whatever I had missed while in Indiana. And to wait for Jenx to give me my next assignment as volunteer deputy. She had promised to drop by later.

By eight a.m., I was at my desk, shuffling every piece of paper I could find in search of phone messages, mail, or any evidence whatsoever that I had missed something while out of town on Friday and Saturday.

There was absolutely nothing new.

Bored, I made myself a pot of coffee. Bad coffee. So bad that it reminded me why I kept Tina Breen on staff. Though prone to distraction, disorganization, and extreme whining, Tina made consistently great java. I rarely drank her brew because we were located right across the street from the Goh Cup, where I liked to take my breaks and catch up on local gossip. Still, it was comforting to know I could get yummy coffee on demand from my own office manager if I ever wanted any.

By now it was almost nine o'clock; I was way too restless to do anything constructive like reorganize my files. Crossing the street to visit Peg and sip her coffee wasn't an option. On Sundays she opened late. So did most other Main Street merchants.

What's a seminauseated, underemployed, dogless single woman to do? I started messing with the computer. To be specific, Tina's computer. I'm not sure why I chose to play with hers instead of mine. I told myself it was because hers was located in the foyer, which gave me a view of the street. That way I'd have something else to look at if the Internet proved boring.

But the Internet didn't prove boring. Far from it.

FORTY-TWO

TECHNICALLY, IT WAS TINA'S email that interested me, not the whole Internet. I never got past her email.

When I'd glimpsed it on Friday, I was stunned by her assortment of saved spam, all of which bore subject lines related to, shall we say, "male enhancement." Most of us don't look at that stuff, let alone save it. I couldn't imagine uptight, goody-two-shoes Tina reading emails from Shane Maverick, Constantine Braver, and Kong. Unless her boredom at work had turned her into a sexual voyeur. Not Tina. Not likely.

Then I got really nosy and discovered something else. Call me unethical, but the computer did, after all, belong to me. So I opened her spam emails and read them all. The subject lines had little or nothing to do with the actual messages.

Maybe that's common spam practice, I thought: catch readers' attention with a sleazy come-on and then sell 'em what you're really selling. Except these senders weren't selling anything that I could see. Even if the messages sounded vaguely sexual, they contained no hyperlinks to other websites and mentioned no products or services for sale. Examples:

For a real big time
Kept me up all night long
Enlarge your demands

Compared to Chester or Brady, I had little computer savvy. But I knew that if I right-clicked the sender's name, I should be able to see "properties": i.e., the sender's email address. Curious, I pointed my cursor at "E. Z. Manning" and clicked.

Imagine my surprise when I recognized the email address. Or, to be accurate, the domain. It was mattimoerealty.com. But the bigger shock was what came *before* the @ sign: a name I didn't know at all. Someone calling himself rocco@mattimoerealty.com was sending porn spam. Or something that looked like porn spam. And for some reason Tina Breen was reading it. Saving it, too. Another question bloomed in my brain.

I clicked on her "sent" files. Yup. Tina was not only reading this crap; she was replying to it. Well, not exactly replying, if by that we mean saying something. Tina's replies were blank. And there were many of them.

Back to her inbox. When I checked the properties of "Rod Wunderly," I uncovered another mattimoerealty.com address. Not *rocco* this time, but *stuart*. Trembling, I right-clicked all the porn spam senders. Every single one featured my company's domain, yet each sender had a different name before the @ sign. I didn't know any of them.

I returned to Tina's sent files. She had answered every porn spam message with a blank message. What the hell? Knowing Tina,

I wondered if this was her weird way of fighting back, of trying to make the world a cleaner place. Bored at work, had she decided to waste the spammers' time and cram their inboxes? That might make sense if these were real spammers. But they couldn't be. To paraphrase that classic horror-movie line, "The emails were coming from inside the house!"

Who were the senders, and what were they up to? What was Tina up to? Maybe this was nothing more than an innocent game played during dull work days by an employee or two who knew more about computers than I did. Someone who had figured out how to set up several email accounts for the purpose of cheap laughs.

But for me that didn't wash. The Tina Breen I knew wouldn't deign to play with smut. Not even make-believe smut.

So what the hell was going on?

I glanced up at the sound of the front door clicking open. There stood the potential answer to my question. If the potential answer was in a mood to cooperate. Since she was holding a gun, that seemed unlikely.

Pushing with my feet, I rolled the desk chair as far back from the computer as I could. As far from Tina Breen as I could. And I raised my hands in the universal sign for "I surrender."

"That gun's not real, is it?"

I stared at the weapon she held in her shaky right hand.

"I'm warning you, Whiskey. Don't make me use this thing." Tina's voice cracked.

I kept my eyes on the small metal revolver. It was either a snub-nose .22 or a toy. I decided to believe it was a toy. Totally bullshitting, I said, "Come on, Tina. I've seen Winston and Neville playing with that thing!"

"No, you haven't!" she snapped. "I would never let my boys play with guns. Not even a toy like this."

She winced and reluctantly dropped the replica into her handbag. It took a long moment for her to regain a sense of menace. Then she approached her computer screen and scanned it to see what I'd been reading. Her next comment caught me completely off guard.

"What do you think you're doing?"

"Me?! How about *you*? Why did you come in here with toy gun blazing?"

"If you're half as smart as I hope you are, you're going to pretend none of this happened," Tina snarled. "You never pried into my email. And you didn't see me this morning when I came in to clean out my desk."

"You're *quitting*? I thought you couldn't afford to lose this job! Friday you got down on your knees and begged me not to let my business fail! You said you and Tim were at the end of your rope—"

When I mentioned her husband's name, Tina's right eyelid pulsed. Then her upper lip twitched, and her breathing turned ragged.

"I never wanted him to do it!" she hissed. "I would have stopped him if I could! But you know how men are, Whiskey. They gotta fix things their own way. Even when things aren't really broken!"

"Do what? Fix what?"

Was she talking about Tim? Or a Mattimoe Realty employee who had been sending fake spam?

"Oh, darn it, Tim wrecked everything!" she said.

Although Tim Breen had never worked for me, Tina would know how to set him up with an email address, or several email addresses, at my business domain. But why would she? What had he done? And did she really intend to quit? If so, I probably wouldn't need to replace her immediately. Not till Odette started selling Big and Little Houses on the Prairie…

This was not the occasion to mentally review my payroll.

"Tina, you'd better level with me. What kind of trouble are you and Tim in?"

"Oh god," she moaned, sinking into a lobby chair. "All Tim wanted to do was be the breadwinner again. Being the laid-off, stay-at-home dad made him feel like less than a man!"

"So he started sending email porn spam?" I asked, trying to find the connection.

"No! He talked to MacArthur about doing the same kind of work *he* does."

"Being a Realtor? Tim should have come to me about that!"

"Not a Realtor, Whiskey! A cleaner! And now you know why I can't stand that man. MacArthur turned my husband into a criminal, just like he is!"

"MacArthur's not a *criminal*…" I wished I could have been more specific, but I really wasn't sure how to defend him.

"Oh yeah?"

Tina had a crazed look that made me want to put my hands on my cell phone. Subtly, I reached toward my sweatpants pockets.

"Somebody you know hired Tim as a cleaner. To make their problems disappear," Tina said.

"Somebody I know?"

Nothing in my pockets. *Damn.* Then I remembered: I'd left my phone in my purse. In the bathroom.

"Oh yeah," Tina said. "You know this person. It's one of your super-rich friends."

"I have no super-rich friends, Tina. Just a few super-rich former clients. Who do you mean?"

Tina shot straight up from her chair. "I know what you're doing, Whiskey! You're stalling for time, hoping somebody else will come by and stop me from doing what I gotta do!"

"What do you gotta do?" My heart thumped.

"I'm really, really sorry, but I gotta take whatever cash you got in the safe. Then the boys and I are going to meet Tim. We're going underground. The four of us gotta disappear—"

Her voice dissolved into choked sobs.

"What does Tim's 'cleaner' business have to do with spam?" I said.

"That's not spam!" she sputtered. "Those are Tim's notes to me about how he was doing. We had kind of a code. If I understood what he was telling me, I replied with a blank message. If I didn't understand or needed more information, I didn't reply at all. Then he'd try again. Tim said sending emails on his Blackberry would be safer than making calls! He didn't think anybody would read them if they looked like spam."

I glanced at the email message that I'd left open onscreen.

"'Enlarge your demands'? What did that mean?"

"Tim wanted me to ask you for a raise. You, of all people, were never supposed to get shot!"

FORTY-THREE

"*Tim* SHOT ME?" I said when I could find my voice again.

Red-faced and sniffling, Tina nodded. "He kept trying to catch Abra—for ransom. But you kept getting in the way. He said you were as big a nuisance as your dog."

I didn't know which was more amazing, that Tim Breen had shot me, or that he had thought I would pay ransom for Abra.

"He only meant to scare you," Tina said. "Shooting from a moving truck is a lot harder than you might think."

I pictured the silver pickup with the splintering windshield. MacArthur had said he couldn't identify the driver. Was that true or false? How much did he know about what Tim was up to?

"Since when does Tim have a truck?" I said.

"He doesn't. He 'borrowed' it from our neighbor who's on vacation."

My head spun faster than a yoyo. If I hadn't already been sitting, I would have immediately sought a chair. As it was, I wanted to slide all the way to the floor.

"Are you saying ... *Tim* shot *everybody*?"

Tina arched her back. "Not everybody! Just four people involved in that dog show."

"Two of them died," I said.

"By accident," my office manager declared. "Tim had instructions to *hurt* those two. But ... they moved." She shrugged. "Mitchell Slater wasn't supposed to take that last step. As for Matt Koniger, well, you know what they say about a shot in the dark? Poor Tim. It's really hard in a blackout to *hit* the target, but not kill him."

"How about Ramona Bowden?" I said. "Was Tim supposed to hit her or miss her?"

At that instant my front door clicked again. Seeing our chief of police, Tina let out a cry of either surprise or relief; I couldn't tell which.

To me, Jenx said, "That's where it gets interesting. Ramona Bowden was Tim's boss."

"No way!" I said.

"Way," sighed Tina. Then she took a deep breath and extended her fisted hands, palms down, toward Jenx.

"What are ya doing?" the chief said.

"Go ahead and cuff me. I'm an accessory."

"Shut up and sit down," Jenx said. Tina obeyed.

I waited for Jenx to make the next move, but all she did was stare at Tina.

"Isn't this the part where you read her her rights?" I said.

"If I was planning to bust her, yeah," Jenx said. "But I think there's a chance we can keep Tina out of this."

"Her husband killed two people!" I exclaimed. "And shot two more, including me!"

Jenx nodded. "He also kidnapped a valuable show dog. And your dog, assuming Abra didn't go willingly."

"Abra always goes willingly."

Tina raised her hand like she was in school. "I threatened Whiskey with a toy gun and told her I was going to rob her safe. Does that count?"

"Did you rob her safe?" Jenx asked.

Tina shook her head.

"Then let's all play Whiskey's game," Jenx said.

"What's that?" I said.

"Denial. We're all gonna pretend nothing weird happened here."

Jenx pointed Tina toward the door and told her not to do anything stupid. I considered those instructions much too vague.

It turned out that Jenx hadn't known about the Tim-and-Ramona connection till she followed up on the pickup truck reported by MacArthur. When she drove to the house where the truck was registered, she found Tim in the garage, cleaning broken glass from the dashboard.

"The son of a bitch ran when I pulled in the driveway," she said. "I got so pissed off my magnetic compass went out of whack! Everything electrical on the block started arcing."

I nodded, imagining the scene. Jenx wasn't a superhero, although her geomagnetic powers were the stuff of local lore. Magnet Springs happened to be built on a highly charged electrical field. Spikes and surges have always been commonplace here. Records dating back to 1820 note that the occasional grazing cow keeled over when it wandered into the wrong part of a wet pasture. A few farmers did, too. But fertile soil and sweeping views of Lake Michigan kept most settlers from moving on. Then along came the Jenkins clan with a genetic predisposition for channeling energy, especially when riled. Don't piss off the chief. She's got a weapon nobody can make her register or put down.

Jenx continued, "A power line snapped loose and fell next to Tim, spraying sparks! I swear, he jumped a foot in the air. Stood there bawling like a two-hundred-pound baby. So I marched him to my cruiser. He spilled everything before we got to the station."

"Everything" turned out to be this: After Ramona's second husband died, and she inherited yet another small fortune, she decided the time had come to pursue personal satisfaction regardless of cost. Personal satisfaction in the form of revenge, that is. Ramona kept score. She wanted payback for Mitchell and Matt having publicly rejected her in front of her dog-show cronies. She wanted to spite Susan, too, for carrying on high-profile affairs with the same two men. Ramona intensely resented Susan's easy egotism, her conviction that—and I'm paraphrasing—her own shit didn't stink. Her dogs' shit didn't either.

Ramona told Tim that Susan had schmoozed her for one reason only: to access her excellent breeding stock. Susan's kennel would have been unremarkable without it.

Why did Ramona do business with Susan? Probably to be able to say that she did. If there's guilt by association, the same holds true for glamour. That was Jenx's theory, anyhow. Susan and her dogs got national attention because she was rich, beautiful, and sexual. On that scorecard Ramona was one for three. And resentful as hell about it. Through a paramilitary listserv she placed a discreet ad seeking a "personal assistant capable of confidentiality and excellent marksmanship."

"We know this much," I said. "Tim padded his resume."

"We also know he bought supplies through that listserv," Jenx said. "Including night-vision goggles and a chemical designed to disguise his scent. Ramona didn't want anybody killed. Her goal was to scare the crap out of 'em. But her marksman screwed up."

"He shot his own boss!" I exclaimed.

"By accident. Tim was supposed to shoot *at* her in order to draw suspicion away from her. But he got nervous because she kept yelling at him. It was Tim that Ramona phoned just before she got shot. He was on a cell phone that Ramona had 'lifted' from Kori, just to confuse things."

Although I didn't know Tim well, I knew now that he was the man I'd seen in silhouette leaving the exhibit hall after the lights went out. And his was the voice I'd heard shouting at people to stay still.

"Was Brenda in on this, too?" I said. "She drives a big black car. The hood was hot when MacArthur talked to her!"

"She'd just come back from the carryout down the road," Jenx said. "I interviewed Brenda by phone—after her attorney sprang her from the local slammer. She got busted for driving drunk. But she had nothing to do with Ramona. In fact, Brenda was the victim of another crime."

"Let me guess. Sandy Slater accused Brenda of wanting Matt dead because he was blackmailing her!"

"Matt *and* his mama were squeezing money out of Brenda," the chief said, "in exchange for not telling her snooty friends and fellow breeders about her sexual preferences. Brenda also had the hots for the Two L's."

"We still don't know whose Cadillac picked up the dogs," I sighed. "If it was a Cadillac."

"It's a Cadillac, all right," Jenx said. "A Seville, not a DTS. Your Amish teen was full of crap, like teens everywhere."

"How did Ramona learn to drive so aggressively?"

"Practice. She's had a slew of citations for speeding and driving without due regard."

"Where is she now?" I said. "And where's Silverado?"

"We assume they're together. There's an APB out for her and her car. It's just a matter of time till somebody sees her."

I comforted myself with the knowledge that Ramona raised dogs, so she wouldn't hurt this one. Tim Breen had told Jenx that Ramona paid off one of the Two L's to get her other dogs safely back to Grand Rapids. She'd also hired Kori to make sure Silverado ended up in her motel room when he took off after Abra. And to "pull the plug" during the final round of judging.

I said, "So Kori was involved! I knew it!"

Jenx shook her head. "Kori thought she was participating in a nasty practical joke on Susan. That's all."

"You talked to her?"

"Not yet. But I believe Tim. He's way too scared of me to lie."

"What about MacArthur? Tina blames him for getting Tim into this business. If that's true, then MacArthur knew what Tim was up to. And he ratted Tim out when he gave you the license of the pickup."

"I don't know what MacArthur knows about Tim," Jenx said. "I haven't been able to find him."

"He drove me home last night, like you told him to, and then he and Chester went back to the Castle."

"MacArthur cleared out of there," Jenx said. "Packed up his shit and left after he put Chester to bed and hired a sitter to watch him till Cassina and Rupert come home."

FORTY-FOUR

I COULD HAVE BELIEVED a lot of things about MacArthur: that he cheated on Avery, turned in Tim, and was inclined to bend the law. But I couldn't believe he would walk out on Chester. Over coffee at the Goh Cup, MacArthur and I had often discussed Chester's need for a father figure. Rupert the Sperm Donor, his frequently absent, usually stoned, sorry excuse for a dad, didn't even try to be paternal. I had assumed MacArthur saw himself filling that role for Chester.

"And then he goes and abandons the kid!" I fumed.

"He didn't abandon him," Jenx said. "He left him a note and got him a sitter."

"He took off! *Adios. Sayonara.* Have a nice life! How is Chester handling it?"

"I think he's—"

Jenx's ringing cell phone interrupted her reply. She checked Caller ID and passed the phone to me. The lighted panel said The Castle.

"That's Chester," I said. "I can't talk to him! He's calling you for help!"

"No, he's not. Chester wanted me to call him as soon as I saw you. He must have got tired of waiting."

"What if I can't think of anything comforting to say?" I hissed.

"Nobody calls you for comfort, Whiskey. Just be yourself."

"Hello?" I answered coolly. My strategy was to pretend that I routinely answered Jenx's phone without checking Caller ID.

"Hello, Whiskey! This is Chester. I was hoping to reach you. I'm afraid I have some potentially alarming news."

"Chester, just remember, no matter how terrible things seem now, they will get better!"

"Thank you, Whiskey. But this is a courtesy call . . . to let you know Avery was here. She's on her way to find you."

"Avery?" I had completely forgotten that my evil stepdaughter was due back in town today. "Does she know about . . . ?"

I bit my tongue before I could mention the missing cleaner.

"MacArthur leaving? Yes. He wrote her a note, too."

Uh-oh. Avery scorned was even scarier that standard Avery. According to her overblown sense of entitlement, people owed her whatever she wanted whenever she wanted it. How dare MacArthur change his mind about being there for her and the twins?

No doubt Avery was looking for me because she expected me to solve her problems—in other words, provide free room, board, and baby-sitting. The concept of full employment didn't figure into Avery's universe. I assumed she'd go straight to Vestige since it was right next door to the Castle. Failing to find me at home would double her frenzy. By the time she arrived at my office, every vein in her neck would be pulsing, and her tongue-flicking tic would be in overdrive.

"How long ago did she leave the Castle, Chester?"

"I called you the minute she left. When you didn't answer, I called Jenx."

"Good man!" I said, remembering that I'd misplaced my cell phone.

"No problem, Whiskey. We'll talk about MacArthur some other time. When you feel up to it."

I'd flipped the call to speaker phone so that Jenx could hear every word. Just in case I needed coaching.

"Stay calm," she told me after I hung up. "It'll take Avery ten minutes to get here. By then we'll have at least one good excuse why she can't move in with you. How about . . . you have a fatal contagious disease?"

"I like that! Name one."

"Malaria."

"Name another one."

"Bubonic plague?"

My front door clicked again, and my heart clenched. I wasn't ready for Avery. No way she'd buy malaria or the bubonic plague.

But it wasn't Avery. Standing in my lobby was none other than Kori Davies. With Abra on a leash.

"I didn't have time to groom her for ya, but here she is."

I'd never seen Abra more of a mess. Her usually glossy blonde coat was not only tangled and matted, it was also caked with mud. She looked like a street mutt. A brown one, at that. Idly I wondered how much a snood might have helped.

"I owe you some kind of reward," I told Kori. What I didn't add was "assuming you didn't help steal her in the first place."

"Forget about it," Kori said, cracking her gum. "I was going this way, anyhow."

As was always the case at our reunions, Abra showed no interest in my presence although she did wag her tail at Jenx. But that was probably because she associated Jenx with Brady and Brady with Roscoe. Abra was always hot for Roscoe.

Where were my manners?

"Uh, let me introduce you two. Chief Jenkins, meet—"

"Kori Davies." Jenx finished the sentence herself and extended her hand.

"How did you know?" I asked.

"I know how she knew," Kori said. "Ya looked me up on NCIC. Right?"

"Right," Jenx said. "You have an impressive criminal record. For your age and parole status."

"Thanks."

I wondered if there was more to Kori than car theft and vehicular homicide. If there was, I decided I'd rather not know about it. Accepting Abra's leash, I said, "Where did you find her?"

"Route 20. Not far from that shit-hole motel. I pulled over, and she jumped in. I took her back to your room, but you'd already checked out. I was just dicking around Amish country, so she was my excuse to come see Big Mac."

"'Big Mac'?"

"That's what I call MacArthur."

Kori tilted her pelvis provocatively. I gave thanks that Chester was nowhere nearby.

"I thought you'd gone back to Chicago . . ."

"I'm never going back there," Kori said. "You think Abra's a bitch? Try living with my aunt Susan. Uncle Liam's going to help me make my dreams come true. He's sending me to school in Vegas."

"UNLV?" I asked.

"Bartending school. I'm a natural."

"I know it's none of my business, but aren't you in a twelve-step program?"

"I am," Kori said proudly. "Not AA, though. I'm addicted to sex. Speaking of which, where's Big Mac? I can't wait to surprise him!"

Jenx and I exchanged glances; I caught a twinkle in the chief's eye. She was leaving this one for me.

I cleared my throat. "Uh, I hate to be the bearer of bad news—"

"Don't tell me!" she said. "He's in jail."

"No. Why would you guess that?"

"It happens. So what's the bad news?"

"MacArthur's gone," I said. "He bugged out last night."

She stopped chewing her gum and stared. "Are you shitting me?"

"No. Sorry. I am not shitting you. He packed up and left."

Kori guffawed so hard that her gum flew across the room and stuck to the glass of my front door.

"You think that's *funny*?" I said.

"Oh yeah. That's what Big Mac said he was gonna do, and I didn't believe him!"

She was still laughing.

"You're not mad at him?" I said.

"Why the hell would I be mad at him? The guy did what he said he was gonna do. That, like, almost never happens!"

"Ya hear that, Whiskey?" Jenx said meaningfully. "'That, like, almost never happens.'"

"Let me get this straight," I told Kori. "Where did Big Mac—I mean, MacArthur—say he was going?"

"Oh, he didn't say where. He just said it was time to move on down the road. He's a rolling stone, that one."

Abra farted, and I laughed. I couldn't imagine why; dog farts had never amused me before. Then Kori took a cell phone call from another boyfriend, somebody named Lance. She promised to "jump his bones" in two hours. They were synchronizing watches as she walked out the door with nary a backward glance.

I couldn't help but admire Kori. She was an awesome Bad Example. If the economy were better, she'd make one hell of a Realtor.

FORTY-FIVE

JENX SAID, "WHAT A bitch."

Stretched out across two chairs in my lobby, Abra snored.

"I'm talking to *you*," Jenx said, getting in my face. "Jeb loves you. Why give him a hard time?"

"Because he's acting like... Jeb always ends up acting," I whined.

"Meaning what?"

"He loves the ladies and his music more than he can ever love me."

Jenx plopped down in Tina's reception desk chair. She put her steel-toe-booted feet, one at a time, on the counter and leaned way back.

"You know what your problem is, Whiskey?"

"I have a strange feeling you're going to tell me."

There's no stopping the law, especially when it takes the form of somebody you grew up with. Somebody who knows you better than your own mother.

Jenx said, "Jeb would do anything he could for you. Anything you'd let him do. Your problem is you don't know a good thing when it wants to move in with you."

"I know my ex-husband! He never grew up. If he hadn't connected with Fleggers and cut that *Animal Lullabies* CD, he'd still be living out of his old Nissan Van Wagon—and liking it!"

"You're right," Jenx said. "It doesn't take much to make Jeb happy. What the hell's your problem?"

"This is about Jeb's problems!"

I recited my usual and customary laundry list of Jeb's faults, starting with his easy attraction to other women. Jenx's eyes glazed over, but I kept talking, building my case against my ex-husband. When the chief's cell phone rang, she stood up.

"Hold that thought," she told me. "Hold it, cuz nobody wants to hear it."

She stepped away to take the call. A moment later she was grinning at me.

"Fleggers to the rescue! That was Deely. They found Silverado and Ramona."

True to their word, Deely and Dr. David had watched for black Cadillacs all the way home from Nappanee. While filling their tank at a Shell station near Union Pier, they spotted an unattended black Seville parked at an adjacent pump and asked the cashier where the driver had gone.

He pointed toward the woods behind the station. "She's chasing her big gray dog. It got out when she opened her door."

In other circumstances, Dr. David and Deely might have cheered Silverado's run for freedom. But they recognized a felony in progress and notified local authorities. Within fifteen minutes, deputies had retrieved and busted Ramona. It took less time for Deely and Dr. David to secure Silverado.

"He came right to us when we called for him," Deely told Jenx.

Dr. David added, "Animals instinctively know that Fleggers are on their side."

Maybe some animals. My Bad Example bitch wouldn't care. Watching her snooze, I doubted she gave a damn about anybody.

If Abra had a heart, it belonged to one human—Leo—and one dog—Norman the Golden, father of Prince Harry the Pee Master. Sure, she'd looked happy loping along Route 20 with Silverado, but Norman was her real mate. Her soul mate.

I explained that to Jenx.

"Remind you of anybody?" she asked.

I didn't answer. I couldn't. I had to dash to the john to barf again.

Afterwards I put the lid down on the toilet and sat there, head in my hands, telling myself that everything was all right. Or would be eventually. Before I could convince myself, however, the cell phone I'd been looking for earlier rang inside my purse. I scooped my bag from the floor, accidentally dumping half the contents.

"Have you finished searching for Abra?" Odette inquired when I answered. "And please note that I'm not asking whether you found her."

"Duly noted. The answer is yes. You'll be pleased to know I'm back at the office."

"Excellent! Anything new at Mattimoe Realty?"

"Aside from the fact that Tina doesn't work here anymore because she was an accessory to her husband, who killed two people and also shot me? Nah. Nothing new."

"I see," Odette said. "Well, I have news from Chicago."

Part of me wanted to make sure she'd understood my news. But a bigger part of me needed to know what was happening on her end, so I listened.

"Last night Liam officially propositioned me, and I officially turned him down. We're still working together, of course. We're both mature adults."

"Of course," I said automatically.

"I thought you had doubts," Odette remarked.

"Not about you. Never about you."

That was almost completely true. I had certainly wanted to believe that Odette would stay true to Reginald... if only as an antidote to my own doubts about Jeb.

Then she pressed me for details about Tim and Tina, so I gave her what I had. She was less surprised than I was by the turn of events—further proof, I suppose, of my tendency to tune out unpleasant indicators. Ignorance may be bliss, but it's the kind of bliss that can cost you.

Happily for me, Odette was in top form heading into her meeting with Liam's favorite Chicago investors. No doubt she would dazzle them with her vision of Big and Little Houses on the Prairie. I expected construction to start before all the leaves were off the trees.

When I emerged from the bathroom, Jenx was gone. In her place sat Avery Mattimoe. My first reaction was to run for my life.

"You look like shit," Avery said, by way of greeting.

I would have returned the compliment except that Avery looked pretty good. For a big girl with bad skin, thin hair, and a permanent scowl. I gave silent thanks that her tongue wasn't flicking.

"Where are the twins?" I said. "Don't tell me you left them with Chester."

"They're with Peg Goh. She was opening her shop early, in case anybody wants a tattoo before breakfast. She couldn't wait to hold the twins."

Something was different about Avery. And it wasn't the hint of suntan on her sallow face or the conspicuous lack of tic. Her voice, usually strident, was pleasantly modulated. Serene. How was that possible? MacArthur had just dumped her.

"Everything all right?" I asked cautiously.

"Wonderful. We loved our Mommy and Me Retreat in Sedona. I learned so much."

"I mean is everything all right *at the Castle*?"

In the brief pause before she spoke, I saw Avery compose her response. Her lips moved silently, as if chanting a newly learned mantra.

"MacArthur is gone. But the twins and I will follow our bliss and find our destiny."

She smiled in a way that made me extremely nervous. Probably because Avery never smiled. At moments like this, she ordinarily threw things.

When I didn't smile back, she said, "You really do look like shit. And you smell like puke. Are you pregnant?"

At that point I responded the way Avery usually did: I burst into snotty, snuffling tears.

"I think so!" I wailed. "I've missed two periods! But I'm scared to pee on a stick!"

At the sound of my sobs, Abra snapped at the air and then sank back to sleep. Avery, on the other hand, took practical action. She reached into her purse and pulled out a home pregnancy test kit.

"You carry that around with you?" I asked.

"If you were as fertile as I am, you would, too."

My stepdaughter placed it in my palm and closed my fingers around it.

"Wow," she said. "I thought you were too old to have sex. Let alone get pregnant."

"I'm thirty-four!" I said.

"Wow," she repeated, shaking her head in amazement. "Just think, if you have a kid, by the time he starts high school, you'll be, like—"

I could see the wheels turning as she struggled with the math.

"You'll be forty-eight! That's older than my dad was when he *died*. When *my* kids start high school, I'll be the same age you are *now*."

She narrowed her piggy little eyes, either picturing herself at my advanced age or imagining my looming decrepitude.

"How does Jeb feel about being a daddy?" she said. "It is Jeb's ... isn't it?"

I watched Avery's mental machinery grind as she ran the known list of Whiskey's Possible Sexual Partners. I allowed myself the pleasure of her apparent self-torture as she considered—and discarded—MacArthur from that list.

"It's gotta be Jeb's," she concluded, more for her benefit than mine. "Have you told him?"

"Not yet. Maybe not ever."

"You gotta tell him!"

"This from the woman who never notified the father of her twins."

"That was so completely different!" Avery said. "I didn't even know that guy. You used to be *married* to Jeb!"

"And then I divorced him. For a lot of very good reasons."

Although now, staring at the pregnancy test kit, I wondered which mattered more: forgiving Jeb or being stubborn enough to raise a kid on my own.

"You're right," Avery said suddenly.

"About what?"

I was immediately suspicious since my stepdaughter had never admitted I could be correct about anything.

She said, "You don't need Jeb. We can do this ourselves! We can raise our kids together!"

"I'm not following you…"

"The twins and I will move back to Vestige. And you'll hire a nanny for all three kids!"

I flicked my own tongue and told Avery I'd think about it… as seriously as I'd think about bungee-jumping from the Mackinac Bridge. Then I located a brand-new box of tissues for her; it would come in handy when the Sedona trance wore off, and she resumed her sobbing, screaming ways.

Moments later Abra was stretched out on the backseat of my car, snoring. I had locked all the doors in case Avery cracked up fast and tried to join us. Instead of starting the ignition, I stared at my cell phone. Jeb had not called since taking off for Chicago with Susan. About now he'd be playing animal lullabies at her fund-raising country club brunch. That meant I could leave him a voicemail message instead of talking to him live. Maybe it would be easier that way to explain my current … situation.

When I speed-dialed his number; the call went straight to voicemail:

"Hey," Jeb's crooner voice said. "What's happening? Tell me now, and I'll call you later."

I opened my mouth with every intention of telling him what I knew: That I was scared to my bones I might be pregnant. Me, the Queen of Denial. A woman who couldn't keep track of a dog much less a child. Just ask Chester, whom I'd lost more times than a set of keys. And I'd accused Cassina of being a lousy mom! How could Bad Example Me ever handle motherhood?

I listened for the beep and opened my mouth, but nothing came out. A recorded voice kindly suggested that I try again. When I remained mute, the voice said to call back later and disconnected me. Probably just as well. I really didn't have a clue how to speak my deepest fears. So I started the car and headed home.

Somewhere along Broken Arrow Highway, my favorite radio station played "Once in a Lifetime" by The Talking Heads. When I was married to Leo, that was our song. In fact, it was the last song I heard while he was alive. A year and a half ago, we were holding hands on a late-night drive home from Chicago, Abra asleep in the backseat just as she was now. With the windows rolled down, and the fresh spring air rushing in, we savored our special tune and our happy time together. Naïvely, I thought those tranquil years would roll on and on. I dozed off, waking when we hit the ditch. Abra was howling behind me; Leo was silent beside me, dead from a ruptured aorta.

Now I found myself sobbing so hard I couldn't keep the car on the road. I pulled onto the berm, shifted into park, and collapsed against the steering wheel, letting my heart break all over again.

"Oh, Leo," I moaned. "Why did you have to go? You should be here with me right now..."

Something gentle yet firm was nudging my neck. I turned my head and made contact with a cold wet nose, followed by a warm wet tongue. Abra was awake and, unless I was badly mistaken, trying to comfort me. She vaulted into the passenger seat.

"Hey, girl," I said. "You got knocked up, too, didn't you? And things turned out all right. Without any help from the daddy."

I stroked her head. Her stately Afghan hound head.

"Oh, sure, Norman came around later. After we gave your babies away. Which isn't an option in this case..."

Then I did something I'd never done before. Something I hadn't imagined Abra ever letting me do: I pulled her close and held her tight in a soothing big-dog embrace. Burying my face in her tangled, sticky, not-so-sweet-smelling coat, I sobbed till I had no tears left. Squeezed between me and the steering wheel, Abra didn't budge. The diva dog patiently allowed me to hold her as long as I wanted to, which was exactly as long as I needed to.

We were both a mess. A couple genuine Bad Examples. But we were also survivors; Abra and I could muddle through damn near anything. Leo had brought us together, and we would carry on. The dog, for one, had decent instincts.

THE END

ABOUT THE AUTHOR

Nina Wright, a former actor and playwright, is the author of five books in the humorous Whiskey Mattimoe mystery series, and two paranormal novels, *Homefree* and *Sensitive*. Nina has enjoyed living in a variety of locales: along the Great Lakes and the Gulf of Mexico, as well as in central West Virginia and in Dallas, Texas.

To find out more about Nina Wright and her entertaining workshops for aspiring writers, contact her through her website or blogs:

www.ninawright.net

www.ninawrightwriter.blogspot.com

www.whiskeymattimoe.blogspot.com